Praise for the novels

For *All Fir*

"Equally hilarious and heartfelt, England has woven not only a fiery hot and emotional love story between two beautifully rendered women, but a wonderful love letter to the power of adult friendship and finding your place and values. I couldn't turn the pages fast enough!"
—CARLYN GREENWALD, author of *Director's Cut*

For *The One True Me and You*:
"A love letter to every queer nerd… Hilarious, joyful, and deeply relatable."
—ASHLEY POSTON, *New York Times* bestselling author of *The Dead Romantics*

"This story is lovingly queer, and shows the differences that set us apart should be celebrated rather than denigrated. England writes with heart and I, for one, can't wait to see what they do next."
—TJ KLUNE, *New York Times* bestselling author of *The House in the Cerulean Sea*

"A sweetly romantic and deliciously queer story about building the courage to embrace your individuality, and love yourself all the way through."
—CALEB ROEHRIG, author of *The Fell of Dark*

"Full of love and hope, and geeky to its core…an incredible story of self-discovery and acceptance."
—JENNIFER DUGAN, author of *Some Girls Do* and *Hot Dog Girl*

"A smart, funny, joyously queer love letter to fandoms, first loves, and the freedom to be yourself."
—JAMIE PACTON, author of *The Life and (Medieval) Times of Kit Sweetly* and *Lucky Girl*

ALSO BY M. K. ENGLAND

The One True Me and You
(written as Remi K. England)

Roll for Love

For additional books by M. K. England,
visit their website, mkengland.com.

ALL FIRED UP

A Novel

M. K. ENGLAND

CANARY STREET PRESS

CANARY
STREET
PRESS

Recycling programs
for this product may
not exist in your area.

ISBN-13: 978-1-335-44860-6

All Fired Up

Copyright © 2025 by Megan England

All rights reserved. No part of this book may be used or reproduced in any manner whatsoever without written permission.

Without limiting the author's and publisher's exclusive rights, any unauthorized use of this publication to train generative artificial intelligence (AI) technologies is expressly prohibited.

This is a work of fiction. Names, characters, places and incidents are either the product of the author's imagination or are used fictitiously. Any resemblance to actual persons, living or dead, businesses, companies, events or locales is entirely coincidental.

For questions and comments about the quality of this book, please contact us at CustomerService@Harlequin.com.

TM is a trademark of Harlequin Enterprises ULC.

Canary Street Press
22 Adelaide St. West, 41st Floor
Toronto, Ontario M5H 4E3, Canada
CanaryStPress.com

Printed in U.S.A.

For Jamie, who has always championed this book.
Love you, friend. You're a star.

AUTHOR'S NOTE

One of the characters in this book, Kira, is a firefighter with the Seattle Fire Department. Her struggles with the internal politics of that organization do not reflect the actual SFD or any real situations I'm aware of there. This is a work of fiction, and no disrespect for the firefighters in Seattle is intended. Every story needs obstacles, and for Kira, several of those obstacles crop up in the career she loves. Extra apologies to any Seattle firefighters named Jared. I'm sure you're perfectly nice people.

The issues Kira faces do exist, however; sexism, racism, homophobia and transphobia, and other forms of discrimination are still rampant in firehouses across the country. As with everything in the world, there is nuance. We can respect and show gratitude for the work of our firefighters even as we demand better. Two things can be true.

If you are a firefighter reading this: thank you for your service. I appreciate you.

CHAPTER ONE

NIC

I have never wanted to set a fire so badly in my life.

The aggressively pink box sits on my doormat like a puddle of gasoline waiting for a match. It's roughly the size of a fancy artisan loaf of bread, made from glossy card stock, and marked with a white label on the side that faces the hallway. I can see her name from ten paces away: Skylar Clark, written in perfect looping cursive on the top.

Who writes in cursive anymore?

I've been back in Seattle for less than a week, sporting a shiny new master's degree in fire protection engineering and a job offer from a local university to run trials in one of their labs. I moved back without telling the group exactly what day I'd arrive, except for Willow, who was kind enough to let me crash for a few days until my lease started. As much as I love the rest of my friend group, there are six of them, and that's just . . . a lot all at once. Even though they're the whole reason I moved back, after two years away at grad school, I really need more than a week to jump back into . . . *this*.

The box eyes me judgmentally, seeing right through my bullshit.

Okay, fine, yes, I specifically need to work up to seeing *Skylar* in person again. Maybe after the stress acne from moving and starting a new job fades. I figured I'll have coffee with some of our group one-on-one first, feel things out, ease my way back in. One shouldn't need to jump through so many hoops just to see one's best friend again.

When one is stupid enough to fall in love with said friend, a few hoops are necessary.

I could just walk around the box. Fumble with my brand-new key that only unlocks the door on thirty-three percent of attempts, go inside my den of cardboard boxes, and leave the beast right where it sits on my welcome mat. Or I could move again. I only moved into this apartment yesterday. I'm not attached, and the hallway does kind of smell like stale corn chips. Maybe I can cancel my lease? Last I heard, Marco has an opening in his building. I could try there.

I tip my head back to look at the crack in the ceiling over my door and take a breath.

Okay. I will not be bested by a box. I joyfully set things on fire for a living. I clap my hands and shriek with pure delight every time something explodes in my lab. And, okay, I also meticulously record the results of my very carefully controlled experiments and spend days or weeks with my face pressed to a computer screen, crunching the data for my professors or employer. But the point is, if I can face fires, I can face this.

Here we go.

Three, two, one . . .

I step forward and look down.

From: Skylar Clark ♥
To: Nicole Wells (my dearest Nic Knack who is finally home again!)

No postage or address on it. Just her name and my name. She was *here*. What if I'd been home? What if I'd answered the door in my "Baking is science for hungry people" apron, covered in the proof of how far I went down the *Great British Bake Off* rabbit hole while I was away? My stomach flutters at the near ambush. I haven't even told her my new address yet. There's nothing on my door to distinguish it from every other slightly chipped door with too many layers of paint. Skylar must've gotten it out of Willow, who is normally a trustworthy accomplice . . . unless they think it's for my own good. Rude.

No—you know what? I don't have to deal with this in the hallway of my new apartment building with Mr. Anderson watching from the peephole across the hall. It's way too much of a thing to have a breakdown outside your own apartment door, and I refuse to capitulate to such a stereotype.

I let myself in with minimal fumbling and nudge the box over the threshold with the side of my foot, then promptly drop my keys. When I bend down to get them, I get a good whiff of my clothes—ugh, you can still smell the accelerant from the burn trials I ran at the lab today. Better change my shirt before lighting any candles tonight. As soon as I hook a pinky through one of my key rings, the *Super Mario Bros.* theme starts playing from my back pocket. Willow calling. I hang there for a minute, looking between my ankles at the pink box behind me with a growing sense of dread.

Why do I feel like there's a meteor headed for Earth and everyone knows it but me? Am I in a disaster movie? Is this

the phone call the lovable but totally doomed side character gets right before they're engulfed in lava/floodwaters/a
tornado?

I backwards-kick the door closed, grab my phone from
my pocket on the way up, and tap Accept before the theme
music can start over again.

"Hello?"

Willow's voice is frantic. "Oh honey, are you okay?"

"Uh, yeah." The dread doubles again. "Should I not be?"

"Didn't you get Skylar's package?"

The pink box glares at me from the corner.

"I did, yeah, but I haven't opened it yet."

A pause.

"Oh. Um. Hey, why don't you pour a glass of wine and
put me on speakerphone before you open it?"

Oh dear god.

"You give me way too much credit, thinking I have wine
here. I'm pretty sure one of these boxes has a twelve-pack of
ramen and maybe an apple?" Though judging by the sickly
sweet smell from the kitchen box, I'm pretty sure it's an ex-
apple at this point. I also have plenty of baking supplies—
flour, sugar, all that—but I have yet to produce anything
edible from them.

"Nic," Will says. "Just . . . open the box, okay?"

Damn it. They'll absolutely stay on the phone until I do
this. Mouth dry, I pull the phone away from my face and tap
the speakerphone icon, then grab the godforsaken box. It
rustles threateningly.

"Okay. I'm doing this."

I set both my phone and the box on the tiny kitchen island and give the box one last wary look. Its sharp corners
and decorative flaps culminate in four interlocking tabs that

form a clover shape, which I struggle to undo neatly before finally tearing one of the tabs off completely. The four flaps pop open to reveal . . .

Rainbow confetti. And glitter.

"Nic? You still there?" Will's garbled voice asks from the counter. Damn my awful cell reception.

"Still here. All I see so far is confetti and glitter. This is the most Skylar thing I've ever seen."

"You have no idea. Keep going."

I sigh. Leave it to Skylar to require us all to plunge our hands into a box of glitter to unearth its contents. It'll be days before I'm rid of the craft herpes. It'll probably end up contaminating my burns in the lab next week. With a scowl, I steel myself and shove my hands into the box, riffling around for whatever is so earth-shattering. My left hand wraps around something cool and glassy, while my right finds something cylindrical.

A tiny bottle of rosé champagne and a candle from one of my favorite Etsy shops. Toasted marshmallow scented.

"Nic?"

I clear my throat. "Champagne and a candle, so far."

"Ooh, she does know you so well. Dare I even ask how many candles are in your collection now?"

I glance over at my dining table, where two empty moving boxes and a veritable hoard of candles sit proudly. The only two boxes I've unpacked so far.

"A few," I say, setting the gifts aside and diving back into the glitter bog. A caffeinated coffee-scented bath bomb (NO GLITTER! says a handwritten sticker slapped on the side. Bit late for that, but bless her for trying), a handful of dark chocolates wrapped in deep red foil, and a tinted Burt's Bees lip balm in the exact color I wear.

Tears prick unexpectedly at the corners of my eyes. She really does still know me, even after two years of me trying my hardest to get some distance.

Then my hands close around the envelope at the bottom. The dread is back tenfold.

With shaking hands, I draw the heavy envelope out and brush the excess glitter and confetti from it, then slide my finger under the shiny silver monogram sticker holding it closed. It gives way with a little pop, revealing a thick stack of card stock. I already know what this is, and I know I can't take it. It has to be a wedding invitation. I'm not ready, not even close to able to deal with this, and—

"Nic, I can hear you panicking over there. Did you read it?"

I shake my head, then remember she can't see me and force words out instead. "No. But I don't have to. I already know what this is. And I can't do this right now."

It could just be a party invitation. Skylar is drama personified. I wouldn't put it past her. But my gut tells me that isn't what this is. How could she have met someone, fallen in love, and gotten engaged all without telling me? Without her mom blowing up my phone about it? Without any of my friends warning me first?

Will's voice goes soft. "I know, babe. But you need to rip this Band-Aid off, okay?"

"I'll rip your Band-Aid off," I grumble, which is incredibly second-grade of me, but I can't bring myself to care. Will, Grace, and I make up the Nerd Half of our friend group. They won't judge me.

I blow out a breath, hold the envelope out in front of me, and rip the pages free.

Thick pearlescent card stock with embossed silver birds stares back at me. Across the top, the word "Farewell!" dances in looping script.

> *You are cordially invited*
> *to celebrate the beginning*
> *of a grand new journey.*
> *SKYLAR CLARK*
> *is moving to Fiji!*
> *The honor of your*
> *presence is requested*
> *for a farewell celebration at*
> *seven o'clock in the evening*
> *on Saturday, August thirtieth*
> *in the year two thousand and twenty-five*
> *at 10 Degrees in Capitol Hill.*
> *Bring your dancing shoes!*

My mind goes perfectly blank.

"Nic?"

"Will," I reply automatically. "Will, what am I looking at?"

"Keep reading," they say, their voice soothing, like they're calming a frightened animal.

I set aside the first paper and read the next.

Skylar's Grand Adventure FAQ

Q: Wait, you're moving to Fiji? Like, permanently?
A: Yes, permanently! I have no plans to return to the
States once I move this August, except for occasional
holiday visits.

Q: What in the hell are you going to do there?
A: It's a SURPRISE, to be revealed at my grand farewell
party! But I *can* tell you that, in addition to The Surprise,
I'll be starting a little farm/short-term rental that is
already so cute in my mind, I can't wait to send you
pictures.

Q: What are you gonna farm?
A: Taro root to start, then coconuts once my trees mature!

Q: Don't you need . . . visas and things? Permits? Written
permission from the pope?
A: Already taken care of, my friends, but thanks for your
concern. ♥

Q: Why does this whole party thing sound like a
wedding?
A: Who knows if I'll ever get married, or if we'll all
be together for a big event ever again? So I may as
well throw myself a ridiculously huge, self-indulgent party
now, while I'm still in the US and everyone can make it!

Q: Are you registering for gifts like this is a wedding?
A: Yes! I know that many people will feel moved to get
a goodbye gift of some kind, but Fiji has super strict
import laws, so I've already registered for a variety of
Fiji-approved necessities, to be sent directly to my new
address.

Q: When are you leaving?
A: The day after the party. Think of it as the honeymoon after the wedding . . . but it's forever! A forever honeymoon! Sounds great, right?

Q: Will you have internet?
A: Not much! I'll be living in a rural area with very poor internet access, though I'll be able to go into town for better service, so we'll still be able to keep in touch!

Q: But . . . aren't you literally a social media influencer? Isn't that like . . . your whole job?
A: It is . . . FOR NOW. I will be deleting my accounts at my farewell party! And, if you're reading this the day it was delivered, I just put in my notice at my radio show gig earlier today! FREEDOM.

Q: Are you really serious?
A: Totally.

Special thanks to Ian for being my test audience for this news and inspiring the elegant wording of these questions.

This is . . . so much to unpack, and I can't right now. I set the FAQ aside without a word and read the third and final card.

My people!
  THIS IS A SECRET.
  For now.
  I plan to make an announcement—a grand announcement, you know me—to all my followers right before I delete my accounts. Since I'm something of a public figure and all, I feel this is the best option for controlling the narrative. Besides, I have surprises in store even for you on my party day. I have to maintain some mystery!

*If you're getting this package, it means you're in my party
fam! Kind of like a wedding party, to continue the metaphor. I
know I could have just put all of this in our group chat, but
this is more fun, don't you think?*

*I can't wait to spend this whole summer planning and
celebrating with you!*

♥♥♥ *Skylar*

More fun, she says.

More. Fun.

As if on cue, my phone chimes its group-chat notification.
I glance at the banner on the lock screen.

GRACE: Ahhhh skylar congrats!!!

GRACE: I mean, obviously we'll miss you, but I love this
for you! 🎉

I let my head fall forward and thunk against the countertop. Grits of glitter embed themselves into the pores of my
forehead, but I can't care right now.

"Nic?" Will says, shrill with worry. "Was that you faint-
ing? Do I need to call 911?"

"I didn't faint, asshole," I say, my voice muffled by the
counter. "I'm trying to meld with this kitchen island. Kitchen
islands don't have to deal with shit like this. I hope you can
accept my new lifestyle choice."

Will makes a sad, sympathetic noise on the other end of
the line. God, I regret ever telling them about my stupid feelings because of stupid vodka. I will never vodka again. They
didn't even do me the courtesy of pretending they'd blacked
out and didn't remember. What kind of friend is that?

My phone chimes again.

WILLOW: yassssssss you are going to be the MOST
fabulous farmer/innkeeper! 🌾🏡
WILLOW: Gandalf and I are so happy for you ♥

Ugh, even as Willow's on the phone with me, being all
consoling, there they are in the group chat, happy and excited.
Just *be mad with me, damn it.* They follow their messages up
with a photo of themself grinning next to their huge, droopy,
wrinkled Neapolitan Mastiff, the aforementioned Gandalf.

"Are you okay, Nic?" they have the gall to ask, just as the
photo loads.

I dash off a brief "congrats" in the group chat and bark a
disbelieving laugh. "No, no, I'm not okay. The girl I've been
in love with since freshman fucking year of college, whose
family has basically adopted me, would rather move to Fiji
forever than be with me. My chance is completely gone, and
her family will probably forget I exist without her here. How
does that even remotely fall into the realm of okay?"

I can't admit it out loud, but half the reason I moved back
was to take one last chance with Skylar. We texted constantly while I was gone, and video-chatted a bunch, because
even when I'm actively trying to get some space from her by
moving across the country, I still can't stay away completely.
I even came back for Christmas with her family in my last
year of grad school because Mama Clark was so furious at me
for missing it the year before. I spent that whole long holiday break with Skylar in what felt like a weird bubble outside of reality. She picked up me at the airport in Seattle, we
grabbed lunch with Willow since they were the only one still
in town, and then Skylar drove me the hour and a half to her
mom's house in Ellensburg, where I stayed for nine very sur-
real days. When I left for grad school, I had completely given

up on anything ever happening with Skylar. But that trip . . .
I don't know. It started to feel different, I thought. And when
I flew back to school, our conversations seemed different, too.

But maybe it was all on my end. Maybe I was seeing what
I wanted to see, just like I did before. Because if there really
was something there and she knew I was coming back to Seattle, would she be moving to Fiji?

My phone chimes like eight more times with new chat
messages, and I flip it face down without reading them. Will
sighs.

"Have you reconsidered just telling her how you feel? With
words? Like an actual twenty-seven-year-old adult?"

The mere thought sends a jolt of adrenaline straight to my
heart. I let out an involuntary squeak, then clear my throat.

"Yeah. Definitely. No, I'm totally gonna. It's part of why
I came back, right? So I will. You know."

"Nic . . ."

"Once the time is right, of course," I blather on. "Gonna
let the wreckage of this whole Fiji thing settle first, but then,
yeah. Totally."

"I know you can do it, honey," they say, followed by an
ominous beat of silence. "But if it's not gonna be tonight,
then you might wanna take some deep, calming breaths and
do a downward dog or something. Because we're meeting
everyone at the bar in about . . . twenty minutes. I'm on my
way to pick you up right now."

"WHAT?" I shout, then wince when my new neighbor
bangs on the wall in protest. "Wait, no—Willow, *why*? I
can't—I'm not—I don't—"

I don't speak in sentences anymore, apparently.

I'm not ready to see her. I need more warning than this.

Especially after this bombshell news. Can't a girl have some time to process?

I let my head drop back onto the countertop. Thunk. Thunk. Thunk.

Willow sighs again. They'll hyperventilate from sighing too much one day.

"At least take off your glasses so you don't break them. I like those new frames. Maybe change into something that doesn't smell like kerosene before I get there."

"Fine," I say, my cheek mashed against the cool stone counter.

"See you in a minute, love."

The phone beeps its call-end tone, and my microscopic new apartment falls silent once again.

I peel my face off the kitchen island and turn to the wall-mounted mirror in the living room. My cheek is red from where it had stuck to the countertop, my forehead is crusted with rainbow glitter, and my mousy brown hair hangs over my pale face in a tangled mess. At least the outside matches the inside. A rainbow disaster.

I take one long look around my mostly bare apartment, then shove the pile of clean laundry off the sofa, faceplant onto a stale Goodwill pillow, and scream.

CHAPTER TWO

KIRA

I can tell something's wrong the second I walk in the door. Grace looks positively ecstatic, which means somewhere in the world, chaos and drama are afoot. She's practically bouncing in her seat, staring at me with shining eyes and lips pursed to keep from exploding.

"What's on fire?" I ask, already done with whatever it is. I finished a twenty-four-hour shift this morning with a structure fire, multiple car accidents, and my favorite: two "something smells funny" calls. And then, of course, instead of coming home and immediately taking a nap like a woman who loves herself, I went to a completely optional continuing education class on the fire risk of abandoned buildings. For *eight hours*. What day is it, even? June . . . eighth? Ninth?

I am the embodiment of tired.

"Come here. Sit down," Grace says, patting the cushion next to her.

"Is someone dead?"

"No, for— Jesus, Kira, just sit down."

With silent resentment, I kick off my flats next to the door, throw my keys in the basket on the counter, and finally flop down on the couch next to Grace and two incredibly bright pink boxes. The TV is on in the background, muted and playing a new K-drama I haven't seen yet. Grace grabs the controller and turns on the subtitles for me, then nudges one of the pink boxes toward me. It's too late for the box, though—I'm already completely distracted by the over-the-top romance playing out silently on screen, exactly what this evening calls for. I can feel myself starting to zone out when Grace pokes me in the thigh with one socked foot.

"What?" I deadpan, letting my head loll in her direction. "Did you buy into yet another subscription box? I already told you to keep your refer-a-friend codes away from me."

She wrinkles her dainty nose. "You brought firehouse stank home again. Gross."

I roll my eyes and offer her a middle finger. I showered at the firehouse and changed into fresh clothes before class. She is one hundred percent imagining things and/or just saying it to give me shit. I move right past it and get to the point. The sooner this is over, the sooner I can cuddle with my pillow and pass out with some Netflix on my phone. I lean forward and snag the pink box with my name on it, eyeing the swooping letters on top with suspicion.

Dear lord, what is Skylar up to now?

"I swear, I love her to death, she's a genius and a sweetheart, my best friend in the world, et cetera," I begin, pulling open the box flaps.

"Co-best friend!" Grace chirps, watching me with a disturbingly hungry expression. If she weren't straight, I'd swear she was coming on to me. But no, this is the look of a shark scenting blood. Or a Grace Ahn scenting anarchy.

"But," I continue, "that girl is the star of her own mental Broadway musical, complete with big dramatic dance numbers."

"Does that make us the backup singers?" Grace asks, whipping out her phone and tapping away.

"Psh, please. I'm the lead dancer. No one wants to hear me sing."

My phone vibrates in my bag, which is still hanging from my shoulder, squashed between me and the arm of the couch. Grumbling at the effort required, I shove my hand inside and fish around blindly until hand and phone are finally reunited. The home screen glows with a notification banner for our group chat.

GRACE: Ahhhh skylar congrats!!!
GRACE: I mean, obviously we'll miss you, but I love this for you! 🎉

I look up at Grace and raise an eyebrow. She blinks sweetly at me, tracing one finger over Skylar's name on the top of her own pink box.

Okay, fine. May as well see what I'm in for. Skylar never does anything halfway.

I carefully separate the slotted tabs and pull the flaps gently back to reveal a box full of confetti and glitter, which I immediately hold out for Grace.

"You do it," I say.

"What?" she protests. "You love glitter!"

"Um, yes, when it's glitter by choice. Or glitter firmly attached to a shirt. This is glitter that I'll be finding in my bunker pants at the firehouse for weeks, and it is not welcome." No one makes lieutenant with glitter in their pants.

Grace folds her arms and shakes her head. "Nope. It's part of the experience. I've already got glitter hands from opening mine. Do it."

I sigh and collect myself as if preparing to enter a burning building, then plunge my hands into the box, pulling out item after item. A miniature bottle of good small-batch whiskey. Nice. A collection of small zip bags of dried fruit, nuts, and seeds, perfect for snacking on shift. My favorite Sephora eyeliner. Star stickers for my planner.

When I get to the envelope at the bottom, Grace lets out an eager squeak.

"Mmm, this is too good, hurry up!" she pleads, practically bursting.

I have never been more worried in my life.

I slice my finger in my haste to get the envelope open, but I'm a damn firefighter; I've had worse. I skim through the silvery embossed pages one at a time, then go back through again, because there is no way I'm reading this right.

Skylar.

Is moving to Fiji.

To start a farm?

Grace makes a screeching sound like a balloon losing air and flaps her hands. "How. Good. Is. This?"

I shake my head, stunned.

"This is the most Skylar thing Skylar has ever done. She's actually out Skylar-ed herself." I shake my head again, like that'll make it any clearer. I get the humor of the situation, I really do, but the humor is quickly being eclipsed by worry.

This is a giant red flag.

I haven't known Skylar as long as the others in our group have, but she and I went through some really serious shit together. She's the closest friend I've ever had in my life, and I've spent the past two years stepping in to save her from herself whenever her grand schemes take a turn for the self-sabotaging. This, though . . . she's already in deep. She must have been sitting on this secret for a while if she already has her visa and business license, and that might be more worrying than anything, since she normally can't keep a secret to save her life.

Right now, she has a decently successful and lucrative enough career as, of all things, a PhD-holding social media relationship counselor, plus a side gig doing a call-in relationship advice show on a local radio station. She has a huge online following, and tons of friends. She knows nothing about farming. She can't cook mac and cheese without one of her neighbors calling 911. She'll be completely jobless if she deletes her social media accounts. She can't swim, and *islands are surrounded by water*. If she goes through with this, she's going to crash and burn. Personally, professionally, and—with her crushing student loan debt—financially. This will ruin her.

This will ruin *me*.

Without Skylar, I'd still be practically living at the firehouse, never seeing a new face outside my weekly grocery run and the bros at work who resent my existence. I'm the one who keeps her grounded when social media expectations start to get to her. She's who I go to when we lose a civilian in a structure fire, or we respond to a particularly bad car accident. I'm her support when the weight of her volunteer counseling clients' struggles gets to be too much. She's the one who's coached me through every promotion I've failed to get. If she leaves, I'll probably *never* get promoted. No one else seems to understand how hard and heavy our careers are at times. I can't do this on my own anymore.

She also gave me a social life and real friends who are more like a surrogate family, especially since my mom moved to Vancouver. Skylar's the main character, the glue of our group. Without her, Willow will forget to leave their house, Marco will drift away and do his own thing, Ian will let his work consume him, and Grace will aggressively cut everyone off before they have the chance to do the same to her. We'll all fall apart, and I'm not ready to let go.

I have to stop this madness.

My phone chimes again, and I glance down to see a flood of excitement from the group, including a message from Nicole, who I haven't met yet but who just moved back to town. A total wild card thrown into the middle of this scenario, and I don't know how to feel about her grand return. Right as I reach the end of the *congrats* train, a new message pops up.

GRACE: Also Kira came home smelling like satan's ball sweat again.

I glare at Gracie over the top of my phone and hammer out a response, putting my feet all over her as I type. She shrieks and wiggles away, slapping my feet with impunity.

KIRA: Hey, I showered at the firehouse! I smell like LUSH Plum Rain and ambition.
GRACE: Alsoalsoalso, Kira says congrats and she's super happy for you and she can't wait to see your plans for the big party.
GRACE: She wants a poofy dress with puff sleeves

SKYLAR: Hahahaha, yeah okay, sure.

SKYLAR: K, I know you're already internally panicking about all of the required social interaction that comes with planning a huge party like this.

SKYLAR: Not to worry dear, most things will be just us.

Yeah, the social events are *definitely* what I'm most worried about in this situation. Not my best friend leaving the country.

SKYLAR: And you will absolutely bag yourself a delicious lover in the gender of your choice while wearing the dress I picked for you. 🔥

SKYLAR: I chose the perfect outfit for each of you according to your own personal styles and I think you're going to thank meeee

And now I have a whole new set of worries. Is it too late to opt out of the "party fam"?

GRACE: SO EXCITED.

IAN: Worried? But excited kinda?

MARCO: I better look fierce bitch

WILLOW: Does Gandalf get a wedding outfit?

WILLOW: <photo of Gandalf with one of Will's bow ties held in front of his neck>

WILLOW: Bow ties are cool

Before I can even think to respond to any of it, a new group chat invitation pops up.

Marco wants you to join: SKYLAR'S EPIC FAREWELL FESTIVITIES 🎉💍🔥

I tap Join and am immediately flooded with new messages.

MARCO: Side chat for planning Skylar things! If this
is like a wedding, then we obviously have to do a
bachelorette party-ish thing, right?
MARCO: But also
MARCO: popcorn.gif
IAN: Lololol god this is going to be SO good
IAN: starwars-AT-AT-walker-crashing.gif
GRACE: 😊
WILLOW: Hey guys, she seems really sincere about this
WILLOW: But yeah, I've got my popcorn ready
GRACE: So obviously we should be throwing Skylar a
"congrats on quitting your job" party too. Tonight.
WILLOW: You just want an excuse for drinks
GRACE: Correct 😈
IAN: Madison?
MARCO: NO
WILLOW: NO
IAN: But the sounders game is onnnnnnn
MARCO: Exactly. Way too crowded, and confused
straight guys always wander in on game nights.
MARCO: No offense
IAN: None taken, I embrace the confused straight guy
label
WILLOW: Crescent, obviously, why are we still talking?
GRACE: CRESCENT YES! 9ish?
MARCO: I'll kidnap Skylar. Be there in 20. NO
KARAOKE, GRACE, I MEAN IT.
GRACE: 😇
WILLOW: Okay I'll go pick up Nic. I know you're

not looking at this chat right now bb but we're all so excited to see you too! Welcome home!

IAN: The whole gang's back together. Seattle is not ready

I'm not ready. But whether I eventually come up with a way to talk sense into Skylar or not, there's obviously no getting out of this party tonight, no matter how tired I am. No matter how much this whole Skylar announcement has me feeling totally flat and dazed. Do I even believe this? If she's serious, do I really think I can change her mind?

With a groan, I haul myself up off the couch, leaving my purse half wedged into the couch cushions, and stagger down the hall.

"What are you doing?" Gracie shouts after me. "We have to go!"

"Chill it out, East Coast, we'll get there. Since you claim I reek of firehouse, I'm gonna go de-stink-ify myself so you can't give me any more shit."

I rip my (perfectly fresh-smelling, thank you) shirt off over my head and stalk into the bathroom, fully intending to take my damn time and enjoy my shower. Skylar and Marco will debate outfit choices for an hour and be fashionably late anyway. As soon as the water is warm, I stuff my close-cropped red curls into a shower cap and climb in, yanking our inexplicably giraffe-themed shower curtain closed. Not five seconds later, the bathroom door cracks open, and Grace pokes her head in.

"What are you gonna wear?" she asks.

The warm water rains over my skin, and I sigh. Heaven. I crank it up even hotter.

"Gracie, I spend my days either in uniform or bunker gear. I fully intend to show as much skin as possible tonight."

"Your purple halter?"

I care exactly zero. Let me cook myself in peace. "Sure, let's go with that."

"Yesssss," she hisses, and slams the door behind her.

I close my eyes and tip my head back, breathing in the billowing steam.

I'll leave Skylar be tonight, let her have this for a bit. It needs to stop eventually, though. Maybe I'll talk to her about it tomorrow.

I can at least enjoy my night off first.

CHAPTER THREE

NIC

I haven't been to the Crescent Lounge since the night before I left for grad school two years ago. That night is a blur (the absolute last time I drank tequila), and I'm honestly glad for it. I'm afraid if I remembered, I'd see a night of me throwing myself at Skylar, occasionally weeping into my shot glass, and making Marco hug me every five minutes because he's terrible at staying in contact and I knew I'd barely talk to him once I left.

I was a wreck the next morning, and not just because of the brutal hangover.

Now, seeing the rainbow glow backlighting the wall of liquor bottles, the string lights, the two guys crooning terrible karaoke, trashed way too early in the night . . . it feels like home. For the first time since I got off the plane, I really feel like I'm back. Then a gruff voice booms from halfway down the bar.

"Nicole Fucking Wells, get the fuck over here!"

An uncontrollable grin hijacks my face. *Now* I'm back.

"Ian, you giant bear of a man, I have missed you the *worst*," I say as he wraps his enormous arms around me.

"Not that kind of bear, folks," he says, holding a hand up for clarification, then hoisting me up off the floor with the force of his hug.

See, this I can do. Ian and I are simple. I can always rely on him to chill me out, and he can always rely on me to keep him from having that last shot that'll make him do things in public he'll regret. Symbiosis at its finest.

"How did the little shitters do at graduation?" I ask, smiling even harder at the confused reaction to the nickname on the bartender's face.

Ian groans and finally lets me go so he can gesture dramatically. "Three years into this job and I still don't understand why we have preschool graduations. Purely designed for my personal torture, I swear. This year's group did okay, minimal crying and pissing, but new year, new crop of shitters. It's a living. At least there's fewer of them in the summer semester."

He turns to order a drink, and I stifle a grin behind his back. He adores his job and those kids, but I suppose being both a burly, beer-brewing woodsman hipster and an early learning specialist is a delicate balance. I swipe my rum and Coke off the bar for a long sip, my eyes drifting to the entrance every few seconds. Still no Skylar.

Willow breaks my staring contest with the door by flopping down on the stool beside me, kicking their sneakered feet and sucking down some kind of dark beer.

"Defense beer?" I ask.

They nod, swallow, and set their pint glass down. "Beer before liquor, never sicker. I couldn't *possibly* do shots now."

They prop flat hands under their chin and tip their head to the side in an angelic pose, short purple-black hair flopping into their eyes, and I have to laugh. The laugh catches in my throat, though, when the door swings open and over Will's shoulder, I see *her.*

Skylar.

She's here.

Her appearance shouldn't shock me. We video-chatted all the time while I was gone, and it's not like grad school kept me from stalking her Instagram accounts, both public and private. I even saw her in person at Christmas six months ago. But seeing her now, knowing that I'm back for good, not just passing through . . . it's like a punch to the gut, leaving me breathless, speechless, wide-eyed, and still. She's laughing as she walks in, honey-brown hair whirling as she turns to give Marco sass over something. He gives her a gentle shove, and she stumbles fully into the bar, her long white dress fluttering around her in the perfect breezy, bohemian style.

She turns away from Marco and scans the bar, smiling as she finds our group . . . then me.

She shrieks.

"NIC KNACK!"

Then she's running, and in my arms, and I guess she's still using that $40 lavender shampoo. With my nose in her hair, it's all I can smell. My eyes fill with tears because god, it's so good to see her again—*so good*—but it *hurts.* I pull her closer, drinking in that uniquely Skylar energy that pours off her at all times, and she rocks me back and forth—almost like she ached for me as much as I did for her.

"Hey, Sky," I whisper.

She squeezes me tight one more time, then pulls back to cup my face in her hands.

"I have missed you *so* much," she says, planting a giant smacking kiss on my blushing cheek. "How in the world did you manage to sneak back into Seattle without me knowing immediately? My mother is going to be *furious*. I hope you're ready."

Hmm, almost like the sneaking was intentional. What a mystery.

"Just wanted to get settled. You know I need quiet sometimes," I say, putting on my best smile for her. "But I'm back now."

She beams. "You're back. And the gang's all here!" she shouts, finally letting me go so she can scan the group.

"Wait," she says, planting her hands on her hips. "Where are Kira and Gracie?"

"Heeeere!" Grace's voice calls from the entryway, where she and a tall white girl who must be Kira are shrugging out of their jackets. Skylar screeches again and darts over to meet them, leaping up on Kira and wrapping all four limbs around her. Something ugly bares its teeth in my chest at the sight—Skylar greeting her new best friend. My replacement.

Skylar slings an arm around both Grace and Kira as they walk back to the group. By the time they reach us, Skylar has her head bent to Kira's ear, talking at lightning speed about some work situation.

". . . and so I told her no, obviously I can't take on your son's case when you and I have slept together before, even if it's pro bono. The money is not the issue. Is this not obvious?"

"And didn't you already tell her this, like, three months ago?" Kira asks.

"YES. You see my frustration."

"Of course I do." Kira makes a pouty face and bops her on the nose with one finger, a guaranteed Skylar-diffuser.

Sure enough, Skylar melts into a smile and whirls away to demand a drink from the bartender. Well, at least if I have to be replaced, it's by someone who knows how to handle Skylar well. She seems happy. That's what's important, right?

Marco's hand lands on my shoulder, jolting me out of my spiral.

"Welcome back, my child," he says, knocking his hip against mine. "You good?"

Does he know? Am I that obvious? Who am I kidding, everyone probably knows. I bump his hip right back and wind an arm around his narrow waist. "I'm good. Missed you."

"Same, darling."

We rest our heads together for a moment, and that's it. Slotted back together, like no time has passed. The shorter hair is the only giveaway. He's always had the most gorgeously soft and shiny black hair, worn on the longer side, a beautiful complement to his bronze-brown skin. I bet he deliberately didn't post a photo of his new cut to Instagram so I would be surprised and shower him with compliments. Which I do, of course.

Marco sips down his Manhattan at a frightening rate and tells me in vague terms all about some guy he's having regular Sunday brunch dates with—*but* they are *not* dates and how dare I suggest otherwise. I say supportive things in all the right places, mentally preparing my I-told-you-so for when he inevitably gets together with this guy. Marco is *not* known for repeated cozy get-togethers with men he isn't seriously interested in. Eventually, Ian bellows Marco's name and gives him some kind of signal. Marco smiles down at me and squeezes my elbow, then moves to throw an arm around Skylar.

"Ladies, enbies, and gentlebitches, may I have your attention please?" he begins with a grand sweep of his mostly empty drink. "We are here tonight to celebrate Skylar's . . ."

He pauses, notices that several of the Crescent Lounge's other customers are listening in and adjusts his words accordingly.

". . . uh, thing." He leans in close, and we all follow suit. "I mean, this is *real*, right? This is really, truly, one thousand percent not just a super long vacation? Or a quarter-life crisis?"

I bite my lip hard, waiting for what feels like an actual eternity until Skylar bursts into a wide grin.

"Oh, you," she says, swatting Marco on the arm. My heart leaps. Is it all a joke? Was the whole thing just a game to get us worked up?

Then Skylar's smile shifts to one I know from college. It's her "big dreams and life plans" smile.

"Of course it's real! Plane tickets bought, property rented, visa acquired, and my passport photo is *so* cute. And just six more weeks to go at the radio station, so cheers to that!" Skylar says, hoisting her drink.

A beat of silence, then everyone lifts their drink with a cheer while I quietly die inside.

"Skylar's doing the thing!" Marco declares triumphantly.

"*Yeah* she is," Grace cuts in with a lewd gesture.

"Oi, let's respect the monk-like celibacy Skylar is destined for, okay?" Ian says.

Willow snorts. "I think her vibrator collection might have something to say about that."

"Hey, what me and my toy box get up to in the privacy of my own home is none of your business, here *or* in Fiji," Skylar says primly, sipping her violently pink drink through a dainty straw.

Kira barks a laugh. "It is when you insist on spilling the details in our group chat."

"Listen, I just wanted to personally recommend a product I believe in!"

Grace arches an eyebrow. "Along with your affiliate code."

"*Besides,*" Skylar continues, "you do know there are women in Fiji, right?"

"But it takes *time,*" Ian says with the air of someone imparting sincere wisdom. "Establishing yourself in a new place, finding your people—"

"Um, excuse me, gentlebitches, is this your speech?" Marco says. "No. Thank you."

I lift a hand to my mouth to stifle a laugh, then stop just in time to avoid wiping the remnants of Skylar's glitter ambush all over my face. Ugh. A sparkle catches my eye in Kira's direction, and Ian's, and sure enough, every single one of us has some amount of glitter we couldn't successfully wash from our hands before coming here. Everyone, of course, except for Skylar . . . and Marco?

"Wait, wait, wait," I interrupt, zeroing in on Marco's hands. "How in the hell are your hands not covered in glitter?"

"Hey, yeah," Grace says, glitter visible in the straight black hair of her ponytail. "The rest of us look like we jacked off a unicorn."

"Collectively, or individually?" Kira muses.

Marco raises his glass in a toast. "Gloves, duh."

The rest of us groan.

Ian wipes his glitter hands off on his jeans, somehow leaving both his hands and his jeans looking more sparkly. "Look, not all of us are nurses who creepily have latex gloves at home."

"Who said they had anything to do with my day job?" Marco shot back with an eyebrow waggle.

The group groan returns. Marco preens, then waves a "fuck it" hand and lifts his drink toward Skylar.

"Oh, what-the-fuck-ever, never mind. Congrats babe, we love you, now let's get drunk."

"Hear, hear!" we shout, glasses clinking all around until every single one has been drained dry. Marco and his soon-to-be-nurse-practitioner salary buys us another round (Willow stares despondently into the shot glass he presses into their hand—so much for that defense beer), and we settle into our usual bar routine.

Only, I don't seem to quite fit like I used to. I still love them, and they still love me, but it's like I've come back shaped differently, my edges not quite matching up with the puzzle anymore. Every time I open my mouth to jump into the conversation, I hesitate. I hover next to Will for the next fifteen minutes, and they rub my back soothingly after every single shot they down.

"It's all gonna be okay. We missed you. Things'll settle."

I shrug and sip my rum and Coke so I won't have to reply, watching the rainbow lights behind the bar shift over Skylar's hair as she sincerely thanks the bartender for putting up with us all. Then she turns her sun-bright smile on me and I quickly avert my eyes, feeling my cheeks grow hot at having been caught staring. Skylar, it seems, either didn't notice or didn't care, because she lunges forward, practically tackling me.

"Oh my god, Nic, you haven't actually met Kira yet! Like, *met* met, proper introduction like real adults and shit!" There's no time to protest. She drags me by the wrist to where Kira leans up against the bar, chatting with Grace, who immediately vanishes like smoke in the wind. Skylar drops my wrist and gestures to Kira with a grand flourish.

"This is Kira!" she says, grinning proudly like Kira is her very own child who just made the honor roll. Kira shifts uncomfortably and offers up a half smile.

"Ah, yes, Satan's ball sweat, right?" I say. "Nice to meet you."

Kira's face falls into something more genuine: a glare. "I am going to *kill* Grace," she said.

Skylar claps her hands three times in rapid succession.

"Oh, this is so perfect! Okay, so *you*," she says, pointing to me, "light things on fire for a living, and *you*—" she points to Kira "—put them out for a living. Discuss!"

She drifts backward into the crowd, waving her hands in front of her like a witch casting a spell, leaving me alone with Kira. She purses her lips at Skylar's retreating form, then glances over at me with wicked humor in the quirk of her mouth.

"I imagine she's like being hit by a bus when you've been away for a while," she says, holding in a laugh. It's enough to shake me out of my daze, and I huff a small chuckle in response.

"You have no idea," I say, resisting the urge to stare pathetically after Skylar and taking in the girl in front of me instead. I wouldn't necessarily guess *firefighter* at first glance, though her vibrant purple halter top reveals a long, graceful neck and strong, toned shoulders and arms all lightly dusted with freckles. She's not a bodybuilder or anything, but you can tell she uses those arms a lot and keeps in shape for a reason. It is . . . *very* attractive. (Yes, I will admit to being one of those people who has spent hours watching videos of that lumberjack lesbian chopping wood.) Her red curls are cropped close on top and shaved on the sides, leaving all the room for her incredible cheekbones and killer eyeliner. Stylish jeans and sensible-but-adorable flats complete her look. She's gorgeous. Normally, I'm happy to channel the casual nerd style, but Kira makes me feel totally underdressed in my long-sleeve V-neck T-shirt, slouchy jeans, and messy ponytail.

"So, yeah, not to be rude but, like . . . do I need to call the police or get some backup or something?"

I yank my gaze to her face. "I'm sorry, what?"

Kira looks at me sidelong. "I mean, you set fires for a living. Are you some kind of arsonist? Cleanup crew for the mob? A hit woman specializing in fire?"

I bust out laughing in spite of my dour mood.

"Oh my god, no, I'm a *scientist*. A chemist and physicist. I study fire behavior. We burn and blow things up in controlled lab environments only, I promise."

She raises a skeptical eyebrow, so I pull out my phone and flip to a video taken a few hours earlier of me and my new colleagues doing a burn trial. We built a scale model of a building constructed using new materials produced by one of the professors to evaluate their fire-resistant rating claims. It was my first time on a project as lab coordinator since finishing orientation, and as a treat, the professor who ordered the test gave us permission to test a new "probably explosive" chemical on what was left of the model when we finished.

We tried to be somber, we really did, but sometimes it's hard to be chill in our lab.

"Watch this," I say, and hit Play.

On-screen, one of my colleagues adjusts one small thing on the model, then darts out of the shot. A shout of "CLEAR!" echoes from behind the camera, and we all count down together. "Three . . . two . . . one . . ."

A huge BANG distorts the audio, followed by assorted cheering and cackling laughter as the model explodes into a beautifully colored fireball, practically liquefying the model. My own voice, louder because I was the one holding the phone, shouts, "Yeeeesssss, burn! Ooh, not so fire-resistant after all, Dr. Murray."

In hindsight, maybe this wasn't the best video to convince her of my sanity and non-danger to society.

Kira covers her eyes. "Please tell me you have a thousand fire extinguishers behind the camera. Or in-house firefighters. Or something."

I stash my phone in my back pocket and wave her comment away. "We're scientists who study fire. We've all been trained in basic fire suppression since undergrad. Hell, some of us invent new fire suppression techniques; I did work on one as part of my master's thesis. Besides, the whole room is rigged with a super fancy system. It's all fine, promise."

Kira peeks out from between her fingers with a skeptical look. "If you say so, pyro."

I grin. "Come by the lab sometime and I'll show you."

Pyro indeed. She has no idea.

She shakes her head (not reassured of my sanity at all, oh well) and changes the subject.

"Anywaaay . . . what do you think of Skylar's whole plan?" she says offhand, like she's asking about the weather. My interest piques. Perfect opportunity to feel her out, see if I might have an ally in my anti-Fiji cause.

I cock my head and study Kira for a moment. "If you're her new best friend, you've probably had to pull Skylar out of the metaphorical fire a few times, right?"

She nods vigorously. "Seems like every other day, she's trying to physically or emotionally walk into traffic. Not that she doesn't return the favor *all the time*. Let's be real. I too, am an out and proud mess—mentally speaking, at least. But it's always something. She's got a new business idea, or a new 'project' to sink all her money into, or whatever else. Am I right?"

A surprised laugh bursts out of me because her words are *so* on point. That's exactly what it's like. I cast a quick glance at the others, then guide Kira a bit further away with a gentle hand on her elbow.

"Do you think this is one of those times?" I ask.

She smiles faintly, some of the tension melting from her features, and glances over her shoulder to make sure the others are a safe distance away. "Yes. Thank god there's another sane human in this group."

"Right?" I say, incredulous. "I know everyone is used to egging her on, just letting her do her, and being there to take her out for drinks and hugs when it all blows up . . . but isn't this a little different? It won't be an easy bounceback. I wonder if they somehow think she won't go through with it."

"Oh, she'll do it," Kira says.

I nod. "One hundred percent, this is happening. She is all-or-nothing. Can you imagine what's going to happen when her followers find out she's planning to delete her accounts?"

"Ugh, yes, she's going to get eviscerated online. I can already picture the clickbait-y headlines. Not to mention, she knows *nothing* about farming, or being a vacation rental host, or *swimming*, for god's sake—"

I lay one hand on Kira's arm and another over my heart. "Okay, stop, that's enough. I'm about to have a panic attack *for* her."

I take a moment and breathe, then realize I'm still touching Kira and snatch my hand back, the warmth of her skin lingering on my fingertips. "All good points though, yeah. And do you know about her student loan debt?"

"Please, I have nightmares about it, and it's not even mine. And you know how she is . . ."

"Go big or go home," we say in unison, then break into snickering laughter again. It's nice, actually—this is the most I've laughed since coming home.

"So, we're gonna do this, right? Stop this scheme of hers? Or at least talk to her about it?" Kira asks, leaning in conspiratorially.

"We have to," I agree. "It's our sworn duty, is it not?"

She grins wickedly and holds out a hand. I take it, and she shakes it firmly. "Okay, Legolas, your oath be sworn. This move shall not go forth!"

"I'm really more of a Samwise," I say, but at least she knows what *Lord of the Rings* is, theoretically?

She raises an eyebrow. "What, no shieldmaiden Éowyn for you?"

"Ah, I would never presume such greatness," I say, blushing. "But she was my first major girl crush. Pretty sure I'm gay because of her."

"Mmm, when I was a baby bi, I was more of an Arwen girl," Kira says, and our eyes meet for a brief moment before sliding away to look anywhere but at each other.

Skylar saves us from our mutual awkwardness by throwing herself between us, an arm around each of our necks, and a dribble of her fresh vodka soda down my cleavage. It's gonna be a sloppy kind of night, I can already tell. I raise my eyebrows at Kira over Skylar's head, and she gives me a tiny salute and mouths *reporting for duty*. My shoulders shake with silent laughter as I rest my head against Skylar's.

"Sky, can we ask you something?" Kira says once Skylar

and I separate. Skylar gestures expansively, and I barely dodge the hand that flails dangerously close to my face.

"By all means! Anything for my two besties!"

Kira and I stare at each other for a second, silently debating who will be the one to ask her. I finally step up, since Kira broke the ice and all.

"We were just wondering . . . *why*? You know, the whole Fiji thing . . . We're just . . ."

I trail off, and Kira swoops in.

"We're concerned, is all," she says. "You don't really like people in your space. Are you sure a rental property is gonna work out?"

"And the farm," I add. "I didn't know you . . . knew how to grow things?"

That sounds bad. Redirect, quick.

"But mostly, we're worried about the money, right?" I say, shooting Kira a quick *save me* glance.

"Yes, the money," she agrees. "If you delete your social media accounts, then you won't have any income from sponsors or ads, right? Do you have a job lined up in Fiji already?"

The last bit had a pleading, hopeful edge. Naive hope. Skylar leans in close, waggling her eyebrows conspiratorially.

"You wanna know?" she says.

We both nod, eyes wide, barely breathing.

"Well . . ." Skylar says, then snorts and bursts into half-drunk giggles. "Too bad! It's a surprise, remember? I'll announce all my grand plans at the party. Look at you two, trying to spoil all my fun."

The words "grand plans" seem to land as badly with Kira as they do with me. Skylar winks and steps back like she's about to leave, and I mentally scramble for something else to add.

"Wait, though!" I shout, then lower my voice with a wince. "Have you considered just . . . not deleting your accounts, at least? You don't have to use them or anything, but they'll still be there. Just in case, you know?"

Not that being a social media influencer is the most stable of careers, but it *is* a career, and her having the option open would at least help me sleep slightly better. Skylar shakes her head, though.

"Nope. Done deal. Deleting forever. Much healthier for me. Besides, with such terrible internet access at my house in Fiji, I'd never be able to use them anyway."

Kira seems to crumple in on herself, and I feel myself doing the same. Skylar always does this, puts up a big brick wall for all of us to throw ourselves against while she does something she knows we won't like. I can't just let it go, though. I don't care how pathetic it makes me—if I have to just straight-up ask, I'll ask.

"What if we asked you to stay?" I force out past the herd of elephants making a home inside my chest.

"Or begged," Kira added. "I *will* beg if it'll help."

Skylar's expression softens.

"My sweet friends," she says, setting her drink on a nearby table so she can wrap both arms around our necks. "I will miss you so, so much. I know it'll be weird and hard. But you showed me, Nic—we can still be the closest of friends, even if we don't live in each other's pockets twenty-four seven."

My heart drops straight through the floor. Is this *my* fault? By leaving for grad school, I somehow gave her the idea to do this? Skylar squeezes us both one more time, then steps back with a confident smile.

"I'm doing this. I promise, all will be revealed in time," she says, waggling her fingers like a magician. "Until then, have a little faith!" She raises her glass to us with a wink. "*And* have fun."

With that, she whirls around and practically floats through the crowd toward the karaoke rig. Kira and I share an anguished look.

"I'm so sorry," I babble. "I never imagined that me going to grad school would turn into . . . into . . . *this*!"

Kira shakes her head and waves down the bartender for more drinks. "It's not your fault. She would have come up with this plan no matter what. We'll just have to find another way to convince her."

I nod solemnly.

"Shenanigans?"

"Shenanigans," she agrees. "Not gonna lie, though—I'm scared shitless. Last time she had a secret she didn't want to tell anyone, it was that she'd spent all her savings launching a new skin care line to promote on her socials. She closed the business like six months later when she got bored."

I wince at the memory. "And before that, it was her 'mental wellness subscription service' that she took a bunch of orders for, then had to cancel because she had no idea what she was doing."

"Then there's the sheer number of unused web domains she has reserved and pays to renew each year for all her brilliant blog/website ideas."

"And the room in her mom's house that's packed with boxes of craft supplies from when she tried to start an Etsy shop."

The fresh drinks arrive, and we both latch onto them with the fervor of parched desert travelers. In one corner of the bar, a bright riff of '80s synths blasts from the speakers. Throughout the bar, heads swivel to catch Marco and Grace flailing in a semi-coordinated dance to . . . Billy Joel?

"Really?" Kira says, then shouts it for them both to hear. "Really, bitches?"

Their matching grins are devilish and charming as they point to Skylar, who shrugs innocently in front of the karaoke rig, and Marco and Grace launch into the first verse in shouted unison. Guess Marco's earlier "no karaoke" commandment has been voided by vodka. In front of the stage, Willow and Ian lock arms and spin in a mad circle. Skylar appears beside us at the bar and slams her drink down on the countertop, then snatches Kira's and my drinks to do the same. Before I can blink, we've both been dragged over to the karaoke corner, where Skylar plants herself between us, throws her arms up, and dances her heart out.

And what else can I do? I slide my hands to Skylar's waist, Kira throws her arms around Skylar's neck, and the three of us shout along with the chorus of "We Didn't Start the Fire" by Billy Joel.

It's everything I've missed. Skylar, warm and laughing in front of me, my hands on her body like a combustion reaction, my friends all around me, drink, and music, and so many hours left ahead of us tonight.

Skylar tips her head back during the next verse, so it rests briefly on my shoulder.

"Welcome home, Nic Knack," she says, just loud enough for me to hear.

I press a kiss to her temple and dance closer, a weight lifting from my chest as I meet Kira's gaze.

We'll stop this. It'll take time, and we'll have to be careful—strategic—but we'll get her to call off this mad plan one way or another.

And when the time is right, I'll tell Skylar exactly why it is I'm so desperate for her to stay.

CHAPTER FOUR

KIRA

My boobs are vibrating.

Even when I'm ninety percent asleep, my brain manages to comprehend there's something wrong about this scenario. Boobs do not naturally vibrate of their own accord. I peel one eye open, glance down . . . and find my phone face down on my sternum, right where I probably dropped it when I fell sleep.

Ah, normal after all. It's a fairly regular occurrence for my boobs to be gently serenaded to sleep by the dulcet tones of some random sitcom or documentary. All my friends and family know not to bother me the morning after a shift, though, so what the hell? If this is some couple trolling through bi women on Tinder for a third (even though my profile explicitly says I'm not looking for that), I will personally track these humans down and spray them in the face with a fire hose.

I lift the phone and the screen comes to life, displaying a string of texts:

NICOLE: Our first challenge has arisen!
NICOLE: Skylar wants me to go cake tasting with her in two days. She's really leaning into the whole wedding metaphor here.
NICOLE: AND she wants to do it at Shelly's Bakery where the cheapest cake is like A MILLION DOLLARS
NICOLE: Help meeeeeee what do I DO? Come with us??

The corner of my mouth tugs up into a smile, then remembers it's morning and falls back down. I normally nap for at *least* three hours after getting off work at 8:00 a.m., but duty calls, I guess. Texting feels like so much effort, though, so I tap her name and hit the Call button, hoping she'll forgive me for this sin. It rings four times, and I'm about to hang up when the call suddenly connects, followed by a sudden BANG. I jerk away from the phone, but there's a scuffle, then Nic's voice.

"I'm so sorry, that was terrible timing," she says, sounding slightly out of breath.

"What the hell *was* that?" I ask, my heart still in alarm mode.

She laughs helplessly. "I'm at work. I swear, not every day is fire and explosions. Sometimes it's a lot of reading and meetings and spreadsheets and other science-y stuff."

"Whatever you say, pyro." I'm picturing her in a white lab coat, cheeks dusted with soot, hair in a tangled mess, standing next to one of those *Looney Tunes*–style detonators. I get to the point to keep from laughing and having to explain. "So, your cake dilemma. I can't come with you. I work that day. I'm twenty-four hours on, forty-eight hours off."

Nic half groans/half sobs her displeasure. Someone in the background shouts something at her—I think I catch the word *extinguisher*? I really hope she's not about to burn up—but Nic says something unintelligible back before moving to a quieter room.

"Sorry about that," she says. "But honestly, who needs saving more? Me, trapped in a boutique cake shop for rich people with a Skylar on a mission, or people with their cat stuck up a tree or whatever?"

I do laugh this time.

"Uh, the people whose buildings are on fire? Obviously?"

"Yeah, but you had to think about it for half a second, didn't you?"

Fair point. I stretch luxuriously, legs sliding against the deliciously smooth sheets. Getting up is hard. Getting up is a terrible idea.

Getting up is inevitable, isn't it?

I sigh.

"Okay, look," I say. "When's your lunch break? I was thinking we should get together and make a plan. Define our goals, brainstorm some possible tactics, decide on a course of action—"

"Wow," Nic interrupts. "I didn't realize a person could actually *sound* like a neatly tabbed binder and a fresh pack of highlighters personified."

I'm silent for a second, caught off guard—is that a good thing or a bad thing?—until Nic breaks out into frankly adorable giggles.

"I kind of love it," she says. "If it were up to me, we'd probably fumble around for three months with some half-formed idea of what to do, then chicken out and curl into a ball with a bottle of coconut rum."

Now *I'm* laughing too, because the image she paints is so vivid. From what the others have told me about her, Nic has always been good at reacting to Skylar's (many) needs, but when it comes to preemptive strikes, it takes her too long to forcibly remove her head from the clouds and gain the courage to step up. Skylar waits for no one. In fact, now that I think about it, they're quite similar—both geniuses, incredibly knowledgeable and methodical in their chosen fields, but disaster kids at everything else. It's a good thing the two of them never dated, because the planet wouldn't survive the chaos. I wipe my eyes and finally sit up in bed, feeling a bit more energized.

"I'll forgive you for the coconut rum, because I hate to judge people I've just met too harshly, but item one on our list might have to involve whiskey."

"Blegh."

I clutch my hand over my heart in mock agony, even though she can't see me.

"You hurt me right in my *soul*. If your workplace didn't involve so much fire and explosions, I'd bring you a thermos of whiskey for lunch, just to prove how wrong you are."

"But it would be a *Lord of the Rings* thermos, right?"

"If it would get you to drink something not routinely puked up by college freshman, then yes, I would bring you a hobbit thermos."

"We're going to get along just fine."

I smile in spite of myself and roll out of bed with a decadent stretch, pressing the phone to my ear with one hand and reaching for the sky with the other.

"So, you've successfully gotten me out of bed—"

"Not my typical goal with girls," Nic quips, then sputters, frantically backpedaling. "I mean, not that I— I'm not trying to—"

I bust out laughing, true and loud this time, even as my cheeks grow hot. My Skylar laugh, Grace calls it. "Oh my god, chill, it's okay. I was sleeping. I am no longer sleeping. Lunch meeting? Yes? Time?"

"Right, right. Uh, let's say twelve thirty? That'll give me time to order food, clean up, and get the grad students going on their next project."

And that'll give me time to pull up a yoga video on YouTube and do one of my readings for the FEMA National Fire Academy course I'm working on. Once I finish this certificate, my résumé will be so incredible, they'll have no choice but to promote me. I can make the most of this unfortunate early wake-up call.

"Twelve thirty, you got it," I say. "See you soon."

"I'll text you the address. Bring your highlighters, legal pads, binders, Post-it flags—"

"—and a hobbit thermos of whiskey. Byeee."

I hang up the phone and stand there for a minute, trying to pinpoint why I feel so weird.

Then I realize: I'm grinning from ear to ear.

The ever-present dread of the whole situation feels a little lighter now. Sure, my life and career will still be doomed if Skylar leaves, but there's hope now. I have an ally. We're going to save the day.

This might actually be fun.

WHEN I ARRIVE, I REALIZE I'VE MADE A RARE error in planning. The Pacton Laboratory Complex is in a remote corner of the sprawling university campus with seem-ingly endless parking lots blocked off by security gates and guards standing at every entrance. I have no idea where to go. I must look suspicious as hell, because a guard finally flags me down and motions for me to roll down my window. It's a manual crank (this car is twenty-five years old and count-ing, a gift from my dad I refuse to get rid of), and it always sticks about two thirds of the way down.

"Sorry, that's as far as it goes," I say with a shrug, but the guard gives me the side eye.

"You lost?" he asks, all friendly smiles, but with an edge to his voice.

"Completely," I admit. "I'm meeting a friend for lunch. She works in the Miller Building, which is . . . somewhere?"

"She's a pyro?" he asks, eyebrow raised. "Good luck with that."

"Well, I'm a firefighter. If anyone can handle her, it should be me, right?"

I can see the moment the words land in the sludgy tar pit of his brain and start sinking down.

"Wait, *you're* a firefighter? You sure?"

Oh my god, am I sure of my own career? Fucking hell. Why always *this* from random dudes?

"Uh, yeah, pretty damn sure I know where those pay-checks in my bank came from," I say, my tone clipped. "The Miller Building?"

The skeptical tilt of his eyebrows lingers as he steps back and points.

"Two buildings down, turn left, then park in the lot on your right. The building has about a hundred fire hydrants out front, can't miss it."

Well, that's something of a relief.

"Thanks for your help. Have a nice day."

Douche.

The last bit is silent only because my mama raised me right, and I'm not entirely certain she can't twist my ear long-distance from Vancouver. The guy says something else, but I ignore him out of self-preservation and drive to the correct building. My car is just starting to overheat as I pull into the lot and beg the car to shift into Park. It begrudgingly agrees with an unhappy clunk, and I shut the engine off just as a fig-ure in white comes dashing out the front. The guard stand-ing watch there dives to one side to avoid being hit by the door as the figure—Nic—jumps up and down, waving her arms as I climb out.

"I'm so sorry!" she calls, then jogs over to my car. "I should have given you directions. I hope the guards didn't bother you much. I'm almost done. You can come on up. Oh, did you bring your ID? You'll need to sign in."

"What are you *wearing*?" I ask as I follow her back to the building. It looks like a chef's coat, high-necked and buttoned over the left breast, but with elastic at the wrists to pinch the sleeves closed over blue gloves.

She looks down at herself, then jumps as if startled.

"Oh, right. Let me finish up in the lab and we can eat. Sorry, James," she says with a weak smile for the guard, then scans a badge and pulls the door open for me. I follow her inside, sign in, and get my little visitor name badge, then follow Nic down hallways that contain increasingly more worrying signs. Eye wash stations, showers, and fire extinguishers are more common than doors in this building. Finally, Nic turns to me, her hand on the knob of a door with a red light next to it. She holds up a finger, and we wait . . . until, suddenly, there's a shout, a "WHOO!", and the light next to the door changes to green. Nic scans her badge and pulls the door open.

"Fire?" she shouts.

"No fire," someone calls back.

"Hose on deck!" is her response. Then she steps back to allow me past. Am I the hose? I shake my head. Just go with it.

My eyes are used to the fire station, where things are clean but worn. Well used, but well cared for. Here, everything is bright white, stainless steel or glass, with fluorescent lights shining off every surface. Everything is precisely in place, which . . . is logical I guess? But somehow, I wasn't expecting it. Though if there's any room in the world I want to be in pristine order, it's a room full of flammable shit.

"Wow," I say, taking it all in. "This is . . . shiny. What are you working on?"

Nic lights up. "I'll show you!"

She beckons me toward a far corner of the lab, past a guy in a giant face shield that makes me very nervous. Should *I* be wearing a face shield? Nic snatches something from the back counter, then thrusts it into my hands. I nearly drop it, half expecting it to be covered in corrosive acid or something, but stop myself at the last second. And stare.

"What am I holding?" I ask, turning the thing—a light-weight flap of bright yellow rubbery fabric—over in my hands.

Nic beams. "It's a new material we're testing here. It was originally developed for something totally different in the culinary industry, but after meeting you last night, it occurred to me that, with some adjustments, it might have applications in firefighting."

My heart does a funny thing in my chest, a sort of warm, pulsing skip. I lug around tons of gear every day, but I've never really thought about where it comes from, or the people who might be working to make us safer. I look from the scrap of material to Nic and back again.

"Like, you could make new bunker gear out of this?"

"Sure!" she says. "It would need extensive testing and adjustment, of course; it's just a preliminary idea. It might also be good for hosing, depending on . . ."

And she totally loses me. I know a lot about fire, but she's talking molecular-level shit here. I knew in the back of my brain she had to be pretty smart, being a scientist and all— but mentally, I'm putting this white-coated chemist together with the girl in the floppy long sleeves who spilled half a rum and Coke on Ian's beard a few nights ago. The whole, I admit, is much more intriguing. Skylar is exactly this kind of nerd sometimes, when it comes to the way human brains and thoughts work, and I can totally see why they were best friends. Something ugly and selfish rears its head at that—*I will not be replaced*, it says—but I push it away. I'm a better person than that. We can share. I can handle co–best friends.

"Kira?"

I blink and return my focus to Nic, who winces.

"Sorry, she mutters. "I know I can go on and on."

"No, no!" I rush to reassure her. "This is amazing, really. I was just thinking how smart you are. I can see why you and Skylar get along. You're more alike than I thought."

A blush colors her cheeks, and for the first time, I register that she has a faint dusting of freckles. It was too dark in the bar last night to notice, but here, under the bright lights of the lab, a constellation of pale brown freckles peeks out from under her very sparse makeup. I wonder if she's one of those people who's self-conscious about them, which I've never understood. I love my freckles, and I'm a total sucker for them on other people. They're cute. Unique. I look back up to her amber-brown eyes and smile.

"So, what's for lunch?"

She smiles back hesitantly, then strips off her gloves and starts wriggling out of her lab coat, the elastic at the wrists apparently requiring great effort. Underneath, she's dressed in simple tan slacks that hug her legs beautifully, along with a black button-down that looks plain at first, but on second glance has a tiny word stitched on the left lapel: "Science!"

Something about this is so unbearably adorable that I have to bite the inside of my lip to keep from grinning. There's an unmistakable tug in my gut as I trace a line from the curve of her waist to the dip of her collarbones, and I freeze.

Uh oh.

Nope, undo, get out of here, brain. Going after Skylar's other best friend would be a terrible idea. Squash it down forever. So she's cute, and brilliant, and fun to be around, and queer. That doesn't mean I have to be into her. We can be friends. I hope. If my damn hormones will calm down. My phone buzzes in my pocket—one of my four dating apps, maybe? As much as I'm looking for a real relationship, something that might actually lead to the family I want one day, a quick hookup could be just what I need right now. I'll check after lunch.

Nic throws her coat onto a hanger in a locker by the door, then twirls around. I arrange my face into what I hope looks like a neutral waiting expression.

"Okay, ready! I'm afraid lunch won't be too fancy," she says, beckoning me out into the hallway. I follow her around several identical blank hallways to an office door with NICOLE WELLS scrawled on an index card taped over the nameplate beside the door. "I didn't know what you might want to eat, and I don't have any food in my apartment anyway, so I just ordered a ton of stuff. Whatever you don't want will be my dinner for the week! I would starve to death without sustenance delivered to my office."

She opens the door, and I'm hit with a wave of delicious smells. Nic has spread a blanket out on the floor of her tiny office, and her desk is loaded with takeout boxes. There's a whole pizza, tacos, Indian curry, and fancy ramen, all vegetarian "just in case." She was *not* kidding—it's enough food to last her several days, easily. She hands me a paper plate, then proceeds to take a little of everything, letting it all mix together on her plate like a heathen. I grab two tacos to start with and arrange myself on the "picnic" blanket (a no-sew fleece blanket with a Princess Leia on it) with my back against the wall. She sits against the opposite wall with her legs kicked out in front of her, wiggling her sneakered feet back and forth. Nervous, or excited? She nods at the notebook sticking out of my bag, giving it a much hungrier look than her food ever got.

"So, let's get this party started," she says with a wicked grin, ticking points off on her fingers. "Our mission: to keep our best friend from totally destroying her life with this dumbass decision. Our time frame: two and a half months. Our reward . . ." She raises a determined fist. "Keeping our best friend, and keeping the friend group from collapsing into inevitable slow death by apathy."

"Hell yes," I say, offering my can of sparkling water up for a toast. "And our strategy: to help Skylar realize her bad decision *on her own*, because you *know* if she gets even a whiff of meddling, she'll move to Fiji even earlier out of spite."

Nic groans, and I can't quite tell if it's from dread over Skylar's inevitable reaction if we're caught, or from pleasure at the bite of taco she just took. Either way, I agree.

Nic thunks her head against the wall, then looks back over at me. "So, how do we do this?"

I polish off a taco and think. How can we make Skylar wake up and smell the reality without her catching on? I nod to myself as I sift through the past two years of Skylar knowledge.

"We need to make her understand how totally not ready she is to do this, and how much it's going to wreck her life. So, we have to present her with evidence, right? What are the specific elements of Skylar's plan that are problematic?"

I pull out my binder and turn to the first blank page, clicking a purple pen as Nic lists them off.

"Farming, because I'm pretty sure she's never kept so much as a houseplant alive in her life. Finances in general, and for the party specifically. She's already thinking way overboard for this thing, and how is she even managing this move to Fiji? Renting property, getting her stuff shipped there, travel, all that. Leaving her family, her friends, literally everyone who loves her and has her back, to move to a place she's never been, totally alone. Completely cutting off her only sources of income. And finally, water, and Skylar's total lack of ability in or on it. Kind of a necessary skill set when one is living alone on an island. Maybe. I mean, I don't know. It *feels* logical?"

I scribble frantically to keep up with the growing list, and when I finish, I study the page in despair. Now that it's all spelled out on paper like that, it looks even worse. Nic must be thinking the same thing, because she somehow manages to make her next bite of her delicious mango taco look forlorn, staring at the ground with her glasses sliding down her nose. I hate that we have to do this, because it's obviously bringing her down. I want to see her smile again, want to see that total nerd-out gleam in her eyes, like when she was talking about her work, or that bit of playfulness that came out at the bar last night.

There's something in the set of her mouth, the downward cast of her eyes, that feels heavy. She's totally lost in thought. I'm sad about this too, both about having to do it and about the possibility that it might not work, but it must be even worse for Nic. She only just got back. She must have been imagining so much time with Skylar in the future, so many chances to reconnect after being gone so long. I know they kept in touch while Nic was gone and all, but even I, as a new person to the group, could see that there was some kind of awkward rift for a while between them that either caused Nic's move or was caused by it.

Whenever Nic's name was brought up in my early days with the friend group, a strange pall settled over everyone, as if they all knew something but no one was willing to talk about it. Nic's back now, though, and everything seems good between her and Skylar. If we don't succeed in our plan, she'll lose one of the big reasons she moved back here. I kick her foot and catch her eye when she looks up.

"Hey," I say, mustering a small smile. "I know this sucks. It feels mean, but the stakes are just . . . really high, for all of us. I'll lose someone I've been through hell and back with, you'll lose the best friend you've only just reconnected with, and Skylar . . . well, you saw the list."

Nic bites her lip, then glances down at her lap.

"What happened to make you and Skylar so close? I mean, I get it if it's too personal," she says, trailing off, but hurt pinches at the corner of her eyes. It must have sucked to see her friendship be seemingly replaced, and by someone who's known Skylar less than half as long as she has. But she's stumbled into something too big for our second day of knowing each other.

"I'll tell you someday. Soon. But not right now, okay? It's a lot of pretty bleak stuff. And we need to turn this around! Yes, we're sabotaging our best friend, and it's kind of a dick move, but it's for her own good, right? And you know how she is. Big! Dramatic! The more fun we have with this, the more likely it is to work. You get me?"

Nic switches from taco to pizza and thinks for a moment, then musters a faint smile.

"Yes, I get you, and I think I have the perfect opening move."

"Oh? What's that?"

My phone buzzes. I glance down to see a text from Grace lighting up the home screen.

GRACE: Soooooooo how's your first date with Nic going?

I snatch the phone up and tap out a quick reply, glancing furtively at Nic with burning cheeks.

KIRA: Not a date. My dates have a lot more skin and a lot fewer flammable chemicals

I slam the phone down on my lap and look back up at Nic, who studies me curiously.

"Everything okay?"

I force an awkward laugh. "Yeah. Just Grace being Grace. Anyway, you said you had an idea?"

Super smooth and totally not suspicious topic change there. Nic rolls with it though.

"Yes, our opening volley," she says, rubbing her hands together. "Target: Skylar's wannabe farmer phase. Here's what we do."

As she talks, Nic grows more and more animated, the mischievous light coming fully back into her eyes as she outlines her logic. She talks through the idea layer by layer, letting it evolve as she goes and incorporating my thoughts until we have a firm plan. Once the plan is fully formed, we fall silent, picking at the wreckage of our huge lunch as the enormity of our task settles over us.

"So, we're really doing this, I guess," I finally say. "I feel like we're supposed to—I don't know, shake hands or something. Isn't that what people do when they form a grand conspiracy?"

"Oh, you're right!" Nic says, hovering her hands over her work slacks like she's about to wipe the pizza grease off on them. She opts for a napkin instead. Once she's done, I hold out my hand, and she takes it, too gently for a business transaction but just firm enough to not quite be . . . more. My stomach can't tell the difference, apparently.

"We're in this together now," she says, keeping hold of my hand after we shake.

"Yes, we are," I agree.

CHAPTER FIVE

NIC

I pull into the Home Depot parking lot the day after Kira and I made our plan, still blinking against the sunlight after staring at my computer all day. I feel like a full-on screen zombie.

Today was my first Saturday shift as the "responsible person in the building in case of unintentional fire," which meant sitting around to call 911 in case someone else's experiment went awry rather than setting fires myself. I passed the time in full research mode, spending eight and a half straight hours poring over academic papers full of math and chemical formulas, scarfing leftover pizza with one hand while I made notes with the other.

My eyes may be ready to crawl out of my head, but my brain is in full Happy Science Mode. It felt a little like being back in my master's program, and for the first time since returning to Seattle, I actually . . . missed grad school a bit? I let myself follow a little tangent in the research today, diving

down the rabbit hole of a question that's been bugging me
ever since I showed Kira that bit of new material. I like my
new job okay, but I'd much rather be doing my own research
than supervising someone else's.

My phone buzzes, and I look down to see Willow's answer
to my earlier texts.

NIC: Need your advice
NIC: Don't get too excited, but . . .
NIC: IT INVOLVES *PLANTS*
NIC: I KNOW RIGHT IT'S LIKE YOUR
ULTIMATE DREAM
NIC: You free this evening?
WILLOW: Sorry, doing a thing
WILLOW: Off the grid tonight
WILLOW: The ONE TIME you wanna talk about
plants, ugh
NIC: You wandering out into the woods?

No reply. Ah, well. As much as I'd love Willow's exper-
tise here, I'm sure between me, Kira, and our creepy over-
lord Google, we can figure this out. When Willow goes all
distant and mysterious like this, there's no getting their attention. They're up to something, for sure, but they'll share
it when they're ready. With Willow, I can at least trust that
it's not a surprise move to Fiji or something else wildly destructive. They're far too cautious and methodical for that.

I hope, at least. I'm already unanchored and in danger of
capsizing at the next strong breeze. I was really thinking
that returning to Seattle would help me get back on solid
footing and rid me of my perpetual out-of-place feeling. I
need something (someone?) to keep me from flying off into

the void of my own chaos, and in the past that's always been Skylar and her family. Without them . . .

Well. Anyway.

It's a standard breezy and cool Seattle evening, and the sunlight peeking through the clouds feels delightful on my skin—a beautiful pick-me-up after living my life under fluorescents all day. I can never get over just how different Seattle is from Central Florida, where I grew up. They may be part of the same country, but they couldn't be more different in terms of either culture or climate. As much as I occasionally miss the sun here, where it's always cloudy or misty, I definitely *don't* miss Florida's dog-breath humid air, daily 3:00 p.m. downpours, eighty-plus-degree Christmases, or instant sunburns. The one thing they do have in common: wildfires. We lost our house to one when I was in elementary school, a few years after my mom died. It kicked off my obsession with understanding fire right around the same time it kicked off my dad's new streak of moving every year and a half.

A steel trap clamps down in my brain at the thought of my dad.

Nope. Not today, Satan.

I take one more slow breath of cool air in through my nose, then head for the doors to the garden department. My phone buzzes and I grin, fully expecting that Willow caved to their curiosity about the plants . . . but nope. It's Skylar's mom.

MAMA CLARK: NICOLE WELLS
MAMA CLARK: When are you coming to see me?
MAMA CLARK: Skylar tells me you've been back in town for a few weeks now.
MAMA CLARK: Which I had to hear from HER. Not

from YOU. You never told ME, your mother who
loves you, what day you were arriving.
MAMA CLARK: I will forgive you, however, if you start
attending monthly brunches again.

Yikes. If I didn't know Mama Clark so well, I'd be crushed
by guilt, but reading the texts in her voice, I can hear the
gentle teasing that they're meant to be. I . . . will admit that
I've been avoiding her since I heard about the Fiji thing.
In fact, I'd been planning to do our monthly-ish check-in
call the very night Skylar announced her grand plans. I was
(understandably, I think) derailed. Brunch could be a good
way to ease back in. Skylar and her mom alternate months:
one month, Mama Clark drives into Seattle to go out to
brunch with Skylar, and the next month, Skylar drives out to
Ellensburg for the weekend. I've always joined Skylar for both,
throughout college and beyond—when I lived here, at least.

NIC: I'm so sorry!
NIC: Things have been super hectic since starting the
new job and Skylar announced her plans
NIC: I will be there for brunch this month. Promise. ♥

I shove my phone in my back pocket before she can reply,
and I scan the garden area for Kira. My hand curls and un-
curls around my car keys in my pocket, a nervous habit I can
never seem to kick. Why am I nervous? I know it's not this
whole Skylar scheme—I've made my peace with that. Maybe
it would be kinder to just let her do her thing and come
home broke in a year, but she's pulled me out of my own self-
destructive nosedives plenty of times. Without her, I would
still be letting my dad drag my entire life down.

She's the one who helped me realize in our freshman year—when I came back from winter break completely wrecked—that sometimes the healthy thing to do is to cut a person off completely. That summer, she brought me home to Mama Clark, and that was the end of it. I haven't been back to see my dad since. Every birthday and major holiday is spent with Skylar, her mom, and her brothers and sister. Baby adult me was totally blindsided by her family's unconditional acceptance. I was just suddenly . . . part of them. A member of the family, expected at gatherings, included in the annual newsletter, teased and scolded like a sister. It was strange, and I was really weird about it for a while. Now I can't imagine my life any other way.

I can't imagine losing them all.

Skylar has to stay, and I feel completely fine about what Kira and I have planned.

Kira.

Maybe that's where the nerves are coming from. Maybe it's that this feels weirdly like a date, even though I *know* it's not. I've only just met Kira, and she's awesome, but it's Skylar I want to be with. I've tried dating other people, I really have. But it's never worked. I've never gotten her out of my head. It would be so perfect, you know? Then I'd *really* be a member of the family. Mama Clark would be so happy seeing us together, I think.

I'm not the best at making friends, but Skylar saw me in our shared freshman-biology-for-science-majors class and attached herself like a barnacle on day one—a beautiful, brilliant, very talkative barnacle who I fell for in a heartbeat. My long-distance high school girlfriend could tell immediately, even over the phone, and broke up with me two weeks into the semester. I didn't even mind, which probably makes me an asshole, but it wouldn't be the first thing to do so. Our friend group came together quickly after that—Marco and Willow (in our lab section for that biology class), Ian (shared a child psychology class with Skylar), and Grace (at the second Queer Student Alliance meeting of the second semester; funny, since she's one of the straight ones). A few others drifted in and out over the years, but our core group has persisted. Skylar gave me a friend family, then adopted me into her actual family. How can I just get over that?

It killed me to move away from them all for grad school, but I had to get some space. Skylar had a ton of girlfriends throughout college, but it was way different when we were living together after graduation, while Skylar was in grad school and I was working as a lab grunt, trying to figure out what I wanted to do with my dual chemistry/materials science degrees. Suddenly, I couldn't get away from her and her girlfriends, our paper-thin walls, and the perpetual reassurances that "oh, no, we're best friends, it's not like that, don't be jealous, she's like my sister." I should have lived with Willow instead, but stupid me thought that maybe, if we lived together, Skylar would see how good we could be if we shared *more* than an apartment.

And then things started to shift. We were on the edge of something, I thought. She broke up with her girlfriend. And just when I got up the courage to make a move . . .

She started dating someone else.

I left. I tried to get over her. I kept in touch, of course. She's still my best friend. My family. But it has to mean *something* that even after two years away, I still want her, right? And now that I'm back, it's all poised to fall apart.

Unless Kira and I can stop Skylar and save the day. This is some straight-up superhero shit.

I find Kira standing by a long, low table packed with greenery and potted flowers in full bloom, chatting with a sales associate who practically has hearts popping out of her eye sockets. I frown. No distractions, Kira—we're on a mission. I slide up a bit too close beside her and shoot a sugary smile at the saleswoman, then beam some apologetic thoughts at Kira. Hate to run cliterference here, but we have to focus on the goal at hand.

"Hey, Kira!" I say, forcing my voice high and chipper. "Where are we at?"

She smiles and steps back to include me in the conversation. "I was just talking to Mel here about challenging houseplants. There is a *whole* lot more to it than I thought."

Mel nods with a polite customer service smile and pulls a few dead blossoms from a sad-looking marigold. "I was saying that lots of plants are difficult to take care of, just because they're fussy or whatever, but the real challenge will come in making all your plants happy in the same environment without getting lazy."

I snort, then cover my mouth, because I'm not trying to be a jerk here. Skylar isn't lazy by any stretch of the imagination. You don't end up with two successful careers and a PhD by being lazy. But when it comes to detailed housekeeping . . . well, I've found underwear in her fridge and apples in her medicine cabinet before, and though I guess the latter makes a certain kind of sense, I could do without a lacy thong on my eggs. I can't believe I actually thought that might be a *hint*. I'm hopeless.

Kira hands me a spindly miniature bush with pink buds dotting its branches. An African violet, according to the tag.

"Get this," she says with an evil gleam in her eye. "This one can't stand having any water on its leaves! You gotta water from the bottom or keep it in a special pot, and it has to get indirect, filtered light."

Mel picks up a droopy fern with long green arms flopping over the side of the pot. "This one wants humidity, and it's gotta be warm, and with the right kind of light, or it gets really pissy and starts dropping leaves all over the place."

"And it gets better," Kira says, motioning me over to the next table down and pointing to a bunch of little succulents. "These ones, right?"

Mel nods her approval, and Kira picks up a pot with several adorable little spikey plants nestled around a larger version of the same plant. The label reads Hens and Chicks. What?

Kira grins. "This one is adapted to survive in super shitty soil with barely any water. You can totally neglect it and it'll live forever."

Surely there's a catch here. "But . . . ?"

"But, if you water it, it'll die," Kira says, walking two of them back to her cart.

Mel laughs. "I mean, it's not *that* dramatic, but yeah, if the soil isn't really well drained, and you water them more than like . . . once a week at most, it won't be happy."

Kira turns to me and gestures expansively to encompass the entire garden section. "Well? You ready?

I rub my hands together, cartoon villain–style. Skylar is *guaranteed* to massacre these plants in a week, tops. Farmer Skylar: foiled.

"Hell yeah," I say. "Let's get some death plants. What else have you got?"

Mel loads us up with two carts full of plants, including peacock plants (must be misted regularly and watered with distilled water), miniature roses (require their own growing light and a fan for air circulation), and Venus flytraps (must be fed live insects regularly—gross). Kira and I cackle all the while, and Mel is kind enough to find us a coupon that will knock twenty percent off the whole total.

This is a hell of an expensive prank, but I keep reminding myself it's for a good cause. My new steady adult job paycheck may as well go to something worthwhile, even if that job is a one-year contract that's likely to get axed if they lose funding. It's steady *for now*. And on the off chance Skylar manages to keep all the plants alive and leaves us anyway, the plants can move in with me or Kira. Who knows? Maybe I have a heretofore undiscovered green thumb? I can't become a cat lady, because *allergies*, so maybe I'll just fill my apartment with plants and candles until I inevitably die by lighting a plant on fire.

Kira and I pay and load the whole mess into the back seat of Kira's car, which she cheerfully calls the Toyonda Civry. It's a Frankenstein's monster of a car, a small black vehicle with a right front fender in a muted gold color, a hood in bright silver, and a left rear fender in blue. The badges on the back are confusing as heck—there's both a Toyota and a Honda logo, and someone spliced together the badges for a Civic and a Camry so it reads Civry in two very different fonts. Kira insists on being the pack mule for this errand since, in her own words, "Toyonda is a piece of hot crusty garbage ready to die any day now, so what's a little dirt?"

I am two hundred percent okay with this arrangement. I may be a mess both physically and spiritually, but my car is the one thing in my life I'm fussy about. She's ten years old, bought used with eighty thousand miles on her, but she's *mine*. My dad may as well live on another astral plane, but my last car was technically half-funded by him, and I couldn't stand the constant reminder, that vague connection. As soon as I could afford it, I traded that generic early 2000s fuel-efficient box on wheels for Stella—a reasonably priced but fun-to-drive manual transmission Mazda3. I love her, and I'm pretty sure we'll be together forever. Another benefit to being with Skylar—she already knows that any relationship with me is necessarily a poly arrangement between me, her, and my car. I'm glad that Kira appreciates my sweet Stella and respects her exalted position in my life. A position that definitely does *not*, under any circumstance, involve dirt on her nearly spotless seats.

We leave Stella in the Home Depot parking lot and head for Skylar's, chatting all the while about our next move after this one. I'm not naive—I know that this one scheme won't convince Skylar of the error of her ways. It'll be a cumulative effect. This is the first step, though, and I can't *wait*.

We arrive, and Plant Strike 2025 commences. Kira and I load our arms up with as many potted plants as we can carry, biting our lips to keep from cracking up as we pile them outside Skylar's door. Once they're all there, Kira produces a spare key to Skylar's apartment. The lock clicks open, and we pass the plants inside like we're in a bucket line, putting out the fire that is Skylar's life. We pile them on her coffee table, every windowsill, her bedside table, and even a few in the bathtub. I'm going back for the last zebra plant when I turn out into the hallway and walk straight into Skylar, who's standing there with the plant in her arms, gazing at it like it's a newborn puppy.

Shit.

"Oh, hi, Skylar!" I chirp, sounding totally unlike myself. Inside the apartment, there's a loud THUNK. Guess Kira heard me. "Uh, what are you doing home so early?"

She raises an eyebrow at me. "They were having technical issues at the radio station today, so my show got canceled for the afternoon. But really, that's the question we're going with?"

She weaves around me and ducks inside the doorway before I can formulate a response, and Kira squeaks as Skylar catches her climbing down from the back of the couch, where she was hanging a planter from the curtain rod.

"Well," Skylar says. "Isn't this a surprise? It . . . is . . ."

I hold my breath, meeting Kira's eyes for a terrified second.

". . . *beautiful* in here!" Skylar finishes with an excited clap. "It feels like Fiji!"

"Yes, totally, that was the goal!" Kira says. "We thought they might help you . . ."

". . . adjust to your future home!" I cut in and finish. "And to your new farmerly lifestyle!"

Kira jumps the rest of the way to the ground and drifts to my side, her shoulders tense. "Oh! And we also thought they could be party decor and favors, you know? At the end of the summer, you can give them away to your party guests, since you can't take them with you."

Wow, yeah, good thinking on your feet, Kira. Though it would have been better if you'd sounded less like the idea had just occurred to you this very second. I force a smile and back her up.

"Yeah, absolutely! I know you're going to take great care of them," I babble. What happens if you water a plant with vodka, I wonder? "We just wanted to . . . show our support. For your decision. Which is . . . a smart one. Yeah."

Okay, so I have no room to criticize in the whole thinking-on-your-feet department. It's fine, though, because Skylar lights up at my words, her eyes doing that crinkle-smile that

I love. She puts her plant down, steps forward, and smooshes my face between her palms, then does the same for Kira.

"I just love you two *so much*," she says, wrapping us both in a joint hug. "Your support means the world to me. And these plants are a genius idea! You're so right, they'll be the perfect decor for the party. Whiiich, I can*not* wait to tell you all about my *plans*."

She actually waggles her eyebrows like a cartoon villain. I feel like I should be very concerned. Mostly, I just want to kiss her right between those eyebrows. Good to know my feelings haven't faded *at all* in the last two years. I almost wish they had. It would have saved me several totally tragic dates while I was away. All the more reason to stay totally committed to the mission. No distractions.

My eyes drift to Kira, to the long line of her neck and the snug fit of her jeans over her hips, the way her lips curve as she laughs at whatever Skylar is saying. Was there ever anything between the two of them? Groups of queer women can be a little messy—everyone's hooked up with everyone else at least once—but our group has never been like that. At least, not to the usual degree. Grace and Ian hooked up once, which feels like it shouldn't count, and Willow and I had a one-time pity party. That's it as far as I know. But Kira and Skylar?

God, they'd be gorgeous together. They contrast in every way—hair, height, body type, temperament—and the differences would only accentuate each other's beauty. I glaze over for a long moment, a daydream unspooling: Kira's long, probably freckled legs wrapped around Skylar's pale shoulders, bare breasts rising and falling with every gasping breath, Skylar's tongue venturing down, teasing at—

"Nic, you okay?" Kira asks, brow furrowed with concern. "You look a little flushed."

I snap back to reality, my cheeks totally on fire. Skylar is biting her lip to suppress a laugh, and I would like to open the nearest window and fly into the sun now, please and thanks. How obvious can I be? Though . . . maybe this isn't totally a bad thing. Maybe Skylar *should* know how much I want her. If the end result could be us together, then . . .

I flick my eyes back to Kira and force myself to meet her gaze. "Just zoned out for a minute, sorry."

She hums an acknowledgment and studies me, her eyes drifting from my reddened cheeks to my forehead to my . . . lips? Like she's trying to figure me out. Skylar, never one to abide a silence, breaks the spell with a proclamation.

"Dinner!" she declares, snatching up her keys and heading back out the door. "The oyster place, my treat, as thanks for all these gorgeous plants. Plus, I have *so* much to tell you about my plans for the party. In? Yes? Great, let's go, I'm driving."

She marches straight out the door without us, expecting us to follow and lock up behind her, I assume. I look at Kira and shrug.

"Mission accomplished, I guess?"

"Maybe?" she replies with a shrug of her own.

"TBD." I grab her by the hand to drag her outside as she stares, puzzled, at the plants we leave in our wake. I get it. Skylar's reactions can never be predicted. I honestly can't tell what she thinks of this whole thing, or whether she's on to our scheme.

What I do know is that Skylar *will* leave for dinner without us if we don't catch up.

It takes me a full minute to remember to drop Kira's hand.

CHAPTER SIX

KIRA

A week later, I've consumed thousands and thousands of words and images from Skylar in the form of texts, emails with dozens of links, elaborate vision boards, and long phone calls full of rambling thoughts about Fiji and her party.

But not. A. Word. About the plants.

Are they alive? Is she taking care of them? Is she living in a mausoleum of plant corpses? Inquiring minds *must know*. Grace has been making terrible hinty plant puns all week since I told her about our "gifts," but Skylar refuses to bite. I never thought serene calm could be so infuriating.

Our next opportunity has presented itself, though: party planning appointments. And by party, I mean a low-key wedding-reception-sized extravaganza with all the Skylar levels of extra. I'm pretty sure Skylar lives on Pinterest now, which I didn't even know people still used, and Nic and I are the unwilling recipients of her efforts. Are we her maids of honor or something? Are we *really* gonna have to plan pseudo-bachelorette and bridal parties for this not-a-wedding? It sure feels like it.

The good thing about this whole mess is that it provides so many perfect opportunities for Skylar to realize how totally bananas this plan of hers is. And that we need each other. And that this friend group she has here is golden, and leaving it is giving up something precious. I might be oversensitive on this particular point, considering the contrast between my life pre- and post-Skylar, but the fact remains. Today we have the opportunity to feel out where Skylar's head is at money-wise and make her see how ridiculous spending thousands of dollars on a fake wedding and leaving your best friends would be.

It is once again the beginning of my forty-eight hours off after a twenty-four-hour shift, and this time, everyone let me sleep like smart humans with developed senses of self-preservation. Skylar, Nic, and I have plans this afternoon to go meet with the manager of her chosen party venue and talk details, and Nic is taking a half day off work for it.

I manage to squeeze in two hours of schoolwork beforehand, slogging my way through a paper on managing officers through community crises. I can outline a paper in my sleep, but doing the actual writing is like climbing to the top of a fifty-story building in full bunker gear. I can do it, but it takes forever, and I kinda wanna die by the end.

This is an important topic, though. This certificate will be the perfect addition to my application for lieutenant, demonstrating the level of thought I've put into leadership strategies and showing that I'm so committed to firefighting, I'm continuing my professional development on my own time. My instructor seems to think I'm plenty worthy of promotion, though she also knows exactly what it's like to try to make it in this field when you're not a cis white dude and might just be trying to help a girl out. She's offered several times to introduce me to folks in other fire organizations, to get me in the door somewhere that will "appreciate my talents."

Look, I know I'm getting completely stonewalled in Seattle, but I just can't give up that easily. They can't pretend I'm invisible forever. My dad was fire chief here, and I'm trying to uphold his legacy, even though the people who hated him are in charge these days. Even though *he* never saw me, either.

Even though he never wanted me to be a firefighter at all.

I have so much to contribute, though, in so many areas where this department is weak. As a woman, I feel like I have a perspective to offer that isn't heard much in the firefighting world, especially when it comes to community relations, inclusive management strategies, and bringing different personalities together. There are some outstanding women in leadership already in the SFD, but not enough. I want to be one of them.

And now it sounds like I'm conducting a job interview in my own head. Maybe it's time to stop for the day.

I shut my laptop and stand with a stretch, already flipping through my mental catalog of outfits. It's a rare seventy-seven-degree sunny day outside, and I plan to take full advantage. Everyone in Seattle will be as naked as possible today, soaking up the sun and warmth while it's available. Summer doesn't really start until July 5 here (we can still get "spring showers" to rain out the fireworks every year), so I may as well take full advantage of this little sneak preview: shorts and a halter top. Nic seemed to really like that purple one I wore on the day we met at the bar, and I have a bright blue one just like it. Maybe that.

Not that it matters what Nic thinks of what I'm wearing.

I deliberately get ready with minimal preening—I've already said no to that particular line of interest—and leave the house without looking in a mirror for longer than it takes to apply some SPF and get my eyeliner done. I give my beloved Toyonda Civry a break and decide to walk to the venue. It's only thirty minutes away on foot, and it'd take me almost that long on the bus anyway, so I may as well indulge myself in the sun. I put on an audiobook, slip on my sunglasses, and set off in bliss. My phone buzzes with a text the second I hit the street:

SKYLAR: Gonna be a few minutes late, last appointment ran long! Nic Knack should be there on time, though. I'm sure you can entertain each other.
SKYLAR: Be there ASAP!

Sure enough, when I turn the final corner, there's Nic, still in her business casual from work, but with her eyes closed and face turned up to the sky like a sunflower. Her hands are shoved in the pockets of her black slacks, and her fitted gray button-down shirt is doing the boob gap thing that keeps me from ever buying shirts with buttons. So obnoxious, but in this case, it affords me a glimpse of the bright pop of color under Nic's shirt. Wouldn't have pegged her as the bright-yellow-bra type, but maybe she too, was feeling sunny today. I allow myself one indulgent sweeping gaze, from the not-so-professional sneakers peeking out from her too-long pants to the layered waves of hair she's currently battling with. Just as she gets a hair tie around it, she finally spots me, jumping in surprise.

"Sorry," I call, hoping she didn't notice my creepy staring. "Didn't mean to sneak up on you."

Messy ponytail in place, she waves the comment away and shoves her hands back in her pockets.

"No, no, sorry, I was just zoned out. It's so nice today! It's not that I forgot what Seattle was like while I was gone, I just let myself get more used to Maryland than I thought. I kept telling myself while I was there, 'Don't enjoy it too much. After graduation, it's back to perma-clouds and daily drizzle.'"

I lean against the wall next to her, watching the people across the street rush past, out of work early to enjoy the weather or dashing out for an afternoon coffee break. The traffic is approaching peak sunny-day disaster level, and I'm so glad I left my car at home.

"I've lived here my whole life," I say, not sure why I'm offering this information. I guess if she's back for good, though, and solidly part of the group, then I should try to get to know her better. "My mom lives near Vancouver now, and I visit her as often as I can, but the weather isn't all that different there."

Really, we're talking about the weather? That's my get-to-know-you plan? Though to be fair, that's all anyone here wants to talk about on days like this. Nic doesn't call me on it, just turns sincere eyes on me and dives straight for the vulnerable point.

"So, your parents are divorced?" she asks, then winces. "Sorry, god, you don't have to answer that, I'm terrible."

"No, it's okay." I tug at the hem of my shorts and work past the initial surge of emotion. I want to make friends. Making real friends requires vulnerability. I'm not great at that. Brené Brown would be very disappointed in me. I'm better than I was, though; being friends with Skylar has done a lot for me in that department. I take a breath and force the words out.

"My dad passed away while I was in college. My mom moved to help out my grandmother soon after it happened."

"Wow," Nic says, shuffling closer. "Wasn't that . . . It must have been hard, being kind of alone after that."

"I don't blame her, if that's what you think," I say, then bite back the instant flood of feelings. Honestly, I *had* blamed her a bit, afterward. But I understood, too. At least the loneliness got better after Skylar adopted me into her friend family.

Once I get my reaction under control, I continue. "Dad was fire chief here. He climbed his way up through the ranks, spent his whole career working for SFD. Everyone knew him. And you'd think that'd be a comfort, but for my mom, it wasn't. She couldn't take being in the place they'd lived their whole lives together, with people stopping her on the street every time she left the house to give their condolences."

"Did he . . . pass away on the job?" she asks tentatively.

"Not exactly," I say, swallowing hard. "Heart attack. It was probably the stress that killed him, ultimately. His time as fire chief was *not* easy. He had a lot of enemies. A lot of people who made his time hell."

"Do they make your time hell too?"

And isn't that just the ultimate sticking point? She zeroed in quick.

"Yes. I've been fighting for a promotion for years, but the same people who tried to keep him down are succeeding with me where they failed with him. His biggest obstacle was history. For me, I've got the history, the boobs, *and* the bisexuality. I'm a triple threat."

Nic barks a laugh, then slaps her hands over her mouth with an expression of pure horror. "Oh my god, I'm sorry. That wasn't actually funny, just the way you *said* it . . ."

I pry her hands away from her mouth with a grin, grateful to have some levity injected into the conversation. "Hey, it's fine. I know I'm hilarious. You don't have to apologize."

She blushes and looks away. "That sucks, though, on so many levels. I'm sorry to hear about your dad, and about the way you're being treated."

I shrug, as if this isn't a huge defining part of my life that I'm constantly battling against. "Some of it is just regular run-of-the-mill politics stuff, too. They didn't agree with some of my dad's policies, and they think I'm just like him. They don't want me in any position where I could make things happen. They have no idea. though. They thought *my dad* was a progressive upstart too focused on changing everything? I'd be their actual definition of hell."

"I dunno, sounds like you're exactly what we need," Nic says, her expression serious. "I haven't known you long, but I already think you'd be an amazing fire chief."

My heart does a funny little leaping dance at that, and I have to look away. She is off-limits, no matter what opinion my clitoris may have on the matter. Her sincerity is totally disarming, though. I feel like she really means it.

"Thank you," I say to my sandals. "I have a *long* way to go before then, though. I'm overdue for promotion to lieutenant, considering I've been working for the SFD since I graduated from high school. I'm applying again really soon, and if I get passed over again . . . I don't know."

My lips press tight, trying to contain the last thing, the thing I hate to admit out loud, but I've said so much already. The pressure valve bursts.

"My dad didn't even want me to be a firefighter. Especially not one in Seattle. He knew this would happen to me, that I'd never make it in this department. So, I don't even know what I'm doing here. Do I stay here and keep banging my head against the wall, putting off real dating and family and life stuff I want for myself while busting my ass to make it out of some sense of loyalty, or legacy, or . . . pure stubborn-ness, maybe? Or do I go somewhere else and have to com-pletely start over in a place where I have no ties to anything?"

Nic hides her expression for a moment, then smooths the loose hair away from her face and looks back up. "I know a bit about that, too. Maybe once this whole Skylar Fiji thing is over, one way or another, I'll tell you about it."

"I'd like that," I say, and it feels . . . true. I want to know more. I want to know everything about this girl who wears sneakers with her slacks, who burns things for a living and has the *Super Mario Bros.* theme as her ringtone. This girl who ran away from the city she called her adopted home, then showed back up and was instantly folded into the group like she never left. They all love so deeply but have a hard time putting it into words. With Skylar, everyone is instantly full of praise for her energy, her excitement for life, her empathy and compassion. With Nic, everyone is like . . . she's Nic. And that's all they need. I'm pretty sure Grace would literally kill a man for her. She's as much a central figure in this friend group as Skylar is, despite her two-year absence, and I'm not sure she even knows it. The air between us grows heavy, and I open my mouth to say some part of this, any of it . . . but of Skylar's many wonderful qualities, good timing is not one of them.

"I'm *so sorry* I'm late!" she says, bursting in on the moment like a confused bird through an open window, feathers flying everywhere. "My last patient was having a really tough day today, and I had to tell them I was leaving at the end of the summer, which was really hard. I know it's just volunteer work, but I've known some of these clients for years, and I'm working to place them with new counselors that I'm hand-picking based on their specialties, but it doesn't make it any easier on them, and I'm *totally rambling*. Let's just go inside and get started!"

Skylar turns and darts up the stairs to 10 Degrees, her chosen venue, letting the door bang closed behind her. Nic and I turn to each other, blink, and bust out laughing, leaning against each other as we follow Hurricane Skylar inside.

10 Degrees is a fabulous small venue attached to a distillery, which, hello, bonus. The people there are super friendly and obviously share Skylar's enthusiasm for party planning. We're escorted to a round high-top bar table that looks hand-finished and are soon joined by a guy in thick black-framed glasses, an incredibly expensive button-down shirt, and a tie with some kind of repeating pattern I can't make out. He introduces himself as Silas, Skylar gets his entire life story out of him within two minutes because that's just how she is, and Nic and I sit back and let them ramble on while we exchange significant looks and raised eyebrows. After a bit, Nic texts me under the table.

NIC: I think it's time we added some gasoline to this fire, yes?
KIRA: Oh yes. Let's make this ridiculous.
NIC: Round Two: Fight!

"So, Skylar," I say, breaking my way into the conversation. "I love that you're incorporating the distillery next door for drinks, and obviously the open bar is an expensive but fabulous idea. But what about a theme drink to commemorate the occasion?"

Nic picks up on my train of thought right away. "Oh my god, yes. You can call it The Solo, and it's literally just straight whiskey in a glass, to symbolize the bold journey you're strik-ing out on *all on your own*."

Damn, *brutal*, but also, I'm biting my lip to keep from laughing at the expression on Silas's face. He's just sitting there with his mouth half-open, brows drawn together, look-ing back and forth between Nic and Skylar, like he's not sure whether he should be supporting this or not. Skylar takes it from there, because *of course* she does.

"YES!" she shouts, startling the poor guy so badly he sloshes a dribble of the house-made whiskey over his tie, which I can now see is patterned with little white goats. "I *love* that so much! Everyone will totally laugh! Though it could be dangerous for Ian. Nic, you'll be on Ian duty that night."

"Ma'am, yes, ma'am," Nic says with a salute and much less enthusiasm. Not even a bump in the road. Skylar rolls on, detailing the colors of balloons she's envisioning for the bal-loon garland that apparently comes with the package, and the placement of all the potted plants we got her. She must be confident they'll all be alive by August.

When they start talking about the super hipster photo booth included in their fee, though, I get my next idea.

"Oh, Skylar! You should get a solo photo shoot done. I mean, if you're really going hard at this like it's a wedding, you may as well take engagement photos. Give everyone something to remember you by once you're gone, right?"

The word *gone* lands hard, just like I'd planned, and Nic grabs the ball and runs with it.

"There is so much potential here," she says, reaching across the table to take Skylar's hand. "You love posing for photos, and I can already imagine the perfect backdrop. We'll rent you a *U-Haul*," she adds with an evil grin. "Seriously, it's a double bonus. It represents the fact that you're moving away from all of us—though I don't recommend trying to drive a moving truck to Fiji—*and* you can also fully embrace the U-Haul lesbian stereotype, minus the actual girlfriend, immortalized in photography! I know it'll probably cost a lot, but I'm guessing you've paid off your student loans if you're spending all this money on a party *and* doing this huge move *and* still have startup capital for your farm. It'll be a fabulous addition."

It's all conveyed with such perfect chipper nonchalance that I almost don't process the details. It lands softer than it should with those facts on the table, but the delivery doesn't change the words themselves. Skylar's eyebrow twitches. Then she laughs, a full head-thrown-back belly laugh that makes poor Silas jump again, so badly he nearly launches himself out of his chair.

"I am *so* glad I have you two around," Skylar says with a giggle, wiping her eyes. Nic and I freeze and lock eyes. Is that . . . what it sounds like? Is she seeing the problems? Is this all it will take, and we can finally return to real life? Skylar giggles one more time, then throws an arm around Nic and pulls her into a tight side hug. Nic blushes and looks up at me with hopeful eyes.

Then Skylar opens her mouth.

"You two just know me so well. Yes, I love this idea. We are doing it, it's happening, done! Do you know a photographer?" she says, addressing the last part to the party planner guy.

Well, so much for that. They chat back and forth about local photographers for several eternal minutes while Nic and I exchange panicked texts under the table.

NIC: Okay, I'm running out of ideas here. How is she just throwing money at all these things? Does she even have a budget?

KIRA: I swear, last time we talked money crap she was still complaining about her huge student loan payments. What is happening???

NIC: Any last ideas to shove at Skylar?

I lean back in my chair and rack my brain for something—*anything*—that could be outlandish enough to trip up even Skylar. When party guy mentions cake, I finally get there.

"Okay, this is totally nuts," I say, hoping the preamble will help Skylar realize that yes, *this really is totally nuts and you should not say yes*. "But hear me out. One of the guys at the firehouse recently got married, and he and his wife got—are you ready for this?—3D scans of their entire bodies so they could be turned into custom cake toppers. They looked so good, but it cost like seven hundred dollars just for a *cake topper*. Can you believe it?"

"Um, *yes*, I can believe it," Skylar says, slapping her hand down on the table. "Because it's sheer genius! I'm doing it. Get me the number of whoever did that, because this is now a requirement."

"And," Nic adds weakly, with a last-ditch pathetic attempt to nudge Skylar over the edge, "you could wear your ultimate power suit for your pose, to represent the successful career you've had here before you leave it behind. Whatever your favorite work outfit is."

Skylar tapped her lip with one finger and a *hmm*. "Maybe. It's a nice gesture. I've totally loved my career, as short and unusual as it's been."

Short, my ass. Yeah, okay, technically she's only been a licensed therapist for two years, but it should have been even less than that. She finished her undergrad degree in three years and went straight into her PhD at the same college, found an internship to complete her clinical hours with no problem, and passed the national board exam on her first try. It was hard not to be annoyed when I first learned all that. And *then*, instead of getting a nice, stable, lucrative job as a practicing counselor, she went full-time with her social media psychologist thing after graduation and just did pro bono work on the side. Unbelievable.

I love my friend dearly. I will never understand her choices.

"That said, though," Skylar continues, "I think I might want to be immortalized atop a cake wearing something that represents me as a whole person, not just my career. You know?"

I shoot Nic a pleading look, but she just shrugs helplessly.

"Yeah," I say. "I get that."

This whole thing is like a snowball rolling downhill, gathering speed and mass and destined to crush someone. If Skylar just keeps agreeing to things, the cost of this party will go up and up and up, and we're trying to make things *better* for her, not be the source of her inevitable financial ruin. I really thought *something* in this meeting would trip her up, that it would be easier than this. From the look on Nic's face, she's thinking the same thing.

I meet Nic's gaze one more time and shake my head, with a gesture like striking an item off a list.

Scratch this plan, I guess.

Obviously, more drastic measures are needed.

CHAPTER SEVEN

NIC

My apartment is full of fire, both intentional and unintentional, and I can't help but see it as a metaphor for my life. The air is thick with the competing scents of too many candles burning at once—at least two per surface—along with the charred smell of completely torched pie crust. The pie stares judgmentally back at me from the oven rack, its top blackened and misshapen, with thick, burned filling oozing from every burst seam. My phone yammers on in the background with a video on-screen: "Troubleshooting Your Pie Crust."

Bit late for that, honestly.

"Fuck you, internet baking princess," I growl, slamming the oven door closed and sending the pie sliding back inside.

"Now, if it doesn't come out right the first time, don't get frustrated, y'all," she says, gesturing with pink floral oven mitts. I stab the pause button and throw my phone in the freezer, then backtrack and take it out again, the plastic case cold to the touch. I don't know why I did that. I'm not thinking straight. My brain is more of a disaster than usual, and now I have a blackened, oozing cherry pie. If I throw it away, I'm throwing away all the money I spent on ingredients and all the time I put into mixing, chilling, rolling, filling, crimping, and swearing. But if I eat it, it'll be nothing but ash on my tongue. I'm about ready to flop down on the tile floor and cry.

"Please tell me you own a fire extinguisher," Ian says from behind me, and I nearly jump out of my own skin.

"FUCK," I shout. One of my oven mitts flies off my hand and right into Ian's face as I whirl around with my hands up in defense. He catches it and lays it on the kitchen island, totally unruffled.

"Guess you didn't hear us come in," he says, deliberately breathing only through his mouth.

Willow leans on the countertop with an apologetic smile. "We did knock, but between your cursing and YouTube girl's lecturing, I'm not surprised you didn't notice. Why do you do this if it frustrates you so much?"

I rip the other oven mitt off and slam it down on the counter, breathing through the urge to scream.

"Because I'm a fucking chemist. Baking should be the easiest thing in the world for me, but all I can ever make are ash pies and cookie rocks."

"Maybe because you only ever bake when you're upset?" Willow offers gently, shaggy hair flopping into their eyes.

I puff up with irritation and start to protest, but . . . well. That's an entirely valid point, actually.

"I just got off the phone with my dad," I say, and Willow nods with a knowing "Ahh, I see."

"What was he on about this time?" Ian asks as he opens all the windows, then flaps one of my kitchen towels at the smoke detector. Much appreciated. Having the entire apartment complex irritated at me for setting off the alarms would be the absolute perfect scorched cherry on top of this turd pie of a day.

I collapse onto one of the stools at the island and sigh. "All the usual bullshit. When he stops talking about his latest girlfriend of the year and how awesome whatever state he's living in this month is, all he does is ask about when I'm going to get a real job and find a husband."

"A *real job*?" Willow sputters, their cheeks flushing red with outrage. "You're a goddamn scientist."

I roll my eyes. "Yes, but nothing is ever going to come of my 'little experiments,' and no man wants to marry a woman in science, didn't you know?"

"He did *not* say that," Willow says, snarling more ferociously than their dog ever would.

"Oh, he did. And he always will. Couldn't he at least say that no *woman* will ever want to marry a scientist? Can he not give me even that much dignity?"

"You could just *not* answer the phone, you know," Ian says. "You're not obligated to speak to him if he always makes you feel like garbage."

I'm silent for a long moment. Willow gives a quiet *tsk*.

"You called *him*, didn't you?" they ask.

I nod, drowning in my total patheticness.

"Oh, honey, I wish you'd stop. You know you're chasing something he's never going to give you."

Well, I learned from the best, didn't I? Not like he can ever stop doing the same thing, looking for some woman, some place, some *thing* to make him feel whole again after Mom. It shouldn't hurt anymore—I haven't seen him in eight years— but it's like a blade in my chest all the same. Fact is, though, if I don't call him, I will never hear from him ever again. And he's the only person in my life who ever knew my mom. Every memory I have of her involves him, too. If I forget him . . .

I used to think it was my fault, that there was something wrong with me that made people not want to stay. But when I was away at grad school, I ended up with the opposite problem—I had a hard time making new friends because I spent all my time up late chatting or gaming with my Seattle group. Willow, Grace, and I had so many late nights playing video games and chatting on Discord, and we even managed to occasionally pull in Ian, though he's awful at video games. Skylar was always texting and video-chatting me at random times. Marco and I fell out of touch as predicted. That's just how he is. He has his own issues. Besides, he's working as a nurse while going to school to be a nurse practitioner, both full time, so his social time is limited.

From the day I met Skylar, she's actively worked to make sure I was always included. She was the one to introduce herself to me in bio, then invite me out with her other friends, over to study, and everywhere else. She chose me. She loved me—as a friend, at least. My own father couldn't do that (and wow, it took a lot of years of therapy to admit that). Skylar's the one who taught me that it shouldn't be like that. That I had a choice.

And now she's leaving.

Willow must sense the spiral, because they take up the oven mitts and pull the destroyed pie out of the oven, then grab three spoons from my silverware drawer.

"You know, I suspect that under this slightly overcooked crust, there is probably some delicious filling. Ian, the evening's entertainment, please?"

Ian flops down on my couch and brings up Netflix on my Xbox, selecting *Queer Eye* from the Continue Watching list. Willow follows, the pie and spoons in hand, blowing out my excessive candles on their way over. Our weekly *Queer Eye* and Cry session is officially underway, thankfully no longer virtual. It's so much better in person. Willow takes the lead, plunging their spoon into the charred pie and pulling out a spoonful of untainted gooey filling.

"Oooh, cherry is my favorite," they say, and take a bite. Their eyes fall closed, and they keep the spoon in their mouth for a long moment with a pornographic moan.

My text alert goes off, and I snatch my phone off the counter, wiping the flour thumbprint off the screen as I walk over to the couch to join them. A message from Kira glows on the screen.

> KIRA: This is my day: 💩
> KIRA: You busy? Wanna save me?

I smile at the screen as I drop down next to Ian. "Hey, Kira's having a bad day, apparently. Do you mind if she joins us?"

"Of course not," Ian says around the spoon in his mouth. Willow grunts their agreement, totally focused on the TV.

> NIC: Oh no, did your interview not go well?
> NIC: We're doing Queer Eye and Cry if you wanna join us
> KIRA: Can I bring whiskey?
> KIRA: I'm bringing whiskey

NIC: Bring it. I have ginger ale.

KIRA: On my way.

KIRA: And thanks. ♥

I smile to myself and grab a fourth spoon from the kitchen. When I return, Willow and Ian pin me with identical raised eyebrows.

"You and Kira have been spending a lot of time together lately. Anything you want to tell us?" Ian asks with a sweet, hopeful smile. I blush and shove my phone into my hoodie pocket, focusing intently on ripping the burned top crust apart with my spoon.

"No, stop," I say, forcing the grin off my face. "She's part of our group now, so I'm trying to get to know her. She's just a friend."

And I realize . . . yeah, actually. She *is* a friend. We haven't known each other long or anything, but we're not just partners in crime anymore, I think. I like her. And I'm looking forward to her coming over.

I scoop out a big spoonful of cherry filling, and what do you know? It's actually delicious.

By the time Kira arrives, the pie is half-destroyed and Willow, Ian, and I are already weeping messes. I open the door to greet her and find her standing on my welcome mat in an oversized, long-sleeved Seattle Sounders shirt, hair still wet from the shower and a bottle of whiskey sticking out of her purse. She summons a weak smile and wipes a tear off my cheek, then hands me the whiskey.

"Fix us some drinks?" she asks softly.

I study the label for a second, then look back to Kira, taking in her tired, red-rimmed eyes, the little downturn at the corner of her mouth. Wordlessly, I throw my arms around her neck and pull her in for a hug, which she returns instantly, clinging like it's just what she needed. The last bit of my own tension unwinds too, and when she breaks away, I beckon her inside, clicking the door quietly shut behind us.

In the kitchen, I clear away enough of the baking wreckage to set down the bottle of whiskey and two science-themed mugs ("I make horrible science puns . . . *periodically*" and "GIRLS JUST WANNA HAVE FUNding for scientific re-search"). What? It's all I have. I live alone; why do I need tea mugs *and* water glasses *and* wineglasses *and* tumblers *and* whatever else supposed adults have in their cabinets?

Kira and I prepare our drinks in silence, letting the heaviness of the day melt while Karamo's soothing voice instructs us through the TV, telling us to lay down our burdens and accept help from the people who care about us. I want so badly to ask for details about what happened, what's got her looking so painfully sad, but that's not what she needs now. She's looking for comfort. I can help with that.

Drinks in hand, we join Willow and Ian, who scoot to the far side so Kira can squeeze onto the couch next to me, until all four of us are basically in each other's laps. A puppy pile of tears, whiskey, and sticky-sweet goodness. My leg is warm where Kira's thigh is draped over mine, and I can't help but grin as she shovels terrible pie into her mouth, burned crust and all, and the first *Queer Eye*–induced tears well in her eyes.

My heart aches pleasantly in my chest.

I'm really glad she's here. I'm glad we're friends. I haven't made a real, genuine friend that's stuck around since college. Since Skylar formed our group, really. But Kira seems like she might be the real thing. She actually reaches out to me, wants to talk to me, and trusts me with her bad-day bruised heart. It's such a novel feeling, after years of utterly failing to connect with anyone, to finally have someone who matters to me, and who I matter to.

I smile to myself and slouch deeper into the couch, into Kira's side.

Look how this day turned around after all.

CHAPTER EIGHT

KIRA

I have such mixed feelings about the Fourth of July. I adore the opportunity to get sloppy and hang with my friends, but the firefighter in me can't turn off the anxious anticipation. To most people, the Fourth is a day for barbecues, fireworks, and singing along to all the country songs they pretend not to like the rest of the year. For a firefighter, it's parades in the morning and a night full of garage fires, grass fires, house fires, boat fires, firework burns, and the worst: drunk-driving accidents.

This year, the Fourth happens to fall on my day off, and I didn't even draw the on-call overtime straw. I'm one hundred percent free. I'm trying to embrace it, but I can't stop thinking about how the three guys who also interviewed for the lieutenant position are all either working or on call. Does it look bad for me to be off on one of our busiest holidays? Is them not scheduling me a bad sign? I volunteered for the parade anyway, because I think it's important for the little girls out there to see someone like them as part of SFD. A lot of the firehouse bros think parades are stupid. They don't see the value. They don't need to, I guess.

Ugh. Obviously, the answer here is another whiskey to pass the time until my pointless Tinder date later.

It's unseasonably warm tonight—yet another record high day. Thanks, climate change. It does mean we get to play outside without lugging sweaters around in the middle of summer, though. There's a huge block party happening in Capitol Hill near-ish to Skylar's apartment, sponsored by one of the neighborhood gay bars, and it's like Pride part two out here. A stage is set up at one end of the blocked-off street, where some of Seattle's most famous drag queens are lip-syncing their fabulous hearts out, while the other end of the street is choked with food trucks of every kind.

"This is heaven," Nic says, munching on fries from a paper cone in Skylar's hand.

"Right?" Skylar says. "I knew you'd love them."

Nic gestures expansively at the line of food trucks, her gestures clumsy with tipsiness.

"This whole thing though," she says. "So far I've had a freshly fried donut, an amazing pineapple taco, vegan mac and cheese, which I didn't think was possible but it *totally is*, a tiny apple pie, and so many delicious beers. How are there so many kinds of beer? Lots. Many lots of beer."

Skylar and I lock eyes and bust out laughing, but Nic doesn't even notice, just dives right into those french fries like they're the most precious delicacy on the planet and are scheduled to disappear at any second. Did someone give her a hit of their weed?

Grace gives a wolfish grin and elbows Ian in the side—

though given their height difference, it hits his hip. "Hey, isn't that the mom of one of your preschoolers over there?"

Ian's eyes go wide and he whirls around, scanning the crowd, then glares at Grace. "Not funny. One of them ambushed me in the grocery store as I was trying to buy condoms last week. I thought I was going to die. I had to pretend I was looking for laxatives instead, because they were right next to the condoms. For some reason, that was better."

"Oh my god, just *buy the condoms*," Grace says. "I don't get it. You're an adult, and safe sex is important! Shows you're a smart guy who's teaching those children well."

Ian covers his face in remembered mortification. "Not exactly a subject that's covered in preschool, Grace. I don't know how to explain it to you. Teachers are held to a weird standard, you know?"

"I totally get it," Skylar says. "Back when I was doing my clinical hours, I ran into some clients of mine three times in one week at the worst possible times. Once while I was holding a box of dental dams, once at the gynecologist's office, and once at a club, just as I was getting ready to take a girl home. I started to wonder if they were stalking me. *So* humiliating. Don't cross the streams."

"Don't cross the streams," Ian echoed solemnly, clinking his plastic beer cup against Skylar's.

"Speaking of taking people home," Willow says, appearing from nowhere. "Where'd Marco go?"

"Yeah, I haven't seen him yet!" Skylar pouts.

Marco's head swivels around a few feet away, where some guy has his fingers wrapped in Marco's belt loops. "You rang?"

"Marco, you live!" Skylar shouts. "How's the glamorous world of nursing?"

"I only had to give *two* awkward sponge baths today, so

pretty good, I think!" he shouts back, then turns to let his maybe-date whisper something in his ear. Something filthy, if his lascivious grin is anything to go by.

"Place your bets," Grace calls, and everyone quickly gives a thumbs-up or a thumbs-down. Grace, Nic, and I are all thumbs-up: Marco is totally going home with this guy at the end of the night. To my surprise, though, Ian and Skylar are both thumbs-down.

"No?" I say, furrowing my brow at them.

Ian shrugs. "Nah. I don't think so."

Skylar smiles up at him and nods. "I agree! Smart man."

The traditional prize is a nice, greasy hangover brunch the next morning, with the check split between whoever guessed wrong. It's been going on since before I joined up with this group, since their sophomore year in college together, I think. I'm pretty sure Marco somehow invented this whole bet system, though, because the result is that whether he goes home with someone or not, he never has to pay for his own brunch. A glitch in the system no one has ever bothered to fix. Ah well. He pays for enough rounds of drinks that I'm sure it equals out.

"Is this about Marco's Sunday brunch guy?" I ask. "He mentioned him that night we were at Crescent. Bit out of character, right?"

Ian and Skylar share a look.

"Who knows?" Ian says with a shrug, then steals a fry from Skylar's cone. She gives an indignant protest, which kicks off a round of the sibling-like bickering that has always characterized their friendship. With the other half of the group distracted, Grace takes the opportunity to pounce.

"So," she says with a wicked expression, "how's Operation Flying Fox going?"

"Operation what now?" I ask, looking between Nic and Grace.

"It's going horribly," Nic laments, collapsing forward to rest her forehead on my shoulder. I wrap an arm around her waist—she's swaying an awful lot for only eight thirty in the evening—and give Grace a one-armed shrug.

"The Fijian flying fox is Fiji's only endemic mammal," Grace says as if that explains everything, which I guess it does. Didn't realize our shenanigans had been given a name, or that between the two of us, we'd told Grace enough for her to *give* it a name. I glance up really quick to make sure Skylar is occupied and won't overhear, then lean in closer to give our report.

"She's still full speed ahead, as far as we know. It's hard to tell if you're getting through to her sometimes, you know? She's so good at breezing past things. But the stuff we've tried so far doesn't seem to have worked."

"You haven't been by her apartment lately, have you?" Nic asks, lifting her head with a hopeful look.

Grace raises an eyebrow. "No. Why?"

"No reason," I hurry to answer, picturing the desiccated husks of a hundred dollars' worth of plants littering her windowsills. "The less you know, the better. We still have time. We'll make it work. And if we don't, well, it's been fun hanging out anyway, right?"

I don't realize until the stab of fear hits me that I actually want to know the answer. Is Nic enjoying spending time with me? Does she mind how much of her time I've been monopolizing? Of course, she'd probably rather be spending it with Skylar, with the possibility of her leaving hanging over us all. Nic seems to be a little in denial about it, though, and Skylar's been MIA a lot lately anyway. Whenever I ask Skylar about where she's been, she gets ultra-mysterious. All she says is, "Lessons." I try not to interpret the word as ominous.

Nic smiles up at me, though, her cheeks flushed from the beer. "Yeah. I wasn't sure what to expect when I came home. I kinda worried you were my replacement in the group. But you're nice. And fun. And pretty." She scrunches up her brow in confusion at that last one, like it just materialized out of nowhere, then shrugs. "It's true. We are officially friends. Crying into my terrible pie solidified it forever."

An uncontrollable smile takes over my lips. I can't meet her eyes.

"Well, good," I say. "If we fail, we'll both be in the market for a new Seattle-based best friend."

A stricken look crosses Nic's face, and I try not to take offense.

"But this is so much *fun*," she says, turning to face me so she can shake my shoulder for emphasis. "Fun is the *best*, and Skylar *always* organizes all the fun. No one will talk to me if Skylar leaves, and her mom will forget me, and I'll just be a sad Casper floating around between a lab full of fire and an apartment full of fire."

There are *so* many things about that sentence that worry me, the phrase "sad Casper" not the least among them, but there's one thing I can definitely clear up.

"*I* will still talk to you," I say, forcing myself to meet her gaze. Intense eye contact is difficult, though, when one party is starting to feel the buzz, and the other is sprinting for mythological levels of drunkenness with everything she's got. "And if the frequency of Mama Clark's texts to you is any indication, *she* will still talk to you, too. We've got you."

But Nic isn't listening anymore. She breaks free of my hold and whirls dangerously around.

"SKYLAR!" she shouts at the volume of the obliviously drunk. "Skylar, you know there's no Fourth of July in Fiji, right? You're gonna miss alllll this *so much*. This whole thing," she says, smacking the stranger next to her with an expansive gesture, "was *your* idea. Who will you have to go along with all your *things* in Fiji?"

Skylar's expression softens, and she steps forward to gently cover Nic's mouth with the hand not holding an umbrella drink. "Sweetie, that's still supposed to be a secret, remember? And I know I'll be lonely at first in Fiji, but you know me. I like people! People like me! I'll find my way. And of *course* I'll stay in touch with all of you and visit as often as I can."

Nic barrels on like she didn't hear a word of what Skylar said.

"And no one will talk to me except Kira, which is great because she smells nice, but I love *all* of you, and I don't want us to drift apart, because Skylar is the glue."

I blink. I smell nice? The look Grace shoots me is positively devilish, but this isn't about me. This is about Nic veering close to dangerous territory.

"Nic," I say, taking her by the elbow. "Why don't we—"

"I'm *trying* to make you see," Nic says to Skylar, insistent, and my eyes go wide. Grace pulls out her phone and brings up a rideshare app, ready to pour Nic into a ride home if necessary. Willow, absolute angelic saint that they are, senses the danger and rematerializes at Nic's side with more food before she can get another word out.

"I got you more tacos to soak up some of those shots you took," they say, shoving the taco straight at Nic's mouth so she has no choice but to take a giant bite.

"When did she even take shots?" I ask, bewildered. "I was with her the whole time!"

Skylar barks a laugh. "Oh, you have to watch her every single second. She's a ninja shotter. You turn your back to say hi to someone, and by the time you turn back, she's downed a shot of Jäger and has tequila on the way."

My stomach lurches at the mere thought of Jäger. Never again.

While Nic happily munches on a mouthful of taco that's probably filled with quinoa, kale, and rare local mushrooms or something, I make pleading eyes at Ian and gesture with my empty cup. I don't want to leave Nic alone holding the bomb that is our Skylar scheme, but I also can't possibly get through this experience without more whiskey. My fingers are itching to pull out my phone and check every 911 scanner app and SFD social media account to see how busy the department is tonight. Ian snatches the cup from my hand and disappears for a moment, then reappears with a cup twice as large, filled to the brim.

"You are a saint among men," I declare, and take a long gulp as Marco rejoins the group.

"What happened to your date?" Nic shouts to Marco, then chases Willow's hand with an open mouth for another bite of taco.

"Wasn't a date," he shouts back. "Just an old friend saying hello. I'm here with you all tonight."

Skylar and I glance at each other, and I raise an eyebrow.

"Marco bailing on someone who's obviously down to fuck? He really has caught feelings for his mystery brunch guy," I say, but she only puts a finger to her lips and winks. Ugh, there is something going on there, and it is going to *kill me*. I must know. Normally, Grace is one who collects secrets like a gossip-hungry decorator crab, but when you dangle something shiny straight in front of my face, I'm gonna go for it.

Marco rolls his eyes and throws his arms around Skylar and Ian. "So, what, are we just gonna stand around all night, or are we gonna go *dance*?"

"Dance!" Grace says, skipping off into the crowd without waiting for anyone else. Marco, Ian, and Skylar all follow, drinks hoisted above their heads so they don't get hit by a flailing partygoer. Nic is nearly done snarfing her taco, so Willow and I split the last one, discard the wreckage, and haul Nic into the crowd. I down half my drink in one go to reduce the likelihood of spilling, but also because Nic is eyeing it like she wants some, and I think she's had enough. Between us all, we manage to pour water into her instead of alcohol for the next two hours. I, on the other hand, make up for lost time until everything is pleasantly blurry around the edges and that thing that normally keeps laughter locked up inside my chest relaxes.

The show is, quite honestly, *magical*. It's sort of a lip-syncing competition/pageant, which I didn't realize before, with a cash prize for best performance. We dance through tons of performances until, at 9:30 p.m., the competitors all file back onstage for a big group number. Then I realize why: as soon as the city's big fireworks show begins in the sky behind the stage, the music kicks off, and the choreographed dance begins. The crowd shouts their approval as the world blurs into glitter, lights, and bass. The mashup of songs builds higher and higher along with the fireworks, and when the beat drops, the drag queens break ranks and stride offstage, straight into the audience, arms thrown over their heads and hips swiveling wide. The crowd goes wild, jumping along with the music in a wild sea of waving hands, forcing the seven of us even closer together. Ian throws an arm around Marco, drawing him closer to his front, while Grace loops her arms around

Ian's waist from behind. Willow, Nic, and I press close around them, and Skylar jumps in a dizzying circle, her hair whirling everywhere in a golden cascade, somehow dancing with all of us and none of us at the same time. Nic edges up to Skylar, trying to draw her closer to the group, but the people next to us crowd her away from Skylar and into me instead. I take the opportunity to pull her close and murmur in her ear.

"We'll make this work," I say, curling an arm around her waist to draw her close. "We'll get her to stay. And even if we don't, if it doesn't work out, then you'll still have the rest of us, okay? You'll still have me."

She turns around in my arms so we're face-to-face and studies me.

"I'm not giving up," she says carefully.

I shake my head. "Me neither."

Then she's hugging me tight, holding me so close our bodies press together from chest to thigh, swaying to the music.

"I'm glad I met you," she says, pulling back to kiss me on the cheek. But she's drunk, and I'm pretty much there myself.

She misses.

She's kissing me.

On the *mouth*.

God.

Distantly, I think I should stop this, that we shouldn't, but with her soft lips moving on mine and her nails dragging through my hair, I suddenly can't think of a single reason why.

Would it be so bad if we got together? Skylar wouldn't mind, I think. None of the others would mind. Why should I deny myself the possibility of being with someone so smart, so driven and passionate? So *beautiful*? I have to at least consider it.

Maybe it'll be awkward later. Maybe I'll regret it. But right now, in this moment, it feels important. Necessary and real, like I don't actually have to wait for a promotion to deserve this. Like it could really work, just because we are who we are, right here and now.

I'm gonna give this a try. I'm gonna pursue this girl.

And I'm definitely gonna cancel my boring Tinder date.

I smile, run my thumb up under the back hem of Nic's shirt, and pull her body even tighter against mine, loving the feel of her breasts pressing against mine and her skin under my hands.

We kiss again.

Again.

And damn, it's *good*.

CHAPTER NINE

NIC

A week passes before we can find a time to make our next attempt, and it takes me almost as long to get over the hangover and embarrassment from the Fourth of July. Ugh. Why do I make bad choices? And yet, it's not like I've never made out with a friend before—several times at parties with Willow, once with Grace when she "just wanted to see," once with Skylar that was almost as painful as it was amazing, and even once with Ian in sophomore year, which we both found hilarious. It's never been a big deal. Why does it feel weird this time?

I run my finger over a cluster of tiny white flowers filling the gaps between a rainbow of enormous blossoms, the feature arrangement in the flower shop's front window. This little Skylar-related errand will be the first time Kira and I have seen each other since the kiss—kisses. *Plural.* Because it went on for a *while.* It wasn't until one of the drag queens marched through the crowd to dance with our group, belting out some Dolly Parton at the top of her lungs, that we finally broke apart. Dolly always deserves full attention. And then there was some late-night greasy breakfast. Then we all ended up at Marco's place somehow . . . It got a little hazy.

Kira seems to be reacting okay, if her texts are anything to go by. She hasn't brought it up, at least, which I appreciate. I am the actual worst at awkward conversations. I stumble over my words, can't make eye contact, repeat myself, a real glorious sight to behold. The kisses weren't bad or anything—on the contrary, they were pretty fucking great—but it's not fair to her for me to be pulling that shit when I'm over here in love with Skylar and pursuing her in the only way I can. Kira is so smart, dedicated, selfless, kind, and funny in her own dry, quiet way. She deserves someone who is one hundred percent devoted to her. Maybe if Skylar leaves . . .

But no. I've tried this. Dating other people has never worked, not in the nine years I've known Skylar. Kira and I would go the same route as every other girlfriend I've had. We'd date for a few months. I'd watch us get more and more distant until she'd finally say something like, "I just feel like we aren't connecting." Then it would be over. But this time, what would it do to the group? Especially because I have yet to master the skill of being friends with an ex.

It doesn't matter. Skylar is my home, my family, and it doesn't help anything for me to get distracted. Besides, in Kira, I have the makings of a really good friend. I should focus on not fucking that up. Plus, I don't want Skylar to get the impression that I'm into someone else. If she thinks Kira and I are a thing, then that gives her even less reason to stay.

I texted her on July 5 to apologize for the night before, but the exchange was brief and cryptic.

NIC: Hey, I just wanted to say I'm sorry for being such a mess last night
NIC: I didn't mean to get so sloppy and almost spill your secrets
NIC: And the thing with Kira.
NIC: That wasn't anything, you know. We're not together and I'm not interested in her that way. I was just sad and I tried to kiss her on the cheek and things went awry which sounds like total bullshit but I promise it's not
NIC: Okay?
SKYLAR: Oh, my sweet Nic Knack, you're adorable
SKYLAR: I'm gonna be busy the next few days but there is a dress fitting appointment in our near future and it'll be EXCITING
SKYLAR: Bye for a bit!
NIC: What do you have going on the next few days?

She left me on Read. I hate it when she gets all mysterious and disappears. I think really hard about texting Mama Clark for intel, but the bell over the door tinkles and Kira rushes in, tucking her keys into her bag.

"I'm so sorry I'm late," she says, looking harried. "One of the guys tried to convince me I had switched my schedule with someone else and that I was late reporting for work. Like I don't know my own schedule. But now I'm gonna be a mess until I go in, because part of my brain will be wondering if he was right instead of just a douchebag."

We hug briefly in greeting, and the scent that always clings to her fills my nose, sweet and light. What did she say it was? LUSH Plum Rain and ambition? Gotta say, ambition smells divine on her, even if it's stressing her out right now. I hope she hears back about that promotion soon.

"Don't worry about it. I'm sure he was just being awful," I say, pulling back to scan for signs of awkwardness. Kira meets my eyes easily, though, a pretty smile lighting her face and tugging at my cautious heart. Not awkward at all, then, I guess. Good. Right?

I clear my throat and look away. "So, have you been by Skylar's apartment this week?"

"No, she keeps finding excuses to meet me other places because she's 'packing and her place is a mess,'" Kira says, scowling. "It's killing me. Also, I didn't realize her lease was up so soon or I wouldn't have bothered with plants at all."

I shake my fist at the sky. "I keep picturing her sitting on her couch in the morning, sipping her tea, surrounded by withered plant corpses. Is that morbid?"

"Same. I *must know.*"

An employee (Everett, according to his name tag) slides into our conversation with the effortless ease of a smooth salesman, smelling not of ambition, but of beard oil and weed.

"I heard 'withered plant corpses' and got concerned, so I figured I'd offer some assistance," he says with a charming smile. "What kind of flowers are you looking for today?"

Kira and I look at each other blankly. I haven't been in a flower shop since I last bought flowers for my mom's headstone ten years ago, a memory my brain flinches away from. Apparently, Kira doesn't know where to start, either. We managed to overlook that little detail when we were texting about this plan earlier in the week. It went like this:

KIRA: Okay, I know we've already done something plant related but hear me out, this is a totally different approach
KIRA: FLOWERS FROM A SECRET ADMIRER
KIRA: ☺
KIRA: RIGHT??
NIC: She doesn't like it when people ask her out, though. It'll be an instant no for her. No intrigue at all.

Right? RIGHT? I got my hopes up ever so briefly that Skylar had changed in my absence, that my problems could potentially be solved by marching up to Skylar and just *asking*. Kira killed it pretty quick, though.

KIRA: Totally true, she says no every time. EVERY TIME, I don't understand it.
KIRA: BUT she DOES like being admired
KIRA: A secret admirer and the resulting social media hype when she inevitably shares the flowers online might convince her that she'll miss out on all the adoration when she leaves.

Which, yes, okay, she was right. Skylar has a bit of a vain streak. It has the potential to be the perfect ploy. But now we're here, staring at bearded guy and a collection of flowers I couldn't name with a gun to my head.

"Uh, Kira," I say. "Tell the guy what kind of flowers we're looking for."

"Pretty ones?" she says.

The guy snorts, and all three of us break down laughing.

"Okay, since you're obviously hopeless, how about I help you out," he says, waving us deeper into the shop. "What do you need them for? You two need wedding flowers?"

My cheeks go hot, and I can't help but glance at Kira, who's looking back at me with her bottom lip between her teeth. *There's* the awkwardness we've managed to avoid thus far.

"No, uh, it's a bit . . ." How do I even describe to this guy what we're trying to accomplish without him booting us out onto the street because a) we're horrible human beings and b) it turns out he's some kind of secret Skylar superfan? It's happened before. Her people are *everywhere*.

"It's hard to explain," Kira says, picking up where I trailed off. "But we need them for a . . . secret admirer kind of situation. For a woman. To be sent with a note."

She cringes, because it sounds so horribly cheesy when you say it out loud. The guy raises an eyebrow, though, and smirks in such a mischievous way, it's mildly concerning.

"So, I have some options. You could go pretty traditional, red roses, blah blah, but I feel like you're looking for something more . . ."

"Loud," Kira says.

"Yes," I agree. "She's got a . . . big personality."

Everett grins. "That I can work with. Price point?"

We actually *did* talk about this beforehand. My new job has left me with more spending money than I've ever had in my broke student life, which is still not much, but it's *something*. And Kira lives a pretty lean lifestyle with good pay and benefits, so we decided we could splurge a bit. Still, it pains me deep in my soul to tell the guy, "Seventy-five dollars is our limit."

"Perfect." He whirls away with a hand to his mouth, then points to an arrangement on the far wall. "This one. What do you think? I can customize it, if you need."

He snatches the vase from the shelf and sets it on a low table for us to admire. It's a dramatic half-moon spray of roses, but they're not like any roses I've ever seen. They must be dyed or something, because each rose is a whole rainbow swirl of color. They're packed in with stems of tiny white flowers, and the whole effect is just . . . way over the top.

"They're perfect," Kira says.

I nod my agreement. "What the hell are they?"

"We call them rainbow roses," Everett says, already moving toward the register. "We dye them here in house. They're very popular during Pride, but we carry some year-round."

"I feel like it's shouting at me. It's the caps lock of flower arrangements," I say, daring to run a finger over the soft petals, then inspecting my fingertip for leaked dye.

Kira bumps her hip into mine. "That's what makes it so on point, right? Are we agreed?"

"Oh, absolutely."

"But we have to write the card now."

"I got this," I say, and plop myself down in the chair next to the service desk to compose the note. Writing a secret admirer note to Skylar should come laughably easy to me, right? I stare at the blank card for a long moment, then look up with wide eyes.

"Wait, you aren't going to send this exact card in my handwriting, are you?"

Everett's smile fades a bit. "I mean, yeah. Unless you'd rather we send a printed one, which—"

"Yes," I say over the cool relief flooding my chest. "Yes, that. Do that, please."

"Well, just write extra neatly so we don't make a horrible typo that'll send your potential girlfriend screaming." He hands me a pen like he's presenting me with a solemn responsibility. "You seem to be taking the *secret* part of this secret admirer thing very seriously."

Buddy, you have *no* idea.

I tap the pen against my cheek for a minute and think. What would intrigue Skylar? Make her so curious that she'd consider not leaving?

And if she somehow discovers that it's from me, what will make her want me?

I compose it in my head first, then put pen to paper.

Skylar,

I know secret admirer notes are a few decades out of fashion, but they seem like your kind of thing, so here I am. Here I always am, for you.

Who knows you the best?

Who's always there when you're hurting?

Who puts your happiness first?

Who could make you feel so good, if given the chance?

I'm here if you want me.

Right here.

Just say the word.

Always with love,

Your secret admirer

When I finish, I hand it to Kira with my eyes averted. Hopefully she doesn't see through me.

"Yes, that's perfect!" Kira says, reading over what I've

written. "It's the ideal secret admirer note. A little mysterious, a little sexy but not creepily so, a little sweet, and a little . . . What's the word? Longing, maybe?"

Welp, I'd like to melt into the floor right now. It's the perfect secret admirer note because it's *coming from a secret admirer.* Those words aren't fiction concocted to convince Skylar it might be worth staying. They're my honest words. My feelings. I wonder how obvious it would be if I suddenly knocked my coffee over on this notecard, then played it off like, *Oh no, I forgot what I wrote! You do it.* The shop owner plucks it from my hands before I can make the move, though, and begins typing into the computer.

"I could see you about to chicken out, so consider this me saving you from yourself," he says, clicking away happily. "Where would you like these sent and when?"

"First thing Monday morning?" I ask, daring to look at Kira. She nods. "Yeah. To the station?"

"Yes." I spell out Skylar's first name and the address of the radio station where she does her call-in advice show, which Everett dutifully types into his computer. If he recognizes Skylar's name, he doesn't betray it, just takes our credit cards and splits the payment. When he presents us each with a receipt, his impish smirk returns.

"I wish you the best of luck with your secret love," he says. "If it works out, you'll have to come back and tell me."

"I will," I say, because if I do end up with Skylar, I'll wanna tell the whole damn world. Why not start with Beard Oil Everett?

Once we step outside, the gray overcast day instills in me an instant and insistent need for coffee. Kira and I stand in the parking lot, where our cars sit side by side, and . . . yeah, now it's gotten a little awkward.

"Do you wanna get coffee?" I blurt out to fill the strained

silence. "There's a place on the next block that's really good. We can plan our next move, in case this one doesn't pan out."

Kira glances over at Toyonda Civry, keys clutched in her hand, looking torn. "Ugh, I really want to, but I need to get a nap in before I have to be on for twenty-four hours. If I don't sleep, I'll be cranky as hell and useless to the crew."

Disappointment tugs in my chest, but I could never blame her. That schedule must be rough, and her job is so demanding. I picture her in full bunker gear, facing down a raging fire with an axe in her hands, her expression serious and fierce. I mean, not to overromanticize what is a seriously difficult and dangerous job, but . . . there is an undeniable appeal to the image.

Yeah, it's probably for the best we don't do the coffee thing. That sounded more date-ish than I intended, anyway, and that's not fair to her. Especially not with a vision of her stripping out of her gear now firmly in my mind.

Skylar. Remember *Skylar*. She's the point of all this.

"How does that even work?" I ask, steering more into friend territory. "Are you allowed to sleep on shift?"

Kira laughs. "Yes, and we do, but it's almost worse trying to sleep than it is to stay awake some nights. If it's a busy night, the alarm is constantly jolting you awake as soon as your eyes shut. I try to catch twenty-minute power naps on busier nights, like Fridays, weekends, and holidays. Other nights, I occasionally get some real sleep, but not much."

"So, basically, I should stop texting you before noon on your days off," I say with a wince. "Sorry about that."

Her answering smile is sweet, and she bumps her hand against mine. "Hey, it's fine. You're officially part of my life once you learn and embrace this essential fact about my existence."

I like the sound of that. Even through all this drama and

chaos, I've gained a friend. A really good one, too. I hope, no matter what happens with Skylar, we're able to keep this up.

"Good to know," I say, then do that awkward sway thing that always happens when you aren't sure if you should go in for a hug or not. Kira takes things out of my hands, though, and steps up to wrap her arms around me.

"Enjoy your coffee, okay? Hope your night is chill," she says, then turns to walk away.

"Yours too," I say ten seconds too late as Kira's car door slams shut.

ON MONDAY MORNING, A BEAUTIFULLY LIT AND filtered photo of the flower arrangement graces the top of my Instagram feed. Below it, the caption is short and sweet:

> @DoctorSky—Look at these flowers I received from a *secret admirer*! Sorry ladies, it's a super sweet thought, but I'm officially off the market. Details to come! #SkylarsSecret

Skylar's fans are going *nuts* in the comments. People tagging each other, asking if they sent the flowers, people begging to know what #SkylarsSecret is and posting their own reaction videos using the hashtag. Seriously, Skylar is one of the few people who can make up a ridiculous self-referencing hashtag and have people start using it instantly. Influencers probably deal with this kind of thing all the time, but with Skylar specifically being known as a radio and social media relationship counselor, the hype is extra high for this. Seattle's Queen of Romance getting flowers from a secret admirer? And saying she's off the market?

We were *so* close this time. She did share them, and the hype is real, but her quick dismissal of her "secret admirer" takes the wind right out of me. Did she realize it was me? If she had, would she have been so casual and public about shooting me down?

No, she would have called. Or talked to me in person. She has no idea.

It probably hasn't even occurred to her that I'm an option.

My heart sinks, and I hit the share icon to forward the post to Kira.

NIC: . . . damn it.
NIC: Back to the drawing board. Again.

The messages show up as read right away.

KIRA: Hey, we'll get there.
KIRA: It's a cumulative effect.
KIRA: Something about a frog in a pot of boiling water
KIRA: Which I always thought was a cruel metaphor
NIC: That's actually a myth! The critical thermal maximum for many frog species is an increase of around 2 degrees F
NIC: They'll get agitated and jump right out long before they actually boil to death
NIC: Omg sorry
NIC: Not the point.

God, why am I *that person*? No one likes that person. Quick, move past it! Skylar is still off doing whatever she does when she disappears, and there are no group plans, so . . .

NIC: Come over tonight? We can get pizza and watch some more Bold Type or something

NIC: Maybe an episode will inspire a genius idea that will solve all our problems

KIRA: I'll be there. All I'm doing right now is looking for some new recipes. I'm on dinner duty tomorrow at the firehouse.

NIC: What are you gonna make? Cooking for a whole firehouse of people sounds hard

NIC: Also, have you ever gotten interrupted and had to leave something in the middle of cooking?

KIRA: Oh, all the time. Just gotta remember to turn off the burner before you run for your gear

KIRA: A lot of it is finding recipes that scale well. Chili is easy, but I only ever make it on a busy night when we'll be out of the firehouse a lot

KIRA: You can't even imagine what it smells like in there afterward. And I don't mean the chili.

I snort and slap a hand over my mouth to keep from busting out laughing. But hey, I'm alone in this apartment, so what am I holding back for? I laugh so hard the lit candle next to my breakfast plate nearly goes out.

NIC: Thanks for the laugh. I needed that.

NIC: Looking forward to tonight

I'm about to head out the door for work when her final reply comes.

KIRA: Can't wait.

CHAPTER TEN

NIC

I know something is wrong with Kira the second I open the door that evening. She stands out in the hall wearing her fire-house shirt and a mid-thigh-length skirt, her eyes bloodshot and puffy, mouth tight and drawn in.

"Can I come in?" she asks, and I scramble back to open the door wider, feeling like a jerk for standing there, staring at her while she sniffles.

"What happened?" I ask. "Are you okay?"

She sets her bag on the countertop and heads into the kitchen, hoisting herself up on one of the stools. With a deep, calming breath, she runs a hand through her hair and says words that seem to weigh a thousand pounds.

"I didn't get the promotion. Again."

Oh no.

My heart sinks, and I stride forward to stand between her legs and pull her into a hug.

"Kira, I'm so sorry. God, that sucks. They are so horrible!"

"My dad was right. I'm never going to get anywhere in this system," she says with a sniffle, muffled against my shoulder. "I feel like I'm throwing myself against a sliding glass door, like a stupid, confused bird ready to knock itself out from sheer stubbornness, and there's always some buff muscle bro named Jared on the other side, flexing his pecs while he laughs at my struggle."

"That's an extremely specific metaphor. Do I need to hunt down a guy named Jared?"

It's a bad joke, but I feel her weak laugh vibrate where her chest is pressed to mine. She drops her forehead on my shoulder.

"Is my professor right? Is it pointless for me to stay? Should I even keep trying?"

I tighten my arms around her and run a hand up her spine, relishing the feel of holding someone even as my heart aches for her and this shitty situation.

"I know what you mean," I say. "The feeling of being trapped, of struggling for something that might never happen. It really sucks, and I'm so sorry you're having to deal with it right now."

She sniffles and pulls back but keeps her eyes on the ground.

"Thanks. Um. Sorry. For breaking down on you the second you opened the door." She wipes her eyes and shakes out her hands, then meets my gaze. "How are you?"

I look down at my red "Baking Is Science for Hungry People" apron loosely tied over my pajamas and covered in flour, and smirk at the accurate summation of my life. I gesture down at myself.

"You know. A mess. And I got some of my mess on you, whoops." I reach out to brush away a smudge of flour below her collarbone, dusting her dark blue SFD shirt. My fingers linger for a moment, suddenly feeling the weight of the job that goes with this shirt more acutely. It's so hard, and so important, and she wants so badly to do even *more*. It's horrible that she's being kept down because of bigoted assholes and politics. It makes me feel ridiculous for stewing in my own bullshit all day.

Something of my thoughts must show on my face, because Kira covers my hand with hers and squeezes.

"Hey. What smells so good in here?"

I smile and look back down at the floor, pleased.

"I'm getting better at pies, I think. I've got a bourbon pecan pie in the oven right now. Kind of got a taste for them while I was out East for grad school. And you're a bourbon fan, right? Thought we could use a treat tonight. And baking usually makes me feel better, even when I'm bad at it."

Her stomach growls audibly, and we both laugh.

"Okay, yes," she says. "That sounds perfect. Is it pie for dinner, or are we still doing pizza with pie afterward?"

"Best of both worlds. I even got ice cream for the pie, *and* there's bourbon left over for drinking."

A smile stretches her tearstained cheeks, less bright than normal, but honest and real.

"You truly are a queen. I bow before you, my lady," she says, taking one of my hands and bowing to brush her lips over the back.

I snort and snatch my hand back, shoving her shoulder toward the couch to cover the flutter low in my stomach. "Go. Sit. Pull up Hulu. I assume we're continuing the rewatch of *The Bold Type*?"

"Uh, yes, obviously."

It's a show we both missed when it was still airing but started watching together soon after the *Queer Eye* and Cry night. Up until now, we've been watching separately in our own apartments, hitting Play together and live-texting our reactions. It's been a nice distraction from everything: from Skylar, from Mama Clark's worried looks over brunch, from the growing seed of a PhD thesis topic that won't leave me alone. Watching together, in person, should be an even better distraction.

The pizza arrives, and we sit side by side with our plates on our laps, scarfing and talking and living vicariously through these TV women our same age, who are way cooler than us. But also, we pick at pieces of my ugly but absolutely delicious pecan pie and bask in the total hotness and heart-melting sweetness of Kat and Adena. If Aisha Dee walked through the door right now, I would drop to my knees and beg her to let me go down on her in an instant. True story.

"Hey, what's on your mind?" Kira asks during the ad break between episodes.

I open my mouth to speak, then close it again, considering. I'd rather not tell her what was *really* on my mind two seconds ago, but I know I've been quiet overall, mulling in turn over Kira's work problems and my own professional issues. I haven't said this out loud to anyone yet, but I find the words spilling out all the same.

"I just . . . I'm thinking about going back to grad school again. Getting my doctorate."

Kira blinks, then puts her plate down. "What, at UW or something?"

I wince. "Um, no. University of Washington doesn't have any kind of fire dynamics–adjacent doctoral program. Not many places do. I'd be leaving again."

I regret bringing it up instantly, because Kira's face falls in total dejection.

"What? No! You just got here! Got back, I mean. We just met. You can't leave already."

She scoots closer and folds her hands in her lap, and I put my pie down, bringing one leg up on the couch to turn toward her.

"I know, I know. I just . . . I'm not entirely sure that coming back was the right decision, or that I came back for the right reasons. I really enjoyed my research, and I've been picking at a side project that really feels like it could be something. This job is fun, but the contract is only for a year, and contingent on grant funding, at that. I'm not sure it would feel like *enough* going forward, anyway. Coming back to Seattle was always the plan, right from the start, and I'm having a hard time letting go of that. But I also can't stay just because . . ."

I realize my eyes are welling up and pause to collect myself. "I can't stay if . . . if what I need to move on with my life is somewhere else."

Kira studies her folded hands for a moment, then pauses the show and looks me right in the eye.

"Okay, look, I'm gonna say something, and I want to be clear up front that I haven't known you that long, and I could be completely off base. I don't mean to be a jerk or anything, but . . ."

She hesitates.

"Are you sure that it's about the research and your career? Are you sure it's not just . . . putting your life on hold again? Is there something you're waiting for?"

I nearly laugh. She has no idea how right she is. On all counts. I *am* waiting for something. Something I'll probably never have, that's about to be permanently cut off. Work is the only thing I can control, and I *can* make sure that I'm as happy as possible there.

"I'm sorry if I overstepped—" Kira begins, but I shake my head to cut her off.

"No, no, you're not wrong. I'm in a weird transition phase in my life, and a quick decision isn't going to do much good. I'm gonna let things settle for the summer, see what happens with Skylar and Fiji, get through all of that before I make a decision. I probably let my dad get in my head too much last time we talked, too. He's good at that."

Kira is quiet for a moment, a far-off look in her eyes, until she speaks again.

"You know, Skylar recommended another counselor she knows after she saw how much the anniversary of my dad's death messed me up every year. It really helped me work through a lot of the complicated shit I was dealing with, both because of his death and some stuff going on at the fire department. Did Skylar ever tell you how she and I met?"

The instant surge of curiosity catches me off guard, but I've been quietly obsessing about this since I found out Kira existed. Play it cool, self.

"No. I've wondered, though. You said you and she went through some hard stuff together?"

"Yeah." Kira nods, then takes a deep, bracing breath. "We actually met while I was on a fire call. I was responding to a structure fire, and it turned out to be an arson case. The suspect ended up being someone tied to Skylar. This was her first year as a fully licensed counselor, and she had just started doing her pro bono work for the city while building up her social media empire. One of the cases she was overseeing turned into . . . this. Someone died. Not her fault, of course, but it was . . . hard."

Kira closes her eyes and flops sideways against the back of the sofa. I lay a hand on her knee and squeeze.

"Hey. You don't have to talk about this. I don't need details."

She nods, her lips and brows pinched tight.

"I know. Long story short, I was the one who found . . . the person. There was a big legal thing, super messy, and Skylar and I both had to report to the courthouse about a million times. When the case finally closed, Skylar did her thing. She just looked at me and said, 'You look like you need a drink.' She dragged me to the nearest bar, we poured our hearts into many shots of tequila, and the rest is history. We've been tight ever since."

I give a quiet laugh. "Yeah, that's pretty much how it works. Skylar doesn't make friends, she claims people. She'll probably have a whole new surrogate family within two weeks of arriving in Fiji."

If only it were that easy for me. I have to cling tooth and nail to keep the few people I have from slipping away.

"Hey now," Kira says, bumping her knee against mine. "That's quitter talk. We still might stop her, you know?"

I shrug. "Maybe. I don't know. I'm starting to feel like this is all pointless. You know how Skylar is. When she's set on something, she's one hundred percent in. Nothing we've done so far has made the slightest bit of difference. Or so it seems. I haven't ruled out Schrödinger's plants yet."

She laughs but quickly turns serious. "Hey, I mean it, though, about you going off to school again. Please don't leave me here with a bunch of firehouse dudes and a giant Skylar-shaped hole in my life unless you're really sure it's what you want to do. I don't want to lose two friends at once unless you're, like . . . following your dreams and shit."

"I'll keep your plight in mind," I say with a small smile, then raise an eyebrow. "Have you ever dated a firehouse dude?"

"Ew, *no*," she says, looking scandalized. "Dating within the firehouse is a terrible idea, but also, scheduling would be a nightmare. Besides, most firemen are a little too beefy for me. My taste in men tends toward the stringy nerd type."

"Fair," I say, then gather our pie plates and take them to the kitchen. "I'm glad you and Skylar had each other through all of that stuff, you know. It sounds so hard."

I can't see Kira's expression, but her voice is soft when she replies. "And I'm glad you came back to town so I could have a friend to go through all *this* with."

I look back at her from the kitchen and let myself enjoy the sight of her for a moment, the golden light of my excessive candles catching on her cheekbones, her full lips, her deep brown eyes that always look just a little sad. More than a little, right now.

Time to fix that.

"Okay, come on, we need a good cuddle," I say with authority. "Put Kat and Adena back on the TV and get comfy."

She obeys, hitting Play on the next episode and slouching down so only the very top of her head pokes over the top of the couch.

"You know there are characters other than Kat and Adena in this show, right?" she says, muffled.

"Yes, there's also all the other queer woman that get to make out with Kat, and I'm disgustingly jealous of them all. I'm in actual love with her. Don't judge me."

With everything put away, I refresh our drinks and bring the bottle back to the couch. We're both in need of some serious comfort. Kira holds an arm up as I approach, and I slide under it, snuggling in close to her side and throwing one leg over her knee. She accepts her refilled drink, clinks the rim against my glass, and takes a long sip as the plot of the episode begins to unfold. We watch episode after episode, and eventually switch from *The Bold Type* and bourbon to mugs of tea and a random string of queer films from Netflix's LGBTQ+ section. Most of them are varying degrees of terrible, but we finally settle on one at random and sink deeper and deeper into our embrace. God, she smells so good. That LUSH shower gel is *her* scent, as far as I'm concerned. It makes her skin soft too, which I thoroughly enjoy as I run a hand up and down her arm. She tightens her hold on me, bringing me closer and brushing her lips over my hair.

Something in my chest pulls tight. This is *so* nice, exactly what I needed tonight, when I've been feeling so untethered. It's a miracle what some basic human contact can do.

Then a sex scene starts up in the movie, and I realize what trouble I'm in.

Yeah, it's been *way* too long since I've gotten laid for me to be this close to someone while a very hot, very *long* sex scene between two gorgeous women unfolds on my TV screen. Kira and I are so close that I both hear and feel her breath growing shallow, the restless shift of her hips underneath me. Dangerous.

So. *Very.* Dangerous.

I'm half in her lap already; the slightest shift would let me straddle her right leg and get some pressure right where I need it. I'm breathing faster now too, imagining it, how it would feel, what she would do, what she would look like as she came. She's beautiful under normal, everyday circumstances; with my name on her lips and her taste on my tongue, she would be a goddess.

My hips twitch helplessly forward at the thought, the slow burn low in my belly driving my body to seek its pleasure, though I try to stop it. This isn't what this night is supposed to be. She isn't Skylar. She's my friend.

She's running her fingers along the waistband of my shorts.

The slight ticklish feeling sends a wave of shivers up my back and a pulse of heat to my center. I can see it happening in slow motion, where this is going, what's about to happen—but will it sabotage my chances with Skylar? Do I want this bad enough to risk it?

(Do I even care?)

The back of my shirt rides up slightly. Kira flattens her hand on the small of my back, exerting just the slightest guiding pressure.

I shift so my knee is on the couch between her legs, putting me in the perfect position to press myself down on her long, bare thigh. I groan faintly with relief, then with the torturous need for more as my knee slides far enough forward to push Kira's skirt up and feel the wet heat of her center.

I can sense it, the way this situation is ready to catch fire, to become a wild blaze before we have a second more to think about it. I have to check, before we're in too deep. I have to make sure this won't ruin everything. I fight to think clearly through the haze of lust and force myself to speak.

"We're clear about our goal here, right? Operation Flying Fox?"

"Yeah, of course," she says, grinding her thigh up between my legs. My eyes flutter shut, and I groan, shifting my hips to rub in slow circles against her.

"And you want this?" I ask through panting breaths.

"Fuck yes, I do," she says without hesitation.

That's all I need.

I let myself fall forward, crashing my mouth to hers.

CHAPTER ELEVEN

KIRA

Hell. Yes.

God, Nic's mouth is amazing, her kisses hot and insistent as she grinds slowly against my leg, putting perfect pressure on her clit. There is something so hot about watching her take her pleasure—but there's no way I can just sit back. I run my hand up the back of her leg, slipping it under the hem of her sleep shorts to tease at the spot where her leg meets her ass. She pushes back against my hand, then forward onto my thigh again, like she can't decide which she wants. I appease her, letting my hand climb higher under her shorts, and my breath catches.

She's not wearing anything underneath. It's all gloriously bare skin.

I grab a handful and haul her closer until our breasts press deliciously together, her peaked nipples visible through her shirt and absolutely begging for my mouth. God, I want to touch them so badly, touch her *everywhere*, and she seems to sense it, because she pauses for just a moment to unbutton her silky sleep shirt and let it hang open.

She's not wearing a bra, and the view of her bare breasts knocks the wind right out of me.

"Oh my god, you are actually going to kill me," I say, and dive in before the smart reply can leave her mouth. I use the hand still gripping her ass to haul her closer so I can tease one tight nipple with the tip of my tongue, wondering if hers are as sensitive as mine are. If the way her laugh immediately transforms into a gasp is any indication, they definitely are.

She holds herself up on the back of the couch so her breasts are right at the perfect level, her shirt falling down from her shoulders to catch at her elbows, so I obey her silent request and keep my mouth busy on that perfect nipple, dragging my lips over the tip and letting my tongue dart out to tease. My free hand cups her other breast, my thumb rubbing gently at the tip, then daring a light pinch. Nic gasps above me, each exhale painted with the ghost of a moan, and I want *more*.

I let my hand slip away from her breast, tracing down over her ribs, the gorgeous curve of her waist, her hip, then use my grip to tilt her hips so she can still work her clit while I get what I want—my fingers tracing around the bottom hem of her shorts again. I reach up underneath and drag one finger lightly over the line where the fabric meets her legs, slipping a finger just underneath to feel the slick lips inside.

"I never would have imagined you'd be the worst fucking tease on the planet," Nic pants, shifting her hips in an attempt to find my finger. I run just the tip of my middle finger over her entrance, then pull back when she nearly succeeds.

"Oh, was there something you wanted?" I ask, pulling off

her breast to kiss up the side of her neck and speak into her ear. "Something you needed?"

"Kira Fucking McKinney," Nic growls, her hands tightening into a death grip on the back of the couch as her hips work, chasing my finger.

"How do you know my middle name?" I ask sweetly. I tease her entrance again, but this time, I don't back off—I stay right where I am as she impales herself on my finger with a moan. The breath punches out of her, along with a cry, and the slide is so easy, so good, that I add a second finger soon after, loving the slick tightness of her, sinking deep into her wet heat.

I swear, I normally go a lot slower than this. I like to take my time with a girl, spin her up nice and slow, giving her whatever she wants with my fingers, tongue, anything. But it's been way too long for both of us, and apparently, what Nic wants is *fast* and *now*. Can't say I disagree.

She fucks herself on my fingers, her hand cupping the back of my neck and holding my face to her chest. I oblige her silent demand, letting her ride my leg and fingers while I hold her to me with a hand splayed across the small of her back, working her nipples with my mouth. The heat pooling between my legs is almost unbearable, and my hips twitch forward, seeking that same friction that's getting her off.

"I'm so close," she whispers, then louder, more frantic. "So close, I'm so close, so . . . so . . ."

I suck harder on her nipple and drop my hand to her ass, grabbing on hard, and her orgasm crashes into her.

I feel it from the inside, feel her clench around my fingers as she cries out, grinding down hard on my hand and drawing out the last of the pleasure, her whole body shuddering.

Her mouth finds mine and we kiss, slow and deep, tongues twining with languid ease as Nic's hips slow and she comes down from the high.

She pulls back just enough to look into my eyes, and if I weren't already at peak spontaneous combustion levels of turned on right now, the sight of her sex-flushed cheeks and bitten lower lip would do it. She quirks a smile and leans in to kiss me again, long, sensual, teasing . . .

Then, suddenly, she's gone, leaving my lips tingling and my lap cold from her absence.

She reappears between my legs, and my brain goes fully offline.

Nic kneels on the floor with her hands sliding up my thighs, dipping under the hem of my skirt. She looks up at me with half-lidded eyes and licks her lips, then ducks to press a kiss to the inside of my knee.

"Yeah?" she asks, her lips whisper-soft against my skin.

The heat between my legs flares white-hot.

"Yes, god, please."

I let my legs fall open wider and feel her smile against the inside of my thigh as she glides her hands all the way up. Her finger traces the edge of my underwear, back and forth, then dips in ever so slightly, just enough to feel how wet I am. God, just that brief touch sets me on fire. I shift, following her finger, aching to feel it inside me, but she always stays just ahead of my movements, keeping her touch light. Teasing.

"Yeah? How do *you* like it?" she murmurs.

I throw my head back against the couch and curse myself. "Payback's a bitch."

She skims over my entrance again, again, sliding through my slickness—but the second I finally release a groan in frustration, she sinks her finger in deep and lights me up from the inside. Oh god, oh *god*, yes, *finally*. My shirt feels suddenly restrictive, far too hot, and I rip it off, arching into Nic's finger as I do.

"Fuck, *yes*," she mutters, taking the shirt from me and throwing it across the room with her free hand as I undo the clasp of my bra. My breasts spill free, nipples begging for attention, and I cup them both and brush the pads of my thumbs over my nipples as Nic works her finger inside me. She watches me, licking her lips as I arch and thrust against her, my own breasts in my hands. There's something that feels so gloriously dirty about being spread open for her like this, having her watch intently, the way her fingers press into me, the way her thumb circles my clit over and over, gently and slowly at first, then *more*. Her mouth drifts closer and closer, tracing a line up the inside of my thigh, then ghosting over thin fabric just barely separating her tongue from exactly where it needs to be. She tilts her head to rest on my leg and licks her lips again, looking up at me from under her lashes with her open shirt hanging off one shoulder.

"Tested?" she asks, and I'm glad she thought of it, because I can't think at all.

"Clean," I gasp.

"Oh, thank god."

She withdraws her finger and strips my panties off in one swift movement, then dives right in.

"Ah!"

The first sweep of her tongue makes my hips buck up off the couch, but her free hand pins my hip down as she moves in again, the tip of her tongue tracing my hot, wet entrance, then moving up to slowly circle my clit.

"Ah, god," I gasp, pushing back against her insistent tongue. "God, Nic, you . . . Yeah . . ."

"Mmm," she says, either in agreement or in response to my taste, and slides her finger back inside me. She seems to sense that I don't want more than that, working that single finger in tandem with her tongue on my clit, starting soft, then increasing the pressure as my cries grow louder. God, I hope her neighbors are out tonight. I can't be quiet with Nic's fingers and tongue working my pussy so fucking well. I pinch my nipples and arch my back, thrusting down against Nic's face and hands as the burn begins to take hold. It builds right in the spot beneath Nic's tongue, a tight coil of pleasure stoked higher and higher, my toes curling tight into the carpet, until I tip over the edge with a cry, riding her fingers through the sensation. I'm making so much fucking noise, I know I am, but Nic doesn't seem to mind at all, moaning right along with me as she tastes my pleasure.

She gentles as I start to come down, easing me through it before I go oversensitive. When my body finally stops moving and melts boneless into the couch, she withdraws her finger and collapses with her forehead resting on my thigh, breathing hard.

"Holy shit," she says.

"Agreed," I say.

Then we both bust out laughing, and it's kind of awkward laughing with her face still near my soaked pussy and my panties tangled around one foot, but I can't bring myself to care. I pull her up on the couch with me, and she tucks up under my arm, lifting her face to share my taste on her tongue.

"I assume you're staying over?" she asks. "You're welcome to, if you want."

"Good," I reply. "Because I'm pretty sure puddles of melted human aren't legal drivers. Also, my legs may not work."

"Not even well enough to stand up in the shower for a bit? With company?"

"I'll manage," I say.

Nic laughs again, and her eyes are so bright, her skin so flushed and glowing, that I can't take my eyes off her. This is clearly the best idea I've ever had, and it looks great on her.

She takes me by the hand and pulls me through her bedroom to the apartment's single bathroom, then guides me into the shower with so much stumbling and laughing that I swear we're going to run out of hot water before we ever get under the spray.

We do run out of hot water, eventually. It's long after our clothes hit the floor, though, and long after we ride the high of our earlier orgasms into more.

By the time we collapse into her bed, an exhausted tangle of endorphins, my brain is buzzing with giddy happiness. Nic falls asleep with her face in my cleavage almost immediately, and I bury my nose in her hair to breathe in her sweet-smelling shampoo and calm my wild heart, which is already swelling and glowing in a dangerous way.

It's still so early. I don't want to get ahead of myself.

But I really, really do.

CHAPTER TWELVE

NIC

Kira is still asleep in my bed when I sneak out to go to work the next morning. At 6:30 a.m. Which is . . . *slightly* earlier than I'd normally leave. For no reason at all.

It's the kind thing to do, really. Yesterday she got bad news, cried a lot, stayed up late despite being exhausted, then passed out from all of the above plus orgasms. Today, she has to report to work at 8:00 a.m. for a twenty-four-hour shift. She needs all the sleep she can get and no distractions so she can get out the door on time.

See? Kindness!

Is it also slightly cowardly? Maybe. Yes. I don't know. For once, I am refusing to overthink.

I don't *regret* it. I know that much. We had a good time, and Kira is an incredible person. And hey, I left a sticky note on her phone telling her to help herself to anything she wants in the kitchen and to text me later. Sadly, great sex and a beautiful girl in your bed isn't a legitimate reason to call out of work. Probably. I still considered it, though.

My phone buzzes on the passenger seat—ah, maybe that's Kira now, just waking up. I don't text and drive, because I want to live, but I *do* glance over just long enough to see *Skylar's* name on the glowing notification. My pulse shifts into high gear.

Skylar. I didn't think about her *once* last night after things with Kira kicked off. I feel weirdly like I've cheated on her or something, like I've betrayed Operation Flying Fox and my feelings for her by forgetting to think of her for twelve hours. The second I pull into the parking lot at the lab, I snatch my phone from the seat and swipe to see Skylar's text.

SKYLAR: Hey friend, I want to come to your place
tonight to talk about something important. Okay?

Instant. Panic.

Who does that? Who *does that*? That's borderline deliberately provoking a panic attack. Bad text etiquette. You can't just drop a "I have something to tell you later." *Everyone* knows this. My brain instantly breaks into stressed-out gymnastics: Is she finally giving up on this whole Fiji thing? Is she staying? Did our shenanigans finally have some impact?

Or is she maybe . . . going to tell me she wants to be with me?

My stomach becomes a circus contortionist at the thought. It's what I've always wanted. It's what I moved back here hoping for. It's what I've been dreaming of since I was eighteen.

So why does the thought make me so *uneasy*?

THE ENTIRE WORKDAY IS A BUST. IT'S A GOOD thing today was a research-and-writing day, not a meetings-and-setting-fires day, otherwise the professor who oversees my lab would have had some serious words for me. As it is, when he comes into my office to ask a question and I talk to him like my head is in a cloud, he assumes it's the usual—a researcher who's been staring at a computer screen for way too long, their brain a soup of numbers and graphs and jargon.

My brain is *actually* a soup of all the things Skylar might possibly say to me, and Kira's skin, and PhD applications, and . . . everything. I manage to drive myself home on autopilot, though I don't remember getting in my car or making any of the turns. That should maybe worry me more than it does.

But it's nothing compared to the sight of Skylar standing in front of my apartment door when I arrive, two bags of Heartbreak Takeout dangling from her hands.

Heartbreak Takeout has been our traditional "sad times" meal ever since Skylar's longest-ever girlfriend (six months) broke up with her in our senior year of college. I ran out and picked up every form of fried cheese available at this little diner near campus, plus a whole-ass chocolate pie from our favorite bakery, and we've had that exact combination of foods a dozen times since then. Jobs we didn't get, academic advisers being jerks, phone calls from my dad, and every other bummer in life was soothed with cheese and chocolate. But not in a fancy French way—in a greasy American way.

All my hopes of this being good news come crashing back to reality.

"Hey, Nic Knack," she says, her voice gentle. "Sorry I'm early. My last client canceled, so I figured hey, might as well beat the traffic! Let's eat. I'm *starving*."

I *was* starving. Now my stomach feels like there's a boulder sitting inside it. I unlock my door and let her in, putting away my bag and shoes in a daze as an uncharacteristically quiet Skylar unpacks the Heartbreak Takeout on my coffee table. Should I light candles? I always light candles when I get home, but in this context, it would feel romantic, and this is . . . apparently *not* a romantic conversation.

The boulder of dread in my gut has little boulder babies until I feel like I might fall to my knees from the weight.

"Come sit down," Skylar says, patting the cushion next to her. Playing host in my own house. That sounds about right. I do a zombie shuffle over to the couch—the couch Kira and I had brilliant sex on last night, awkward—and drop into its overly squashy embrace. When I look up and force myself to meet Skylar's eyes, she smiles sweetly.

"Take a bite of pie," Skylar commands. I do as I'm told. I dig a spoon directly into the middle of its pristine chocolaty surface and scoop out the perfect amount of silky-smooth mousse, letting it slowly melt on my tongue. Perfection. It's even a little soothing, just like Skylar knew it would be. I take one more bite, then sit up straight and take a deep breath.

"Okay. Get it over with," I say, squeezing my eyes shut.

A hand curls around mine and squeezes, and Skylar waits to speak until I open my eyes.

"I know what you and Kira are up to," she says, and the words are like a lightning strike to my heart. Which thing is she talking about? The Fiji shenanigans . . . or the sex?

"I know," she says again. "And I need you both to let it go."

My confusion deepens. Let what go? The shenanigans or the sex? I can't ask without revealing whichever thing she *isn't* talking about.

"Oh," I say, hoping that will be enough to make her talk again. Thankfully, talking is one thing you can *always* count on Skylar for.

"I'm going to Fiji. It's happening. And I need you and Kira to be okay with it and support me."

My breath leaves my body all in one big rush.

What . . . am I feeling?

It's so tangled. There's sadness. Grief. I expect those. But also . . . I'm weirdly relieved? Maybe relieved that this isn't about Kira?

There's also a healthy helping of guilt over getting caught.

"I . . . I'm really sorry, Sky," I say. My body finally catches up and floods my eyes with tears. I try to turn away, but Skylar pulls me into a sideways hug, my ear resting on her shoulder and my nose pressed into her neck as my tears drip down her collarbones.

"It's okay, love. I understand it. I just need it to stop now before you spend more money on another scheme. I want to have an awesome last month and a half together, and we can't do that if this secret is hanging between us," she says, running her fingers through my hair.

I sniffle and lean back, wiping my eyes. This is humiliating. I gotta pull myself together.

"Can you at least tell me why?" I ask, voice watery. "I just . . . I don't understand how you could leave—"

Me, I think.

"—all of us," is what I actually say.

She smiles, and it's not the smile I expect. Not sad, not pitying; it's the Proud Skylar smile.

"I will tell you *if* you can swear to keep it a secret from the others for now. Well, everyone but Kira, I suppose. I wanted it to be a surprise I could announce at the party, but I can see that the two of you need to know to be able to let this go. So . . . are you ready?"

She sounds . . . almost nervous. What does *Skylar* ever have to be nervous about? She takes a deep breath in through her nose and blows it out slowly between pursed lips.

"I'm going to admit something that scares me, and it will sound unrelated, but just hang with me, okay? I . . . have . . . a paper being published in a major psychology journal!"

I blink, my mind completely blank. Her words speed as her excitement spills over.

"Two years ago, around when you left for grad school, I started up a new research project with my old adviser from my PhD program. The project and paper were on the effects of climate change on interpersonal and community relationships, and I loved it, and it put me in touch with other researchers around the world, studying similar things. I wanted to continue the work, so we all applied for a joint grant together. And we got it. We'll be looking into the psychological needs of people under the direct stress of climate change . . . in Fiji."

"Wow," I say, still too stunned to fully process. "So it's . . . not a whim. You aren't just moving out there to start a vacation rental farm thing?"

She laughs. "No, no, that's just a pet project. You know I always have to have a pet project!"

Tragically, yes, that is true. Her pet projects have nearly killed us both plenty of times.

"There are six of us, and we're using Fiji as a home base for the research team," she continues. "But we'll be traveling between lots of small island nations that are the most impacted by climate change. Since the house will be empty so much, I may as well make some money from it, right?"

That sounds really great, actually. I'm fully on board with the idea behind the project. Which leaves the question . . .

"Why didn't you tell us?" I ask.

She gives me a self-deprecating grin.

"I was too afraid," she says with a shrug. "Look, I know what you all think of me. I know I have a lot of disasters on my résumé. I thought you all would think I'm too much of a mess to take this seriously. And . . . I kind of feel that way about myself sometimes. Especially since I graduated from my PhD program."

"No!" I say, even as I visibly wince. It sounds so bad when she says it out loud like that. Maybe we've all been shitty friends. But she really *does* fall into disaster after disaster.

She waves my protest away. "It's okay, I get it. School was so easy for me because there were specific goals and deadlines, all set up by someone else. After graduation was just . . . a mess. I couldn't focus on any one thing. So I did the social media because I was good at it, and the radio because it was offered to me, and the pro bono work for the city because I felt like I needed to do something *good* with my degree and it was flexible."

Skylar's mouth presses into a thin line, and she blinks over and over again—chasing back tears, I realize with horror.

"I just wanted to make sure this wasn't going to become another big public Skylar failure," she whispers. "I wanted to make sure I could do it."

And now I'm crying for a completely different reason. I throw my arms around her and squeeze so tight, like I can force those bad thoughts out of her, like I can make up for all the times I've been too focused on my own feelings to see how much my best friend was hurting.

"Oh God, Skylar, I'm *so* sorry. I've been a completely shit

friend. I've been so selfish, so focused on my own bullshit . . .
but you just always seemed unaffected by everything. Every
time something went wrong, you just bounced right back,
kept on going, like nothing could ever get you down. Nothing could ever stop you."

"And I worked *really* hard to make it look like that," she
says simply. "So don't blame yourself for not seeing through
my cover-up. There's a reason every therapist has a therapist
of their own, you know? Very few get into this field because
we're perfect examples of mental health ourselves."

I huff a laugh, flipping back through my memories of Skylar in college. I knew this about her. She had terrible anxiety
in our freshman and sophomore years, but has always been
able to muscle through it with a single-minded determination, like it was a thing she could physically beat. I never
questioned it.

I *should* have.

"I can't believe I've been calling you my best friend for almost ten years and didn't realize you were struggling," I say,
squeezing her hand. "I'm so sorry. I should have been there
for you, and I wasn't."

"You had your own things you were struggling with," she
says, flopping sideways against the back of the couch. "You've
always had much more working against you, considering your
family situation. I never thought badly of you for it. And that
brings us to the other thing I have to say."

Oh god, there's more? I don't know if I can handle more.
Skylar folds her hands in her lap and frowns, rubbing one
thumb over the other.

"There's no easy way to say this, so I'm just going to say
it and know we'll be okay afterward. You and I are family,
and we're stronger than anything, right?" She takes a deep

breath and meets my gaze with red-rimmed eyes. "In the interest of clearing the air and making sure we're on the best possible terms when I leave, I have to tell you, Nic: I don't see you in a romantic way. I love you deeply . . . but we are never going to be together in that way."

I shove fried cheese in my mouth. In this moment, I truly don't know what else to do.

I . . . knew. I've known all along, apparently, because there's no surprise in the pulpy, beaten mess where my heart lives. Just hurt. Grief. Sadness. A thousand other bitter things, all bleeding together.

The fried cheese doesn't help. It goes down like a mouthful of gravel.

Skylar grabs my chin and tilts my face up until I'm looking at her.

"Here's what I don't get, Nic Knack," she says, letting me go once she knows I'm listening. "I honestly don't think you see *me* romantically, either. I'm not trying to discount your feelings here, or tell you about your own emotions, so if I'm completely off base, feel free to shut me down. I know you like staring at my boobs and all, but can you really tell me the love you feel is romantic?"

"I . . . I just . . ." I cover my face with my hands and groan. This whole conversation might be the worst experience of my life. "I don't know, Sky. I just want to be family, you know? I want us to be in each other's lives forever."

"I want those things too, Nic Knack. And the great news is, we already have them! You *are* part of my family. My mom texts you more than she texts me! She's worried to death over you, by the way. *Please* call her. And you spend every holiday and birthday with my family. My mom is already dreaming of your grandbabies, since she knows you want them and I don't. You don't need to be with me romantically for those family ties to be real. And I don't need to live in Seattle for them to be real. So, why, Nic?"

"Because if we were married, then . . ."

Oh *no*.

The bottom falls out of my world as I look the truth right in the face for the first time. It's lurked in the corners of my mind, only ever spotted in flashes from the periphery of my vision. But now that I'm forced to put words to it, it's undeniable.

"Because if we were married, then my family couldn't leave you," Skylar finishes for me, so quiet and gentle I feel like I'm made of glass. "Then you'd officially and legally be family, and they couldn't walk away. And neither could I. Oh, Nic."

"Don't," I warn, swiping angrily at the tears spilling down my face. This is *humiliating*. This whole fantasy life I've built in my head, where Skylar and I get married and Mama Clark cries at our wedding and we're in each other's pockets forever . . . it's all crumbling to ash and dying embers. And I have no idea what to replace it with. The yawning emptiness feels like it wants to swallow me up.

So of course, the fire alarm chooses that exact moment to go off.

We both groan, slumping against the couch in despair.

"Are you fucking serious? Now?" Skylar shouts. "I swear to God, if someone chose now of all times to burn their popcorn . . ."

"Grab the pie," I say. "We can eat it in the parking lot."

We shuffle into the hallway with a dozen other irritated residents, wincing at the strobing lights and pointedly ignoring the looks we get. Yes, we are red-eyed, covered in snot and tears, and carrying a chocolate pie. What of it? Mind your own business, *Brad*.

"Last time it only took half an hour to get back in," some girl my age with a baby on her hip says to her neighbor, covering the squalling baby's ears as we stomp down the steps. "Maybe we'll be lucky."

Our herd pours into the parking lot and walks the requisite distance from the building, some people heading straight for their cars to go somewhere else for the evening. I open my mouth to suggest the same thing to Skylar . . .

But then I see the very real flames pouring out of a first-floor window.

Not so lucky after all.

Considering the way my life is currently going down in flames, I deeply do *not* appreciate how literal this metaphor has become.

CHAPTER THIRTEEN

KIRA

I hate lifting weights in front of firehouse bros.

They aren't all bad, obviously. I do have male co-workers I like. I rarely see my female and nonbinary co-workers at all; they seem to deliberately spread us out between shifts and fire stations, like too many of us on duty together will bring down the team or something. And I do like lifting weights in general, especially when I've got something on my mind— like Nic. I've tried other types of exercise and found them all boring as hell. But some bicep curls, some deadlifts, and my mind clears, leaving all the space wide open for memories of Nic's skin.

But these days, every time I go to pick up a barbell, suddenly, there's Jared.

Sorry—*Lieutenant* Jared now.

I hate Jared.

"You only do fifteens for bicep curls?" Jared says as he piles plate after plate onto a bar. Any minute now, this place will be filled with manly grunting and shouting as he lifts.

"I'm going for low weight, high reps to prioritize stamina," I say primly. "Also, I don't want to go so hard that I'm useless when we get a call. Can't carry a kid out of a burning building with noodle arms."

"Ha, I never get noodle arms," Jared says, lying back on the weight bench.

"Well, then, you aren't really challenging yourself, are you?" I grumble. But just as he's about to lift the bar off the rack—

The intercom clicks on, and all the bullshit falls away. Three long beeps indicate a structure fire, and the robotic voice on the intercom provides details.

"Engine 25, please respond to a structure fire—"

Gear on. Downstairs to the apparatus. Grab my bunker jacket from where it hangs on the door. Pull myself inside.

"Apartment fire," says Mark, our driver, as he settles in the seat and fires up the engine. My gut twists as I flick on the lights and buckle myself in, prepping us to leave. Apartment fires are always worrying because of the sheer number of people packed inside one building. But I stay focused. This is my job. I know how to do it, how to breathe and get my head in the right place to respond.

Then the dispatch loops back around, and this time, I catch the address.

Nic's address.

Oh, god.

I want desperately to call Nic, to see if she's okay, to call everyone and rally the group. But I can't just whip out my phone while I'm responding to a fire call.

I'll just have to do what I do best: fight the fire, work with my team, and save what I can. Stay low, be safe.

Mark eases the apparatus out of the garage, I flick on the siren, and we're off.

THE NEXT HOUR IS A BLUR. I DO A QUICK HALF-second scan of the crowd beyond the caution tape for Nic's face when we first arrive, but don't find her. There's no time for anything more.

Instructions come down from the chief: we're making an interior attack, I'm leading the hose team, and we're first in. From there, it's all about properly deploying the hose, managing the stretch, evaluating our interior path and angles into the active fire zone. My breath rasps in my respirator as time dilates with the adrenaline and focus. Seconds stretch into minutes, then an hour, feeling the scorch through my sixty pounds of gear as we beat the fire back to its origin point in one of the first-floor apartments. Other response teams sweep the building floor by floor, looking for anyone still needing evac.

When Nic's floor is finally called clear, I spare another half second for grateful relief. But it isn't until a full hour later, when the fire is completely out and we've moved on to site duties and cleanup, that I spot Nic in the waiting crowd and my body finally releases its coiled tension.

She's okay. She's okay. She's not even being treated for smoke inhalation or anything. She's just standing there with Skylar beside her, rubbing her upper arms for warmth.

She's *okay*.

I, on the other hand, am sweating my tits off and smell *very* bad. I can't wait for a shower. I pull my helmet and respirator off, and even though my hair is relatively short, I still feel it when my soaked curls slap back against my forehead. Gross.

Once our engine is finally called to return home, I search the mess of vehicles and flashing red lights for the lieutenant— *Jared*—and ask for five minutes to check on a friend.

"Oh, shit, you have a friend who lives here?" he says, glancing back at the blackened brick exterior of the building, harshly lit by flood lamps and dripping water. "Could have been a lot worse. I'm glad they're okay. You got five."

I nod, fighting the thought that maybe Jared isn't a total asshat, and jog past the three engines, two ladders, and ambulance, over to where I caught a glimpse of Nic and Skylar earlier. When I don't see them right away, I worry they've left. But finally, there, just beyond the caution tape, I spot the two of them huddled together, cradling what looks like . . . the wreckage of a pie? With my helmet under my arm, I approach the line, ignoring the whispers and stares of the other onlookers.

"Kira! Oh my god, Nic, look!" Skylar says, clutching Nic's arm and shaking her. Nic seems to wake up out of a fog, looking up and blinking until her eyes focus on me—the first time we've seen each other since I fell asleep in her bed, soaking up the feeling of her skin. Not exactly the reunion I'd imagined, but the relief at seeing her okay and with a friend to care for her overrides any weirdness I might otherwise feel. Nic's eyes flash through a series of unreadable expressions . . . then widen, scanning down my body.

"I know, I'm a mess," I say, shifting my helmet to the other arm self-consciously. "I don't want to get too close—I stink. I just . . . had to see you. Make sure you were okay."

"We're glad *you're* okay!" Nic says. "Skylar said your station would be one of the ones responding, and we were so worried."

"I'm okay. See? All in one piece," I say, rubbing the dripping sweat from my forehead. I'm sure it leaves a streak of soot behind, but I'm not exactly posing for the firefighter calendar here. "The building is *not* okay, though. The lower floors won't be habitable for a few weeks, at least. Structural inspection, smoke remediation . . ."

"Yeah, someone came over and talked to us," Nic says, picking absentmindedly at a piece of broken pie crust. "So I guess I'm homeless for a while. And I don't have any of my stuff."

"I told Nic she could have stayed with me if I hadn't just moved back in with my mom," Skylar says. "I'm staying one last night to do the last 'please give me my security deposit back' cleaning, but I have no furniture or bed."

Nic and I lock eyes, and the same crazed look crosses her face that I imagine is on mine.

The plants. What happened to the *plants*?

"Yes, before you ask, I took all your plants with me. And they're all still alive, ye of little faith. I have a spreadsheet." Skylar taps her lip and shrugs. "Well, except the hens and chicks. I really did manage to water those to death somehow."

My mouth hangs open, and I glance between Nic and Skylar. Does she know about . . . ?

"We have a lot to talk about," Nic says, a complicated expression shadowing her eyes. "I'll fill you in tomorrow, Kira. Well, maybe. I guess I need to figure out where I'm staying first."

"Oh, this is an easy one," Skylar says, ticking off each point on her finger. "You could stay with our family, of course, but that's an hour and a half away. Fine for me, but terrible for a daily commute. Willow is a reclusive woods witch who I'm not sure I could locate if I tried—they might live in a tree for all I know. Marco can't handle sharing his space long-term, and Ian has that dudebro roommate none of us can stand. So that leaves . . ."

She lets the sentence hang until I finally get the point.

"Oh! Uh, you could stay with me and Grace! We don't have a spare room, but our apartment is pretty big, and the couch is more comfortable than my actual bed. I'm sure Grace would be okay with it."

Nic's eyes bore into me, her head tilting to one side as she thinks. She raises her eyebrows as if to say, *Are you sure?*

I purse my lips and look away, avoiding Skylar's gaze. She doesn't know what happened between me and Nic. She doesn't know that twenty-four hours ago, I had my fingers buried inside her, feeling her clench around me as she came. And now I'm supposed to share my apartment with her for some unspecified length of time, with Grace there as chaperone.

But . . . maybe this is a good thing. I wanted to pursue her, after all. I wanted to see if she was willing to give us a shot. Temporarily living together is an intense way to start, but at least we'd see pretty quickly if we're compatible outside of sex.

"I'll check in with Grace," Nic says, hesitant. "I really appreciate the offer."

I smile in what I hope is a reassuring way. "No problem at all. I gotta get back, but text if you need anything, okay?"

"Thanks, Kira," Nic says, her voice so quiet it's nearly swallowed up by the rumbling engines of the two ladders pulling out of the parking lot.

I really hope this isn't a mistake. Too much pressure on something so fragile and new, something that isn't even really a thing yet.

But if the way she's looking at me in my full firefighter gear is any indication . . . it might *be* a thing soon enough.

CHAPTER FOURTEEN

NIC

I don't realize I'm staring after Kira like a space cadet until Skylar's snicker pulls me out of it. I flush and shove a chunk of pie crust into my mouth to cover my reaction.

"Come on, you," Skylar says, grabbing the pie out of my hands. "I'll drive you to Grace and Kira's place. We can come back for your car tomorrow. I assume you aren't going to work tomorrow?"

Oh god, work. I'm gonna have to thrift a whole new wardrobe just to have something to wear, unless they let us back in soon. I better not have to pay rent next week, or I'll be pissed. And broke.

"Yeah, I feel like 'my apartment building almost burned down and I'm currently homeless' is a pretty good excuse. Though, considering my field, I think 'Are you okay?' is probably going to be the last question I get."

I went into a strange sort of dissociative state while we

all stood across the street watching the fire burn. My mind was automatically observing it like one of the fires in my lab, noting burn rates and estimating temperatures and making guesses about material components and accelerants each time we saw a flare-up or minor explosion. In a way, I'm grateful—my horrified fascination kept me from thinking about the conversation with Skylar and the evening's double heartbreak.

Now, as I climb into Skylar's car and shut out the noise of the scene, it all comes rushing back. Kira and I slept together last night. We got caught in our scheme. Skylar is unquestionably leaving. And she didn't want me anyway.

And maybe . . . I never really wanted her either.

That one is still hard to accept. I've know I've been attracted to her . . . but there's a world of difference between being sexually attracted to someone and being romantically attracted to them. The world is filled with people who experience one, the other, neither, or both.

And, as I'm learning, it's painfully easy to confuse deep friendship for romantic feelings when you've had shitty role models and relationships your entire life. *Trauma response*, Skylar said as we stared at the flames eating through my apartment building. *Understandable. Normal.*

She made it sound so logical. But now I can't even trust my own feelings, and no amount of logic can fix that.

"Hey," Skylar says, poking me in the leg to get my attention. I look up, and some amount of what I'm thinking must show on my face, because Skylar's eyes soften. "You're going to be okay, you know. I'm sure it feels like the puzzle pieces of who you are have just been jumbled up, but you still fit together. I'm going to recommend you a great therapist, and this is all going to work out for the better in the end. Trust me?"

I huff a helpless laugh.

"I always trust you," I say. Trusting myself is the real problem.

Skylar waggles her phone at me. "I called Grace while you were zoned out. She's so on board with you staying there that it makes me a bit worried for you? Like, when Grace is this hyped, something chaotic is brewing. But you have a place to sleep, so . . . yay?"

Did Kira tell Grace what happened between us? No, there's no way she had time. Unless she texted her after she got to work this morning. But would she? Should I text Kira and find out, so I know what I'm walking into?

I thunk my head back against the headrest and squeeze my eyes shut. Brain crispy. Too many feels. Too much happening.

"Hey, I see you spiraling," Skylar says as her electric Mini Cooper starts up in near silence. It's an adorable little thing in a gorgeous shade of ironic "Island Blue," but . . .

"You must be selling this thing before you go," I say, quickly changing the subject before Skylar can pry any more secrets out of me. "You love this car."

"I do," Skylar says with a sigh. "But she can't come to Fiji with me, so she'll need a new loving owner. She's not the most practical car for me while I'm living with my mom either. It's far enough I have to stop for a charge. I thought about selling her early, but . . ."

"But?" I prompt, curious. Skylar normally forges right ahead once she has an idea.

Skylar taps her fingers against the steering wheel and hums. "I was hoping Kira might be in a place to finally let go of the Toyonda Civry. I'd offer her this car for whatever she could afford, and she could even just make payments to me. But since she got turned down for that promotion again, she'll probably be clinging to that car tighter than ever. I can wait until the end of the summer, but I *do* have to get rid of it before I leave."

Something in her words breaks through the last threads of dignity I've been clinging to. *Before I leave.* She's leaving, and here I am without a home, life in shambles, can't trust my own brain, with a grant-funded job that could disappear at the end of the academic year and half-formed ideas of running off for grad school again. I let my head flop to the side so I can stare out the window and watch the headlights of other cars whiz past us while I utter the most pathetic sentence of my life.

"Can I please come with you? To Fiji?" I whisper. "Not in a romantic way or anything. I'd be a great research assistant. I can help tend the farm and rental."

I squeeze my eyes shut against the wave of shame that swells up within me. What am I *doing*? What am I *saying*? How pathetic can I get? I'm just . . . lost. I don't know what I want.

Skylar pulls into Grace and Kira's apartment complex and parks in front of their building, then shuts off the car and turns to face me.

"Nic, I'm going to say something hard. I know this has been a whole night of very hard things, but this one might be the hardest." She reaches out and takes my hand. "You can*not* just drift through life from port to port, looking for something to anchor you down and give you meaning, and structure. Cutting your terrible father off was the right thing to do. That particular anchor would have eventually drowned you. But then . . ."

She squeezes my hand.

"Then you latched onto me. *I* became your new anchor. And that's great! I love you, and I'm so glad that we share a family now. But Nic . . . you've *gotta* take some time and fig-

ure out what you want out of life on your own terms. You
need to be your *own* anchor."

For the thousandth time tonight, I sniffle and dash my
tears away. But I nod along with her words. They ring true.
She's completely right that I feel helplessly adrift, with *or*
without her. Even when I was in grad school, away from her
for two years with a master's degree to focus on, I felt rud-
derless. Like at any moment I might just float right off the
ground and drift away.

I need to be my own anchor.

Skylar gets out of the car, so I follow suit a moment later,
letting her wrap me in a hug and rock me until I feel almost
normal again. As I watch the taillights of the Mini Coop
disappear back onto the main road, I feel . . . almost okay.
Lighter, in a way.

The air is clear. This awful secret I've been carrying is
out. Now Skylar and I can just be best friends without all
the weirdness hanging between us. We can enjoy the time
Skylar has left in the country. Maybe, eventually, I'll even be
able to call her "sister" like Mama Clark is always wanting.
It already sounds more right than the idea of "girlfriend" or
"wife" ever did.

And in the meantime, I'll be sleeping on Kira's couch. It
will be totally fine and not weird at all.

I'm sure Grace's evil supervillain cackle when I walk in
the front door means nothing.

CHAPTER FIFTEEN

KIRA

I sleep through most of the first full day of Nic living in my apartment.

I don't mean to. I fully intended to be a better host, help her get settled in instead of leaving her to Grace's tender mercies. But fuck, that shift was brutal.

We were at the site of the apartment fire for hours, and when we got back, there was paperwork, reorganizing gear . . . and another call, this time for a motor vehicle accident. I got zero sleep.

And so, after being awake for twenty-four hours . . . I crashed. Then I woke up, showered again because I still felt gross, chugged a smoothie, and then forced myself to stay awake in a zombified state so I could get back on a normal schedule. I interacted with Nic in some minimal way that was mostly muttering and watching some random show I didn't retain any memory of, but the whole experience is foggy. Needless to say, I went to bed early.

Not every shift is like that. The extended recovery was warranted. But still, the timing sucked.

I make up for it the next day by offering to go with Nic when her apartment building is cleared for residents to return (By appointment only! With escort only!) to recover belongings before the repairs begin. The landlord provides us with masks to help with the smoke smell and walks us along an approved, structurally sound path to Nic's door, then leaves us standing in silence in the open doorway with a box of supplies. Flashlights, since the electricity is shut off, gloves, industrial garbage bags, cleaning supplies, and extra masks, all sitting on top of a pile of folded-up moving boxes.

Everything looks okay. This part of the building didn't burn, which is the only reason we were able to come back. But I know that looks are deceiving after a fire, and most of this stuff will either be garbage or need professional cleaning. Luckily there's no water damage here, but the smoke, combined with two days of no air conditioning, will have everything porous smelling pretty nasty.

"Have you called your insurance company yet?" I ask, mentally cataloging everything in sight. "They may be willing to pay for smoke remediation for your clothing and furniture. There are companies that specialize in all that."

"Uh . . ." she says, trailing off. Uh-oh.

"Please tell me you have renter's insurance," I say, turning to her with wide eyes.

"Well . . ." She winces. "I haven't exactly gotten around to it yet? I didn't know my unit number when I first moved, and things have been so chaotic since I got back in town, and renting an apartment by myself is so expensive, I didn't think I could really afford it . . ."

I cover my face with both hands and sigh inside my mask.

"Well, this sucks a lot more for you, then," I say, closing the apartment door behind us. "Most of this stuff will be trash."

Nic sighs heavily.

"I mean, I knew, but I guess I was hoping that the smoke wouldn't have penetrated so deeply this far from the fire. I, of all people, should have known better, though. I'm so sorry, Planet Earth," she says miserably, shaking open a trash bag. "Because I decided to be a cheapass, all this is heading for a landfill. Do you think anything can be salvaged?"

I grimace. "I guess let's dive in and find out."

THE ANSWER IS . . . NO, NOT REALLY. EVERY-thing reeks of smoke. All Nic's books are discolored and stinky, her wooden furniture is unusable without complete refinishing, and her thrifted couch is no longer suitable for even a thrift store. You'd think plastic and metal would be safe, but that's extremely not true; most plastic is super porous, and without immediate cleaning, many metals corrode after smoke exposure. All Nic's kitchen utensils and plastic containers go, along with any pots and pans that weren't buried deep in the cabinets. Food, medication, everything made of wood, cosmetics, soaps and hair products—all of it goes in the big black trash bags while Nic chants apologies to the planet.

She takes pictures of a few things she wants to make sure she replaces—some favorite books, a few trinkets from favorite TV shows and video games—but I can see how every item that gets thrown out steals a little more of the light from her eyes, makes her shoulders creep a little closer to her ears.

Once we finish the bedroom and bathroom, I grab Nic's arm and pull her in for a tight, silent hug break. She wraps her arms around my waist, buries her face in my shoulder, and just clings for a few minutes. When she pulls away, her eyes are red, but she heaves a big sigh and shakes out her arms.

"Okay. Let's keep going," she says.

In the end, all we salvage are the mattress, three boxes, and two big trash bags: most of Nic's candle collection (anything in glass could be wiped down and the top layer of wax scraped off), a box of important documents that were sealed inside a filing cabinet, some old keepsakes that were essentially ruined but too precious to throw away, and all her clothing and bedding, which we're hoping will be able to be washed. The mattress *should* be trashed too, but it's too expensive to replace without at least trying to salvage it. As we turn to leave, Nic looks so beaten down—hunched posture, watery eyes, and a frown that refuses to give up weighing down the corners of her mouth.

I can't let this stand.

"Okay, let's go. This calls for bubble tea and snacks," I say, picking up one of the boxes and starting down the hall. "My treat!"

When Nic doesn't immediately follow, I turn to check on her—and there she is, standing in the middle of the hallway, staring down at one of the boxes on her doormat. When she looks up, her eyes shine with tears.

"I'm okay," she says. She takes a deep breath and blinks until the tears recede. "Bubble tea sounds great. I have a lot to talk to you about, actually. Skylar updates."

I want to push, want to say, *Tell me now before I crawl out of my own skin*, but she looks so heartbroken that I let it go. We have all day, and she deserves some space to process.

We make several trips to get everything into the Toyonda,

which always vaguely stinks, so I don't mind the smoky smell. Once everything's packed, I drive us to my favorite bubble tea place near the University of Washington campus, then lead us on a rambling walk through campus toward Union Bay.

"Did you go here?" Nic asks as we walk. "I never saw you around. I mean, I guess there are like thirty thousand undergraduates, so of course I didn't."

"No, I got my degree online so I could be a full-time firefighter at the same time," I say. "Took me five years, but I got there. I ended up with a degree in emergency and disaster management. For all the good it's done me."

"Why are they the *worst*?" Nic says with a groan.

She's silent for several long moments, her feet clearly wandering some well-traveled route on autopilot. Once we reach the Center for Urban Horticulture, she leads me onto the winding paths through the botanical garden that borders on the wetlands of the bay, her silence taking on that heavy sort of quality when someone has something to get off their chest. Once we're well into the garden, away from everyone else, Nic finally speaks.

"I didn't tell you this yesterday because . . . well, you know, you'd just put out an actual dangerous fire and were exhausted from work," she says. "But . . . Skylar knows. About our scheme. She's definitely going to Fiji, and she wants us to stop fighting it and support her. And . . ."

She pauses and looks out over the water, wrestling with the words.

"This feels really weird to tell you after . . . you know, what happened between us the other night. But I need to start being more honest with people. And myself." She takes a deep breath and blows it out, thumbs rubbing rhythmically at the hem of her shirt. "I'm in love with Skylar. Or . . . I guess I thought I was? Ever since freshman year of college. But after talking to Skylar last night, I know it's never going to happen. And . . . I'm not even sure now that I ever really felt that way about her. I'm questioning *everything* now."

It takes me a solid minute to shove down my riot of feelings, all my visions of dating Nic, of repeating that night we spent together, crumbling to dust and carried out on the bay breeze. There have been so many secrets in this group lately. Our shenanigans. Willow's disappearances. Skylar's plans. Marco's brunch guy. Whatever's been giving Ian that pinched, sad expression lately. And now this. A secret I really didn't want to know.

"Wow," I finally say, sounding too flat, but it's the best I can do. "That's why you were so desperate to keep Skylar from leaving. You wanted a chance to be with her."

"I mean, all the things I said before about being worried, and about her being the center of our friend group, those were true, too," Nic says, yanking so hard at her shirt hem now that it stretches out of shape. "But also . . . yeah. I thought I wanted her to stay so we could be together. But she thinks—no, actually, I think too, now—that I was more afraid of her and her family forgetting about me once she wasn't around to drag me to holiday gatherings. That I wouldn't be part of the family anymore. That I'd lose . . . everyone."

I laugh, shaking my head as I watch a long-legged bird pick their way carefully across the marsh. "Nic, the few times I've spoken to Skylar's mom, she's talked about you more than Skylar's actual blood siblings. I don't think you have anything to worry about."

Nic nods. "That's what Sky said. And she's probably right. She usually is about this kind of stuff. But it's hard to make my brain believe it, you know? I'm just so *used* to thinking this way that it's automatic. Default."

Well, that's one thing I have firsthand experience with. I know logically that there's nothing wrong with me—or the job I'm doing as a firefighter—that's stopping me from getting promoted. I've solicited feedback from supervisors, done mock interviews, and taken careful notes at every annual evaluation. But it doesn't stop my brain from whispering in the quiet moments before I fall asleep, *What's wrong with you?*

"I get it," I say, quiet as the distant tide.

After another heavy beat of silence, Nic turns to me, forcibly replacing her frown with a bright smile.

"Hey, we were supposed to be going out to cheer ourselves up, and look what I did instead. I made bubble tea sad. That's just wrong."

"How do you propose we fix that?" I ask, resisting the urge to lean in closer.

Nic thinks for a second, then thrusts a finger in the air with a "Ha!"

"I have an idea," she says. "Let's go on a random ramble."

"A random . . . ramble?"

"Yes. We're going to head back to 15th Ave and start wandering. I'll set a random timer on my phone. When the timer goes off, whatever we're standing in front of, that's what we have to do. Sound good?"

I mean, I'm normally the type to plan out routes and read menus in advance . . . so yeah, this'll probably be good for me. Push me out of my comfort zone a bit, force me to give up a little control. Trying to control every variable in my life hasn't worked out all that well up until now, so what the hell? Let's try something new.

"Okay, you're on. Lead the way," I say, summoning a weak smile. "Let's see what happens."

CHAPTER SIXTEEN

NIC

I was really hoping our first random stop would involve an affordable-yet-chic sit-down restaurant with some manner of cheesy appetizer. Alas, the timer gods have a different fate in store for us:

A tarot café. Inside, it mostly looks like an average café, though with decor that tends toward the modern witchy, crystals-and-houseplants sort of spectrum. The real difference is with the staff: there are two baristas working the front counter, taking and preparing orders from their very thin menu of coffee shop basics, but then there's another pair of employees shuffling and laying out cards at the bar, and traveling table to table with a mat and deck of cards.

"I didn't even know this place was here!" I say, taking the place in with wide eyes. "I've been up and down this street a thousand times."

"I'd say it's probably new, because there's always something new, but it sure *looks* like it's been here a while," Kira says, glancing both ways down the street like there might be some kind of explanation lying around.

Regardless, it's kind of the perfect stop. Willow has read tarot for me a few times before, but it's generally not something I vibe with. Right now, though, I clearly need outside input on my life. I've not been doing the best job of running it myself, and I can't trust what's happening in my own head, so why not see what the cards have to say? Maybe it'll shake something loose.

Or maybe I'm just doing the same thing all over again: putting my life and fate in something other than myself. Letting someone else tell me what to do.

I shove that little bit of unwanted insight back into the dark corner from whence it came and grab Kira by the elbow.

"Let's go in," I say. "The timer has decreed."

We pull open the door and place orders at a front counter overflowing with houseplants and cracked geodes, then take a little tarot card table marker to a small table next to the front window. Each table is hand-painted with a card from the Major Arcana, and our table shows the Fool: a cheerful-looking figure with a dog at their heels, poised at the very edge of a cliff. A vining plant in a decorative basket hangs over the table with three pink crystal pendants dangling from its edges by thin silver chains, the light catching the facets in a hypnotic way. After a moment, a barista brings over an iced mocha for me, a London fog for Kira, and two enormous, fluffy, flaky crescent moon croissants that we absolutely couldn't resist. I already have a giant bite half sticking out of my mouth when the barista asks a question.

"Would you like to reserve a tarot reading with your visit

today?" they ask, tapping into a reservation system on a little handheld card swiper tablet thing.

"Yes!" I say, then shoot a look at Kira. "For me, I mean. Do you want one too?"

Kira shrugs.

"Sure, why not?" she says. "Life is kind of a mess right now."

"My thoughts exactly. We'll take two," I say, looking back up at the barista and their very cute nose ring.

"And how long would you like your reading to be?" they ask. "We book in fifteen-minute increments. We recommend a minimum of fifteen minutes per detailed question you want to ask."

"Just fifteen for me," Kira says. "Nic?"

"Can we get two fifteen-minute blocks back-to-back?" I ask.

"No problem. Your reader will be over shortly," the barista says, tapping a few things into the tablet, then smiling as they depart. I look down and find my napkin in shreds and drop the tatters like they're electrified.

"Ah, sorry, I made such a mess! I guess I'm nervous," I say, sweeping the scraps into a little pile and shoving it under my croissant plate.

"Why nervous?" Kira asks, tipping her head with a little smile. Something about that smile makes me flash back to the moment just before she took my nipple between her lips the other day, and I look sharply down at the table, shoving a piece of croissant in my mouth—a very *large* piece. Once I've dealt with the fallout of *that* decision via an awkward minute of vigorous chewing, I glance up with an apologetic grimace.

"I dunno. I guess my life is just such a disaster zone right now that I'm worried I'll hear yet another thing that will crumble some fundamental pillar of my existence. Maybe this was a bad idea."

"Or, maybe you'll hear just the thing you need to start re-building," Kira adds, removing the bag of loose-leaf tea from her weird tea latte thingy. "I'm very ambivalent about the whole tarot thing, but whenever Willow has pulled cards for me in the past, I've always walked away with a new perspective and some insight I couldn't have gotten to on my own. It's a little like therapy in that way."

"You're right, you're right. When we walked in here, that's exactly what I was thinking. I'm not sure my psyche can handle any more insights, but I'll stay open-minded."

"I'm glad to hear that," someone says just behind me, and I jump, whirling around.

"I'm so sorry!" the person says, holding up their hands. "Didn't mean to eavesdrop. My name is Gabe, my pronouns are he/him, and I'll be your tarot reader today. Are you ready for me to join you?"

"Yes, please," Kira says, scooting our mess of cups, plates, and napkins to the far side of the table as we introduce ourselves. I scoot my now empty croissant plate over, immediately revealing a trail of shredded napkin, which I gather up once again (*on* the plate this time).

Gabe sits in the third chair at our table and lays out a black cloth adorned with green embroidered botanical designs. Multiple glittering silver rings pop against the dark skin of his hands, matched by a line of silver studs on the shell of his ear. He peeks inside a small brown bag, then studies us both for a moment. It feels like he's seeing straight into my brain . . . but that could just be the flawless eyeliner effect, I suppose. After a few seconds, he nods and withdraws a box of cards from the bag.

"Just trying to pick a deck," he says, withdrawing the cards from the box and tossing them in an easy shuffle. "This one seems right for you two. It's a little modern for some folks, but I find it very gentle and relatable."

"The box literally says 'This Might Hurt' on it," I say, eyeing the deck with much skepticism.

Gabe chuckles, looking up at me through long lashes as he shuffles, hands perfectly sure in the motions.

"I know, I know, but trust me," he says, "it's a loving sort of hurt. More of a *healing* hurt, if that makes sense. Like how a cut stings when you first apply the medicine."

"We'll take your word for it," Kira says, but even she looks wary now, arms folded and leaning slightly away from Gabe.

Abruptly, Gabe stops shuffling, cuts the deck into three piles, and reassembles the deck. With one last glance between us, he lays out one row of three face-down cards at the top of the mat and another three at the bottom of the mat. His eyes flick up and linger on my face briefly. Then he lays out one last card in between the two rows, linking them.

"I know you reserved two separate fifteen-minute readings, but it's feeling right to me to give them some shared context. Is that okay?"

Kira and I shrug at each other.

"Sure, why not?" I ask. "Is one row for me and one for Kira?"

Gabe nods, fingers hovering over the first card of the top row. "That's my thought. This top row is Kira's. Can we start here?"

We both nod, and I notice Kira's hands dropping to her lap, twisting restlessly. I expect Gabe to flip over one card at a time and go card by card, but he flips all three in quick succession, looking back and forth between them, reading the spread as a whole.

The Eight of Swords. The Six of Swords. The Ace of Cups.

"Well, that's wonderfully specific," Gabe says, smiling down at the cards. "It's nice when things are so clear and consistent."

"Uh, if you say so," Kira says with a grimace. "All I see are lots of very sharp knives. Well, and the hand of God holding an overflowing teacup, I guess."

"I got you, I got you, don't worry!" Gabe says with a laugh. "But I'm gonna say something you aren't gonna like, which is that you'll need to get out of your head for this reading and try to feel your way through."

From the way Kira winces, that's apparently a direct hit. Gabe continues.

"You are your own worst enemy. More specifically, your thoughts and ideas are your enemy. See the figure in this card? She looks so stuck, right? What do you see that's keeping her there?"

Gabe flips the card around for Kira to squint at.

"She's all tied up and blindfolded," Kira says. "And surrounded by a circle of swords or daggers or whatever, of course."

"And yet she could be free any time she wants to be," Gabe says, raising an eyebrow. "Look again."

Kira shakes her head, clearly getting frustrated . . . and then her expression clears.

"Oh my god, her feet aren't tied. And there's a big gap in the sword circle right in front of her. She could just get up and walk away."

"Exactly," Gabe says, gently setting the card back down in its place on the table. "The swords are the suit of thoughts, ideas, and the voice. In this case, specifically the ways our inner voice keeps us trapped. You're stuck, Kira. But it's only you keeping you there. You can get up and walk away at any point. And that's exactly what this next card is encouraging you to do."

He taps the next card, which has a figure in a boat and six knives of varying shapes.

"You're being called to leave something behind. Again, because this is a swords card, we're talking about a way of thinking, an idea, an intellectual pursuit, or something else of that nature. But there's a level of physical movement in this card. It's not just changing your perspective or letting go of something intellectually, but actively leaving behind the structures in your life that have been built up by those ideas. The figure in the boat is sailing out of choppy waters into a horizon of calm, with a variety of new potential paths before them. But you have to be willing to cut your losses, leave your trauma behind, and get your ass in the boat. And you can't just shove your thoughts down and pretend they don't exist either. That's a good way to get stabbed. Don't fall for the sunk cost fallacy."

He taps one more element on the card: the snake swimming right behind the boat. "And don't be tempted to turn back, either."

Kira's hands are visibly shaking. She must notice me looking, because she quickly drops them into her lap and summons a weak smile for Gabe.

"Please tell me the last card is a good one," she begs.

Gabe shrugs. "I mean, I'd argue they're *all* good ones. You have the power and agency in this situation. A new path is yours for the taking, if you can be brave enough to make the hard calls. But yes—this last card has some potent new beginnings energy. If you're willing to follow through on the callings of the previous two cards, then a whole new emotional landscape opens up for you. Your cup runneth over, as you can see. The aces contain all the essential energy of their suit—in this case, emotions and human connection, among other things—and they often represent a new opportunity opening up before you. So you're sailing out of the choppy waters of your rigid thoughts and ideas, right into a new and brighter emotional landscape. And those things are indelibly connected. There's no getting the Ace of Cups, your shiny new outpouring of love and connection, without going *through* the Eight and Six of Swords. You gotta clear out some space before you can bring in something new."

Kira sits back in her chair, lost in thought and looking exhausted. I don't blame her. I'm emotionally exhausted just hearing all that . . . and I haven't even seen my own cards yet. As if hearing my thoughts—*can* he hear my thoughts?—Gabe turns to me with a gentle smile.

"Ready?" he asks.

I shake my head with a helpless laugh. "No, not really. But yes. Let's do this."

I squeeze my eyes shut for a moment as he flips my three cards, but a sharp inhale from Kira has them flying open again.

Lightning striking a lighthouse. A grim reaper figure on horseback. Anubis the jackal-headed Egyptian god holding scales as souls float skyward in the background . . . laid out upside down.

The Tower. Death. Judgment reversed.

"Breathe and forget every preconceived notion you have about these symbols," Gabe says, laying a hand gently beside mine without touching it. "Hear what the cards have to say, okay?"

Gabe pauses for a moment, seemingly collecting his thoughts, his eyes flicking back and forth between the cards. Finally, he nods.

"You have three major arcana cards here. That's a lot of big-picture energy, life themes and grand patterns and such. The Tower here is past, not future, so don't panic. You've very recently been through a massive upheaval, the kind of event that changes the context of your life in a very big way . . . and that event happened because you had a chance to change your old patterns, but couldn't—or wouldn't. So, they were changed for you. Ultimately, that's a *good* thing. The worst is behind you. You had your Tower moment. Now it's time to figure out what to do next."

He puts one finger on the card with the grim reaper and slides it up an inch from the rest, tapping it.

"The Death card isn't literal. There's no grim reaper hovering over your shoulder, waiting to take you or a loved one." He cocks his head, then adds: "Not that you should walk into traffic or anything. Important disclaimer: this is not carte blanche to do something dangerous."

"Oh, no," I say, waving my hands in denial. "I'm more the overly cautious type. No danger of that here."

"Yeah, I'm kinda seeing that," he says with a wry grin, tapping the first two cards of my spread. "With this Death card, you're being called to pick up the pieces from your Tower moment and build something new. The old way of being, of doing, is dead. It's gone, and there's no bringing it back."

My throat goes tight, blocked by a sudden painful lump. It's . . . true. And it hurts. And damn, that's a blunt way of putting it—but not a *bad* way. Sometimes, you need an out-side perspective to tell it like it really is.

"I'm sorry if that's hard to hear, but it's what you need to accept to be able to move forward. The Death card is just as much about new beginnings as it is about endings. Something is over, but with that comes the opportunity for change and growth, a new direction. A total transformation, even. You're entering a new phase of life, and that's scary, but it's also exciting. Death calls you to purge toxic bullshit—which can include both things *and* people. Break out of your bad habits or patterns and look at yourself as a fertile garden ready for new growth."

Wow. And . . . now I'm gonna cry? This is wild. This is the most intimate and intense interaction I've ever had with a stranger, and that includes random one-night hookups. Gabe shoots me a small smile.

"Do you need a minute?" he asks. I take a long breath in through my nose, then shake my head.

"No, I'm good. I need this. What about the Judgment card?"

He picks up the card and flips it in one hand, seeming to study the artwork.

"This is another card that, on its surface, feels kinda doomy. Makes you think, ahh, I'm being judged! Again, it's not that literal or straightforward. Here, I think you're being called to honestly and deeply learn from the experience you just went through and live in alignment with your highest self. What does it mean for you to live according to your values? What would your life be like if you allowed yourself to be the person you wished you were—*truly*—and held yourself accountable? You have a lot of soul-searching to do to find what that version of yourself looks like, and this card showing up reversed feels a lot like blocked energy in that department. You need to do this sort of deep contemplation, this sort of tough love look at your past, your reality, and the core of who you are, but something in you flinches away from that."

As if to confirm, I literally flinch away from him. This is *brutal*. I *know* I'm terrible at looking directly at myself, at my own behavior and all the ways I'm complicit in my own issues. But, exactly as Gabe said, I don't like to look at it. I don't want to acknowledge it. I just want it to be someone else's fault, something outside of myself I can blame or rely on. But as the saying goes: wherever you go, there you are.

Fuck.

Gabe picks up his tablet, and I sit up with a start. Is he leaving already after dropping these bombshells? I'm about to ask about the final card linking our spreads that he hasn't flipped yet . . . but beneath his tablet are two more cards, face down. How did he lay them there without me noticing?

"These cards are optional," he says with a sheepish grin. "It's completely fine if you don't want to flip them. With these cards, I asked for a warning for each of you. What's something you could use a heads-up about? What awaits if you don't change course? That's what's here—a warning for each of you. Do you want me to flip them?"

"Yes," Kira says immediately. She's the brave one, after all, charging into her burning buildings.

"Yes," I agree, not wanting to be shown up, but the quaver in my voice gives me away. Also, if I'm going to . . . you know, live up to my highest self or whatever, I guess I need to know how I'm most likely to screw up.

Gabe nods and flips both cards without hesitation.

The Ten of Swords on top for Kira. The Three of Swords on the bottom for me.

"Oh goody, more swords," Kira says with a groan.

"Hoo-yeah, and these are some good ones. You managed to get the two bloodiest cards in the deck. But we're not talking literal blood here or anything, promise."

Gabe zeroes in on Kira first, tapping the Ten of Swords, which shows a figure lying in a puddle of their own blood with ten swords sticking out of their back. Does *not* look like a good time.

"This card is a crisis point. It's learning the lesson you're called to learn in the hardest possible way. You could have changed course but chose not to, doubling down on your rigid way of thinking instead. The only good thing about it is the clearing clouds and rising sun in the background. There's nowhere to go but up when you've got ten swords in your back, you know? Everything will collapse one way or another. If you choose to stick it out as long as possible instead of burning things down yourself, then this is the result."

Gabe's eyes slide over to me, and I slip down further in my seat, hands at the sides of my face, poised to cover my eyes.

"Rip the Band-Aid off," I say, eyeing the card with trepidation. It shows a bloody goose falling out of the sky, its heart pierced by three swords. "How bad is it?"

"I mean . . ." Gabe says, drawing out the word. "It's pretty much the same as Kira's. The Three of Swords is often called the heartbreak card, but you've already been through your big heartbreak."

He taps the first card in my spread, the crumbling lighthouse that's literally on fire, with a sympathetic look.

"With this one, I'll ask you to remember that the swords also represent your *voice*, the way you *communicate* your thoughts and ideas. You're being cautioned to use your words carefully and in alignment with your highest self—" he taps the Judgment card this time "—or else you'll be breaking your own heart next time instead of having it broken for you. And that's no fun! Very avoidable! Remember, both of these are just warnings, not predictions. Nothing is set in stone. You have free will, and your fate is always in your own hands. No card is ever a certainty."

Finally, Gabe turns to the lone card still face down on the table, the one that links our two card spreads.

"Hey, let's end on a good note, shall we?" he says, slipping his thumb under it, ready to flip.

Kira sucks in a breath and draws back, wary. "But how can you be sure there's a good card under there?

Gabe shrugs.

"Eh, call it a vibe. But like I said before, they're *all* good cards because they deliver something you need to hear. It just depends on the context and how you act on their messages." He cocks his head, then laughs. "Also, you've already gotten most of the worst cards in the deck! If this is the Ten of Wands, I'll eat my words."

Before we can stall any further, Gabe flips the card with a swift, decisive motion. A brilliant smile blooms on his face.

It's the Star. The card features a nude woman with one foot in the water and one leg kneeling on land. She holds a jug of water in each hand, carefully pouring from both so one stream runs over the rocks and the other splashes into the pond. Eight stars shine over her head.

"I love this card," Gabe says, his look soft. "It's so much more complicated than it first seems. The Star often gets simplified to a single keyword: hope. And that *is* accurate in a very straightforward kind of way. But more specifically, it's a card of rebuilding after trauma. When you line up the major arcana in order, it's the card that comes right after the Tower."

He taps the Tower card again, his finger covering the tiny figure leaping out of the burning lighthouse.

"The Star is finding your way again. It's regaining your equilibrium, regaining the balance between the emotional and the practical that's needed for healing. But it's not a passive card. You can't sit back and wait for things to work themselves out. It takes a lot of active effort for the woman on the card to maintain her balance, to keep those streams of water hitting right where they need to be. It takes focus and belief in yourself, enough inner strength to embrace hope, and a willingness to adjust and let things go when they no longer serve. But if you're willing to do the work, the energy of the Star is there to meet you both halfway. Remember, this is a shared card. So, it's not just that you're receiving the same message, but that this is a shared work. There is vulnerability in the aftermath of crisis, in hope, and in rebuilding. If you can care for each other in that vulnerable state, build together instead of staying siloed, you can avoid constructing an exact replica of your previous cage. You could balance each other. You could build something entirely new *together*."

Silence reigns over the table as Gabe's final words resonate between us. I glance up and catch Kira's gaze, then look away immediately, back down at the cards. It's too intense, this moment, the intimacy of everything we've just shared. But as I watch the cards disappear back into the deck one by one, I also feel a tiny flicker of that Star energy. A little hope. An urge to rebuild.

I leave Gabe a larger tip than I can really afford. He deserves it.

I have a whole lot of thinking to do.

AFTER HAVING OUR SOULS PLUCKED FROM OUR bodies and tacked up on the wall for all to see, Kira and I resolve to move on with the evening as if none of it happened. We don't actually say that, of course, but by unspoken agreement, we exit the tarot café, set the timer for five minutes, and stop at the closest restaurant when the timer goes off. Then we go to the Vietnamese place next to it instead, because thirty dollars a plate is not our speed.

But we don't talk about the tarot reading.

The food is incredible, and the company is good, of course, but it's like there's a gray cloud over our heads the whole time. It's hard not to silently play Gabe's words over and over as we eat, as we walk to Kira's car, even as we arrive back at Kira and Grace's empty apartment and stand awkwardly in the living room, our keys nestled together on the low table just inside the door. There's a weird tension in the air that takes me a moment to identify.

I don't want Kira to go. She'll go to her bedroom, I'll crash on the couch, and a taut thread of *something* will keep me awake with its insistent pull, I can already tell.

What we shared today was intense. We picked through every possession I've accumulated in my adult life and trashed most of it. We walked the campus of my former university as I admitted my secrets. We had the depths of our psyches plumbed by a tarot reader. A fantastic dinner, good conversation on the ride home . . .

And now, we've gone back to the same apartment . . . but not to continue that closeness. Not to cuddle and talk more over a drink, which would lead us back into dangerous territory. Not to sleep together. Just . . . to separate and pretend the other isn't there. To let this little bubble of intimacy pop and sleep off the effects. That's how it has to be for now, though.

I'm too much of a mess for anything else.

"Good night," I make myself say.

My voice comes out rougher than I expect, but if Kira notices, she doesn't mention it. All she says is:

"Good night, Nic."

CHAPTER SEVENTEEN

KIRA

Two days later, I've just woken up from my post-shift power nap and am watching Grace play a very intense story-driven video game in a glazed-over state when Nic hobbles through the door.

"I thought this wasn't supposed to happen until I was thirty," Nic groans, holding her lower back with a grimace.

"Maybe you're just an overachiever," Grace says. Impressive how she's able to summon snark even while engaged in an intense boss battle—research for her work as a game developer, but also for fun.

"What happened? Did you get hurt?" I ask, the fog instantly lifting from my brain as I leap off the couch, going into triage mode.

"No, no, nothing like that, I'm *fine*," Nic insists.

She is clearly *not* fine. She is, in fact, hunched over like an eighty-year-old and making a face like she just licked a hot stove. I grab her elbow and let her lean on me as she hobbles to the couch, lowering herself gingerly into a sprawl. The overly soft, semi-broken couch envelops her, and she sinks into it with a groan that's half pain, half relief.

"So, Nic, how was your day?" Grace prompts.

"It was good," Nic says, gasping as she attempts to change position. "I think . . . this couch might be bad for my back, is all."

I'm instantly flooded with guilt. I was so entranced by the idea of having her here that I neglected to mention a critical fact: while *I* find our couch incredibly comfortable, it is also incredibly *soft*, and that's not always great for a full night of sleep.

"Riiight," Grace says, tapping her bottom lip with the controller. "When my friend from DC visited at the New Year, he hobbled through his last two days sleeping on that couch. There's clearly only one solution here."

It takes a second, but the penny eventually drops.

"One solution . . . oh. *Oh*, right. I guess you could, uh . . . share with me? Unless that makes you uncomfortable or something."

I barely let half a beat of silence go by before I crack.

"You know what? I've been thinking we need a new couch anyway," I babble, giving the couch a thump for good measure. "I wonder if there's anywhere still open that could do same-day delivery? Or at least tomorrow. I guess it's too late for today, but—"

"We can just share. Really, it's okay," Nic cuts in. But she won't meet my eyes. Is she worried I'll come on to her or something? Is she thinking about that one night . . .

"See? It's *okay*," Grace says, clapping me on the shoulder. "Sorry, Nic, I'd offer to share *my* bed, but I don't want to."

Nic and I blink at each other, then bust out laughing, shaking our heads as if to say, *oh, Grace*.

"I guess sharing is the only option that will keep us both fit to work," I say, shrugging *so casually* because there's absolutely nothing wrong with this scenario. No problem. Why *would* there be? Because I was all ready to pursue this girl, right up until I found out she's getting over a ten-year crush on our mutual best friend? No, that's nothing. We're just friends who slept together once, and this is going to be no trouble at all.

I just love getting the chance to help a *friend*.

THAT NIGHT, AS NIC SETTLES INTO BED NEXT to me, I realize just how critical my error was.

My terrible, traitorous brain chooses to dredge up the memory of the tarot café evening and replay it in detail as Nic sighs into her pillow. Straight-up sexual fantasies would be better, rather than throwing all this feelings stuff into the mix. It wasn't a date, but it *was* better than any actual date I've been on in the last . . . god, I don't even remember.

All my dates in recent memory have either been awful or intentionally brief. That evening with Nic was everything I'd always hoped to find via my twelve thousand dating apps: honest conversation, good chemistry, a fun time together, and a genuine connection that leaves me wanting to see someone again. I *have* been looking, I swear, no matter what Skylar says. My job gets in the way a lot, but I know what I want long-term, and I really have tried. For me to have found it completely by accident with Nic . . .

But that's not what the evening was. That's not what *we* are. This is just me inviting a friend with a bad back to share my bed so she doesn't hurt anymore. She wouldn't be up for anything sexy anyway, feeling the way she does. And I'm not sure I am, either, given all the recent revelations. Her history with Skylar. I need someone emotionally available, and Nic seems the total opposite right now. It's *fine*.

It's . . . definitely not fine. My body is acutely aware of her shape beneath the covers, her hair fanned out on the pillow, the scant inches of space between us.

It takes me two hours to get to sleep.

This is going to be hell.

NIC TAKES THREE DAYS, MUCH IBUPROFEN, and an awkward amount of stretching to recover. And sleeping in my bed, of course. The key to it all, keeping the whole thing from getting worse.

Well, the back pain situation, at least. My sanity, on the other hand, is *suffering*. It's a good thing I was away at the fire station for one of those days, because the constant low simmer of my libido is making this arrangement a rough hang. Even worse is the fact that we've taken to watching TV at night, the tablet propped up on our chests as we straight-up cuddle in bed.

Tonight is especially bad, because Nic's head is nestled just above my breast while I hold the tablet, her arm slung low over my stomach, and I can't stop picturing a scenario that begins with me arching against her until my nipple is in her mouth. I *have* to stop this, have to get it together. Nic is a guest in my house, and she's only in my bed because she got hurt. I don't want her to feel pressured or taken advantage of—plus all the other reasons it would be a terrible idea that I . . . can't remember at the moment.

The episode ends, and I shut off the tablet and set it on my nightstand. It's going to take me an hour to fall asleep when I'm this keyed up, so I may as well get started.

"Good night," I murmur, turning onto my side so my back is to Nic. I expect her to do the same, facing away, but she leaves her arm in place as I roll over. Instead of getting space, I've instead rolled over in her arms, my ass nestled against her hips and her breath on the back of my neck. Her hand dangles just above the waistband of my shorts, not touching, but an electric buzz crackles between the tips of her fingers and the bare inch of skin between my tank top and shorts. I want her to slide her hand down, slip a finger through my slickness and circle my clit the way I need her to so badly—so badly my nipples are peaked against my shirt and—

And my hips press back against Nic, all on their own . . . just as she grinds forward into me, her thumb resting on the waistband.

"God, sorry," she whispers against my neck, dragging her hand back from the precipice in a way that's probably supposed to show restraint, but that skates over my skin and turns into a hold on my hip instead, hanging on instead of pulling away. "I'll stop. I'll go somewhere else. I—"

"Don't," I gasp, grabbing her hand and pressing it against my side before it can go too far. "Unless you want to, I mean. But—"

The rest is cut off in a gasp as Nic's hand slides straight inside my shorts without a second's hesitation. But not down the front where I want her hands to go. No, she dives straight down the *side* of my shorts, blunt fingernails dragging over my hip, the side of my ass, my upper thigh, taking my shorts partway down along with her hand.

"Oh, thank god," Nic says with a graze of teeth on my shoulder. "Sleeping in this bed with you has been torture."

I laugh, grabbing her hand and guiding it up under my shirt. "Torture for you? I've been lying awake every night trying to get my body to calm down while you sleep peacefully like a sociopath!"

"That's because I was having incredibly vivid dreams about all the things I wanted to do to you," Nic says. "Very awkward, waking up on the edge of an orgasm next to your sleeping roommate."

"Next time, wake me up," I say with a hitch in my voice as Nic's fingers find my nipple.

"I will," she promises. "All I wanted was to roll over behind you, just like this, and—"

Rather than finishing the sentence, she shows me, grabbing my entire breast in one hand and hitching her leg up over mine so she can grind against me. She catches my nipple between two fingers as she cups me, and the heat of her center bleeds through to my skin. Suddenly, I need nothing more in the world than to feel that heat on my tongue. I haven't gotten to taste her yet, and that's criminal.

I turn over in her arms and capture her mouth in the kiss I've been desperately wanting for days, pouring every ounce of my pent-up need into her with a muffled moan. Her leg slides up over my hip again, the perfect opportunity for me to roll her over onto her back with me in between her legs. She scoots back for a second, and I freeze . . . but she's just getting enough room to take off her shorts, which I *fully* support.

"Can I see your utterly perfect boobs, please?" I ask *so* politely, motioning for her to strip off her shirt as I take over sliding her shorts down her legs. "I want the nice view while I work down here."

"Only if you do the same," Nic says, ripping off her shirt. I get distracted halfway to taking off my own shirt at the sight of her bare breasts, bigger and rounder than mine, with nipples that are begging for my tongue.

"Shirt," Nic demands, and I shake out of my breast-induced daze, artlessly yanking my shirt over my head.

"Hell yes, thank you," she says, leaning up to grab me around the waist and pulling me down with her. I fall forward, forearms braced on either side of her, and take her mouth in a long, intense kiss. It's . . . *more* than I mean to make it, too much spark, too much of that *need* that has nothing to do with sex. But I can't help it. I angle my head, deepening the kiss as I run a hand from her collarbone to her hip, shifting until the flickering pleasure of her nipples teases against my own. Beneath me, I feel her hand snake between us to circle her own clit, and that is something I *have* to see.

I break the kiss, pausing for a brief second to take one of her nipples into my mouth before leaning up to watch Nic touch herself.

"Sorry, I . . . I can—" she stutters, but I grab her wrist as she starts to pull her hand away.

"Keep going," I say, my voice low and gravelly. She arches against the bed at my words, her hand going back to work, and she's so sexy, so beautiful, so . . .

I cut the thought off before it can go any further, shuffling back on the bed so I can lie between her legs. Focus on the here and now. Trying to make it anything else is a bad idea, *such* a bad idea . . .

But then my tongue slides inside her, and everything else falls away.

THE NEXT MORNING, WE BOTH STARTLE AWAKE to the dulcet tones of Jerry Lee Lewis singing "Goodness gracious GREAT balls of fire!" Normally Nic wakes up before her alarm and turns it off, so I've not yet had this particular experience. I don't recommend it.

Well . . . maybe not *that part*.

But then there's the part where Nic buries her face in my neck with a groan of complaint after it goes off. The feel of her fingers curling over my hip, as if holding on to me can prevent the day from starting. The slow slide of her body against mine as she reaches over to silence the alarm. Her nipples poke through the baggy shirt she threw on last night before we fell asleep, and it takes all my willpower not to push that fabric up and put my mouth to work on her. She needs to get ready for the day, and she'll be very late if we start on that. But when she pulls back, something of my thoughts must be on my face, because she grins and leans down for a long, lingering kiss.

"I gotta shower," she says, then pauses for another kiss. "But we should talk after, right?"

Well, that's like being thrown into the bay in January.

"Uh, right," I say, sitting up with the covers held over my bare breasts. "Talk. Yeah. I'll make breakfast."

"You're the *best*," Nic says, then bounds out into the hallway with an armload of clothes, heading for the bathroom.

Well then. Guess I should put on some clothes and make good on my promise.

I throw on a pair of leggings and a slouchy T-shirt, then go about my morning routine of coffee, brushing teeth, and breakfast prep. Normally I'm a smoothie person, especially on shift days, but thanks to Jerry Lee Lewis, I'm up earlier than normal, and I don't want to wake Grace with the blender. I run through my mental catalog of breakfast recipes, cross-reference with what I find in the fridge, and end up going for an Everything Frittata. As in, everything left in the fridge. Whatever leftover vegetables we have, that half can of leftover black beans in the fridge, the butt ends of three different blocks of cheese, all of it seasoned and then dumped in a cast-iron skillet and baked into a crustless pie type thing.

The frittata has about five minutes left to bake when Nic comes out, damp, clean, and smelling good, with wet hair drying in loose waves over her shoulders. I pass her a cup of coffee prepared just how she likes it (maple syrup and so much oat milk it's practically lukewarm), and she looks down at the cup like she's been waiting for it all her life.

"You're incredible," she says, having a spiritual moment with her coffee while I check on the frittata, then pull it out of the oven to cool. Nic's eyes go wide.

"Oh my god, did you actually *cook something* for breakfast?"

I shrug, suddenly self-conscious. Is this too much?

"It's barely cooking," I say, waving it away. "It's just a bunch of leftovers dumped in some egg. Lower your expectations, please."

Nic shakes her head with a small smile and opens the cabinet, pulling down two plates.

"I don't think you know how good of a cook you are," she says. "I've eaten your dinner on two separate nights since I moved in, and it's always delicious."

And *there's* the awkwardness I've been waiting for. The second she says *"I've eaten your . . ."* both of our minds immediately plunge into the gutter. We're both acutely aware of what she's *eaten* recently, if her blush is anything to go by. She sets the plates down and walks me back into the counter, pinning me there with her hips as she leans up for an intense kiss. My brain goes completely blank as I let my hands drift around her lower back, tracing skin just above the waistband of her pants with my thumb and letting the kiss wipe out my fears, just for a moment. I know that, at any second, we'll have to actually talk about this, but for right now . . .

Nic breaks off, then visibly forces herself to step back, hands in the air.

"Sorry, sorry, got carried away," she says, lips and cheeks flushed from the kiss. "I gotta leave soon, and we're supposed to talk."

"Yes, talk," I say. I take a few slow breaths in through my nose as I slice the frittata and serve it up, letting myself slip into something akin to firefighter mode. I'm an adult. I can have an adult conversation with this girl I like, who I just slept with for the second time. Drawing boundaries is a good thing. I sit down at the table with my plate and glance over at Grace's door. Pretty sure she came home super late last night—the studio she works for is in major crunch mode—so we should have privacy for a while. Nic takes a bite of frittata, hums appreciatively, then sets her fork down.

"I just want to make sure we're on the same page about this . . . thing we're doing," she says, gesturing between us. "I feel like we've both been through a lot lately, and I'm only *just* starting to untangle the Skylar stuff. I'm not sure I'm in a good place to be falling into something new. That makes sense, right? I'm not an asshole?"

"No, you're not an asshole," I say, even as my heart pulls in on itself for protection. "Probably smart to give yourself some time."

It's weird now if I put it out there, right? If I come out and say, *I'm developing feelings for you, but I can handle it*, that'll multiply the awkwardness exponentially.

No, I can keep a hold on my own heart. I've done it this far. Nic really *is* smart to focus on herself for a while, figure

out who she is and what she wants. It would be very *not* smart
of me, in fact, to try to be with her before she has a chance
to do that work. Nic smiles down at the table, then looks up,
meeting my gaze.

"So, it's okay to keep this casual for now?" she asks.
"Keep . . . you know, hooking up when we want to, and just
making sure to talk if things get weird?"

Oh. *Oh.* That is *not* where I assumed we were going with
this. I thought we were heading for "this was fun but it
can't happen again" territory. Instead, we've landed in the
"friends with benefits" zone. But . . . do I want that? Can
I stand having Nic in my bed knowing I can't have anything else? There's also the matter of her job only being a
one-year contract, and her possibly leaving again to pursue
a PhD. Leaving is the one thing I truly *can't* do. If it comes
to that, then it's over for real. I haven't spent the past ten
years fighting to make it in the Seattle Fire Department,
struggling for every inch of progress, to just give up on it
completely. I grew up here. My whole life is here.

A brief memory of the Ten of Swords tarot card flashes
across my brain, that figure lying in a pool of their own blood
because they couldn't change their ways. But how am I supposed to know what it's referencing? Which changes should
I be making? Maybe it's Nic that'll be the sword in my back.
Maybe we're only meant to help each other, not be together.
Or maybe I really am supposed to give up on SFD and go
somewhere else, like my instructor wanted . . .

I shove it all away. It's irrelevant to the decision in front
of me: Can I be chill with Nic? I look at her across the table,
remembering how it felt to have my legs thrown over her
shoulders and my fingers buried in her hair as I fully rode her
face . . . then cut myself off, my cheeks burning hot.

I can make this work. It's not like we can *never* be together. I just need to be patient. Give her some time, wait until she's ready . . . and have fun until then. "Yeah, okay. I can do casual," I say.

It's not until Nic has housed the rest of her breakfast and flown out the door for work that I can admit to myself: *I have never done a single casual thing in my life.*

CHAPTER EIGHTEEN

NIC

This thing with Kira is *so* casual and fine.

I mean, we've had dinner together every night Kira hasn't been on duty, complete with post-dinner TV and cuddles. And then there's the sex, of course, which is frequent and blisteringly hot. But no one is falling in love or anything, and it'll probably end when I move back to my place at the end of August, so what's there to worry about? It's August first. I can stay out of trouble for a month.

I don't sound convincing even inside my own head.

I just have to keep being careful. Kira is cool and smart *and* funny *and* brave *and* sexy and my brain could easily get *confused* by all this closeness. So I have to watch myself. Like Skylar said, I need to be my *own* anchor, and that's exactly what I'm doing.

Even when I'm standing in a bridal shop with Kira by my side.

"Hello!" a frighteningly chipper saleswoman says, grinning at us like we're adorable kittens or something. "My name is Darcy. Are you here for a wedding consultation?"

"No!" I yelp, panicked, then realize that was maybe a *bit* too intense when Darcy and Kira both fix me with strange looks. "I mean, kind of? We're meeting our friend Skylar here. The appointment is under her name."

Darcy's face clears, expression sliding back into customer service mode. "Oh, wonderful. We're so looking forward to hosting her! I'll be handling your fitting myself. Let me show you back to the fitting suite and pour you some champagne while you wait. Will Ms. Clark be here shortly?"

I check my phone to see if there have been any updates. "Ah, looks like she got held up. She'll be about ten minutes late."

"No problem. That's *completely* fine. You just enjoy yourselves until she arrives!" Darcy says, leading us into a back room filled with mirrors, clothing racks with curated dresses, and—most important—a tray of fruit, cheese, and chocolate, with three glasses of champagne perched atop an enormous ivory ottoman.

"Of course it's *completely fine*," Kira murmurs in my ear once we're alone. "She knows the opinion of 872,000 of Skylar's followers depends on it."

A shiver runs down my spine at the feel of Kira's breath on my ear. Good thing we're here to watch Skylar try on dresses, not us, because I'm not sure I'd be able to handle the thought of Kira getting undressed just on the other side of a flimsy door.

"I don't even want to think about how much the dresses cost here," I say, looking around at the tasteful decor and luxury fabrics. "Do you think they even have price tags?"

I snag a champagne glass and wander over to a waterfall of white satin, checking every hem for a tag. Nothing.

"Yeah, that doesn't bode well," Kira says with a wince. "I don't suppose that, during your giant heart-to-heart with Skylar, you asked about her finances?"

I shake my head, staring at the little bubbles rising through the pale gold liquid in my glass. "No, we'd barely gotten through the basic heart destruction portion before the fire started, and then I was . . . well, distracted."

"Understandable," Kira says. "I guess this is one of those times when we have to practice trusting Skylar more. I still feel really bad about the Fiji thing."

"Me too," I agree, taking a sip of champagne to cover how much the whole situation still bothers me. "We really didn't give her enough credit. Now that she's mentioned it, I can see that she's been doing better the past year. I was just so used to seeing her a certain way."

Kira shrugs, joining me by the dress rack to look at the samples. "Hey, she always says she's living proof that the pre-frontal cortex doesn't finish developing until twenty-five. It's not like your fears were unfounded. Old habits die hard, and I witnessed plenty of Disaster Skylar over the last two years."

I turn to Kira, mouth open to say something, but the thought goes right out of my head. She's standing much closer than I realized. And I didn't expect her to be looking at me.

My mouth is on her before I can think better of it. I lean up and kiss her bottom lip, slow and lingering, and her mouth *pulls* against mine, everything slow as molasses. I just *barely* stop myself from renewing the kiss, some part of my brain reminding me that Skylar could walk in at any minute.

Oh, fuck, *Skylar*.

"Hey, um, not to make it weird after just randomly kissing

you," I say, grimacing. "But have you told Skylar about . . . us? This arrangement?"

Kira shakes her head. "No. I thought . . . well, it's not a good idea, right? She'd probably be so excited for us, and if we tell her it's not like that . . ."

I nod, unnerved by the emotion creeping into my chest. It almost feels like . . . disappointment? "No, you're right. I haven't told her either. I just wanted to make sure we had our stories straight before she gets here. Sorry for kissing you like that. I shouldn't have."

"You're good," she says, taking a quick look over her shoulder, then pressing one last quick kiss to my lips. "It's okay so long as we know where we stand, right?"

"Right," I agree, taking a small step back to stop myself from drifting into the warmth of her body. "No problem at all."

Thankfully, Skylar has good timing for once, flying into the room like a very chatty shooting star, with Darcy trailing after. Skylar gives an excited double clap once she spots us, squealing as she pulls us both into a hug.

"I am *so excited for this*," Skylar says with a slightly strangling squeeze. "Don't worry, none of these dresses are for you two. I asked them to hold your outfits in the back as a surprise! I wanted to be here when you saw them."

"Outfits for *us*?" I squeak like an actual mouse.

"Skylar, I don't think we can afford anything in here," Kira says in a panicked whisper.

Skylar waves her protest away. "No, no, it's my treat. Please, don't worry! Don't you remember me saying way back at the beginning that I picked out outfits for everyone?"

"I do *now*, but—"

Skylar's not listening, already swept up in her excitement. "Darcy, could we please see the fits I called about?"

"Yes, of course! Be right back," Darcy says, trotting out the door on her mission. The second she's out of the room, Skylar turns back to us.

"Besides, I'm getting my dress for free and your outfits at cost," she says with an eyebrow waggle. "Can you believe it? And unlimited champagne while we're here too!"

She sighs as she bites into a tiny chocolate cake from the snack tray. "I will not miss ninety percent of what goes into being an 'influencer,' but I *will* miss these perks. Have you had one of these yet? They're *life-changing*."

I bury my stress with a tiny chocolate cake as instructed, which is a fantastic decision, then scramble for a napkin when Darcy comes striding back in with a wheeled rack. I am covered in icing and crumbs and cannot touch these expensive clothes until I know my hands are pristine. Skylar runs over to block the view as Darcy hangs each outfit in a dressing room, then closes the door. Once Darcy departs to give us privacy, Skylar turns to us with a fierce grin.

"Oh, I'm so excited to see you both in these outfits," she says. With a dramatic flourish, she whips open the door to the first changing room, revealing a short purple dress hanging from the door hook.

"Kira, for you, I am obeying your insistence that every off-duty outfit show at least *some* skin by giving you a dress that shows a *lot* of skin," Skylar says, taking the dress down to show us the back. "Lucky us, right, Nic?"

"Ha, yeah," I say, *so* awkward it's like the first words I've ever spoken in my life. "Lucky us."

Really though. It will be a *gift* to see Kira in this dress. I can already picture her in it. The halter-style neckline plunges *low*, below the bustline, and goes even lower in the back. The ruched sheath hits above the knee, showing the perfect amount of leg. The whole thing is plum purple, but it seems to contain more colors than that, with the way the light slithers over it.

"Oh," Kira breathes, stepping up to run a hand over the dress with reverence. "I absolutely would have chosen this for myself."

"I know," Skylar says, flipping her hair over her shoulder. I'd call it smug, but . . . nah, she actually nailed it. Doesn't mean I'm any less nervous for myself though. Skylar turns to me with a knowing smile, moving over to the next fitting room.

"Nic, I am continuing my almost ten-year search to find formal wear you feel comfortable in. No poofy dresses, I *promise*. For you, I've chosen . . ."

She throws open the door to the second fitting room. "This marvelous piece! This shop actually works with the custom suit place next door to provide suit options for any body, no matter its shape, so I've taken the liberty of ordering you this three-piece outfit in New Moon Black."

My eyes go wide. The outfit *is* gorgeous, and for once, I actually have hope that I might not hate wearing it. I've never been comfortable in dresses, really; they just don't feel like *me*. But I've tried wearing suits before, and they didn't feel right either. This outfit manages to nail a strange middle ground that I am *here* for. It's a pair of crisp pants with a lacy plum-purple shirt and . . . I don't even know what to call it—a dress-coat? It's like if someone cut out the entire front of a formal satin gown, then belted it at the waist like a coat. All the billowy drama of a dress, but with pants!

"Oh!" I gasp, grabbing Skylar's forearm. "I hope it feels as good to wear as it looks. You might have actually done it this time."

Skylar pumps her fist in the air with a whoop. "Yes! Go, put it on quick. I gotta see this!"

We both dart into our dressing rooms to try on our outfits. I slip into the pants and top with my back to the mirror so I can see the effect all at once, loving the sensation of the smooth, cool fabric against my skin. Expensive fabric definitely feels different. I'm going to be paranoid about messing it up until it's back on the hanger. Finally, I spin around and . . .

Wow. It's so *different* from anything else I've ever worn, in a *very* good way. Comfortable pants, a top that makes my tits look *phenomenal*, and a belted flowy coat/skirt thing spilling down from my waist that is, frankly, majestic. I don't often notice or care about the way I look—it's just not something that ever crosses my mind—but I can't *help* but notice all the best features of my body in this outfit.

Kira's door clicks open next to me, and Darcy and Skylar both gasp and squeal in excitement. This I've *gotta* see. I open my own door and slowly peek out . . . and am stopped dead in my tracks by *that ass*.

"Oh my god," I blurt, then slap a hand over my mouth. Skylar bursts into laughter, full-on doubled over with her hands on her knees, as Kira turns to face me. I'd like to say I have a dignified reaction or give Kira a tasteful compliment . . . but the front is just as bad. And by bad, I mean *perfect*.

I finally wrest my eyes away from Kira's chest to see her cheeks stained with flush under her freckles . . . as she looks straight at *my* chest. We're doing so good at this "hiding our relationship" thing.

"Oh, Nic, that's exactly the reaction I was going for, *thank you*," Skylar says, wiping tears from her eyes. "Here, stand next to Kira. I want to see both of these outfits together."

She waves her hands at us until we shuffle next to each other, shoulders brushing. Kira leans in close to whisper.

"You look amazing."

I smile, bumping my elbow against hers.

"You too. Obviously."

"Oh, this is too perfect," Skylar says, snapping a dozen photos with her phone. "Kira, obviously I knew that dress would be perfect on you, but Nic, this is a *triumph*. Are you comfortable? Do you like it?"

"I love it," I admit, swiveling my hips so the skirt thing swirls a bit. "I've never seen anything like it before. And it's actually comfortable."

Skylar launches herself toward me, throwing her arms around my neck. "Ah, we finally did it! We found you formal wear you can tolerate! Come on, both of you, over here to the big mirror so you can really see yourselves."

We do as instructed, standing side by side before the giant mirrored wall . . . and it takes my breath away.

We look *fucking hot* together.

The purple of my lacy top is the precise shade of Kira's dress, and the satiny black of my outfit brings a certain level of drama. I couldn't tell in the fitting room, but the inside of my skirt is a liquid flash of silver, a perfect contrast to the black. I meet Kira's eyes in the mirror and see a heat in her eyes that feels almost indecent with spectators in the room. But I get it.

We look *so* good. And more than that—we look good as a matched set. Like we belong together.

That thought should scare me more than it does. Instead, it just makes me want to get Kira out of that dress as soon as possible.

Skylar clears her throat delicately to get our attention, then directs us into a series of photo ops that quickly turns ridiculous. We send a stream of increasingly wild photos to the group chat, only stopping when Darcy pops back in to see if we need anything.

"Okay, friends, I'm going up front to settle things with Darcy," Skylar says, shooting a wink at the saleswoman. "Meet me outside once you're changed?"

"Wait, don't we get to see yours?" Kira protests, looking around for an expensive, ostentatious Skylar dress somewhere. Skylar shakes her head with a Grace-like grin.

"Nope! I want it to be a surprise. You both know all the other surprises I have in store for that night, thanks to your *shenanigans*," she says with a pointed look. "I have to hold something in reserve to surprise you! I love it *so* much, though, and it feels good to wear, too. Trust me, you'll agree."

"I don't doubt it," I say, glancing over at Kira. For all her flaws, Skylar *does* have a well-honed sense of what will make a person look and feel great, herself included.

"See you out front in a few!" Skylar says, waving as she disappears, closing the door to the private suite behind her.

We disappear into our respective changing rooms to *very carefully* remove our new and extremely expensive clothing. I manage to undo the belt holding the dress-coat in place—though wrangling it back onto the hanger is another story—and get myself back into my jeans. Just as my hands drop to the bottom hem of my top, Kira lets out a frustrated groan.

"Nic, can you help?" she calls. "This dress has one of those tiny hidden zippers you need a pair of tweezers to find, and I'm extremely stuck."

"Yeah, I got you," I reply, slipping out of my dressing room and into hers before the reality of the situation hits me.

Kira stands with her back to me, one hand bracing herself

against the mirror while the other tugs uselessly at the tiny zipper, which is at the small of her back. The fortunate/ unfortunate part is that I can see right down the front of her dress with her bent toward the mirror like that, and she has the bottom of the dress hiked up around her upper thighs like she tried to get it off that way before I came in. With a slow breath, I shove down all the tempting scenarios my brain presents me with and focus on the task at hand.

"Stop before you break it," I say, swatting her hand away from the tiny zipper. "I got it."

I step closer to get a better look, but it's like the closer I get, the more intense the buzzing energy between us becomes. The second I raise my hands to the zipper and my fingers brush skin, I know I'm in trouble. I meet Kira's eyes in the mirror, and she stares back at me, lips slightly parted. Oh, this is a *bad* idea. My breath goes shallow as I watch Kira's tongue dart out to wet her lips, her body shifting restlessly under my hands. *Just unzip the zipper, Nic, just do what you came to do and leave, just . . .*

The zipper parts with painful slowness, dragging down to the base of her spine until it reveals a line of stretchy black lace.

I should let go now. The zipper is done.

But then her hips rock under my hands, a small, uncontrollable movement.

I drop my hands to her thighs and wait for a reaction, maintaining eye contact in the mirror the whole time. When she doesn't tell me to stop, I drag both hands slowly, *agonizingly* slowly up her thighs until I touch the rucked-up hem of the dress. A quick check-in . . . then I keep pushing, up, up, until the dress reveals just the bottom curve of the round swell of her ass, on perfect display and begging for my hands.

I slide my palms over her, taking in the view as I push the dress up even further, revealing the rest of the stretchy lace thong she wore today. My breath hitches. God, this is a terrible idea, right? I shouldn't? Not here, at least?

But it would be so fun to wind ourselves up and finish off at home . . .

I let my left hand drift back down over her ass and skate a single finger over the scant fabric covering her scorching-hot center. I can tell how wet she is even from the outside . . . but when I hook a finger just under the fabric to slide along her lips, I can *really* feel it. In the mirror, I see her bite her lip to muffle a gasp as my finger traces over her; she's slick and ready, *so* ready for my fingers. When she starts to move restlessly against my touch, I raise my eyes to hers once again, positioning my finger right at her entrance. Then I cock my head in a silent question.

She eases back ever so slowly onto my finger in answer, her mouth falling open in a soundless gasp. *God.* I watch my finger disappear inside her, just holding it still for her to use as she flexes her hips, slow at first, then faster, faster, until her ass bounces on my hand as she full-on fucks herself with my finger. I can *feel* the image of this being burned into my brain for the rest of time—and as Kira reaches up under her dress to circle her clit, I know one thing for certain.

We are *not* finishing this at home.

With my free hand, I tug open my jeans and slip my fingers inside, nearly crying out with how good it feels. I'm dying to get on my knees and let her ride my face until she comes twice, but this has to be quick and quiet. Someone could come back here any second. I gather my own wetness on my middle finger and work my clit slowly at first, then faster, the slide so easy, so good, even with my jeans restricting my movement. Kira watches me in the mirror, our hands working between our legs together as we ride this wave higher and higher—until I feel Kira begin to clench around my finger.

"Ah," she whispers, then bites her lip to stop anything else from coming out as her hips buck, taking my finger as deep as she can and squeezing her eyes shut against the wave of sensation. Her loosened dress finally loses its war with gravity, falling down the arm still tucked between her legs to reveal her tight nipples, chest heaving as she breathes hard in the wake of her orgasm. I know exactly what that nipple feels like on my tongue, dragging over my skin, and it's this thought that finally makes the rising fire in my belly snap.

I let my finger slip free from Kira's wet pussy and fall back against the wall of the changing room, taking in the view of her and chasing that last inch until the pleasure *breaks* over me, every muscle curling tight with the electric sensation at my center, surging again and again until I see sparks behind my eyelids. God, I never thought I could come so hard from rubbing one out inside my jeans. With Kira in that dress, apparently anything's possible.

When I finally come down from the high, I open my eyes to find Kira leaning back against the mirror, flushed and short of breath. I can't believe we just did that. I shake my head in disbelief, and Kira's mouth quirks at one corner.

"Well, uh . . . your zipper is done?" I say.

I can't help but join in when Kira laughs.

SEVERAL MINUTES LATER, AFTER A QUICK wash-up in the bathroom and a lightning-fast change of clothes, we slink back out to the front, Kira about ten seconds ahead of me, so we don't walk out together all sex-flushed and buzzing. Skylar waits for us next to the front door, staring down at her phone.

I give Darcy a little wave and a "thank you" on my way to the door, but she signals for me to wait before I can escape. God, I hope there weren't security cameras. Am I about to get in very embarrassing trouble? But Darcy smiles like everything is normal, pulling open a drawer under the register.

"Here," she says, slipping a business card across the table with a wink. "For when it's your turn."

She shoots a significant look at Kira, who's laughing at something Skylar says on her way out the door. My heart does a painful, unwelcome flip-flop, and an unexpected prickle of heat creeps into the space behind my eyes. What the fuck? I've gotta get this under control.

And I can never let Kira see this card.

I mutter something vaguely polite and flee the scene without meeting Darcy's eyes.

Outside, I catch up with Kira, who's waiting for Skylar to be done on the phone.

"What's wrong? What did she say?" Kira asks, brows knit in concern over whatever is showing on my face.

I paste on a smile and throw the business card in the nearest trash.

"Everything's fine," I say. "Let's go home."

Kira looks like she wants to say more, her eyes soft and . . . pained, maybe? But all she does is reach out and squeeze my hand, dropping it immediately as if burned by the touch.

"Yeah," she says. "Let's go home."

CHAPTER NINETEEN

NIC

August 13, 2025

Dear Ms. Wells,

*Good news! We would like to inform you that your
apartment is now fully restored and has passed inspection by
both the City of Seattle and the Seattle Fire Department.
Repairs continue on the lower floors of the building, but
engineers have declared the building structurally sound.
You may check in with the front office and return to your
apartment any time after 9 a.m. tomorrow.*

*Please contact us via phone or email by August 31 to
inform us of your intent to move back in, or if you would
like to discuss the possibility of ending your lease. August's
rent has been fully waived. Should you decide to move back
in, your next rent check will be due September 5. Once again,
we appreciate your patience and understanding as we navigate
this difficult situation.*

THE EMAIL HAUNTS ME ALL DAY.

I text Kira to let her know right away, of course, but it takes me a full five minutes to compose the message and hit Send. I try very hard not to think about why that is, but every time there's a break in between meetings and lab work, all other thoughts are fully evicted.

This shouldn't be hard. Staying with Kira and Grace was always going to be a temporary arrangement. Sure, it's about two weeks earlier than expected, but that should be a *good* thing, right? Back in my own space. Back in my own bed, if the "odor-controlling mattress enclosure" I bought actually contains the smoke stink.

Pretty sure the "back in my own bed" part is the real problem here, though.

I take a late afternoon break and wander into the grad student break room, which is dominated by posters on "The Chemistry of Coffee's Aroma" and artfully rendered caffeine molecules. There's an entire countertop full of coffee- and tea-making devices, and a cabinet above it with the leaves, beans, and grounds. There's everything from an electric kettle with instant coffee to elaborate pour-over systems and French presses with single-origin beans to use in the coffee grinder. I find the whole setup endearing, which is part of why I use this break room. Technically I could use the one for faculty, but I'm only *just* out of grad school myself. It feels weird. Most days, I'm sure that at any second, someone will find out I'm actually three toddlers in a lab coat with a baking soda and vinegar volcano instead of a master's graduate with a real science job who knows what the hell she's doing. Maybe one day I'll feel like a big kid.

I opt for the most complicated coffee I can make, using a replica nineteenth-century contraption that involves a little burner and a vacuum flask. I feel very old-timey and fancy whenever I use it, and it makes a great cup of coffee. While the coffee brews, I froth up some oat milk, staring into the creamy bubbles like they might hold the answers to life. And Kira.

Should I just be honest with myself, or will that only make it worse?

The number of times I've asked myself that exact question in my adult lifetime should probably concern me. This is what Gabe the tarot reader was talking about, probably—my default mode of only looking at my feelings out of my peripheral vision, ready to avert my inner gaze at the first sign of discomfort. I'm zoned out for too long, apparently, because hot milk and foam splatters onto my hand, overflowing its vessel.

"Ah, shit!" I hiss, dropping the frother and diving for a towel. That's what I get for indulging my traitor brain. There's nothing to think about here. Yes, I feel weird about leaving Kira and Grace's place, but who *wouldn't* miss living with someone who's an excellent cook *and* an excellent eater of things that are definitely not food? I'd be a fool not to feel *some* kind of way about it. And even if there *is* something vaguely in the general region of *feelings* developing, I've got to ignore it for now. Skylar's not-a-bachelorette party is in a week, and her grand not-a-wedding party is the week after. I should be focusing on spending time with my best friend before she leaves the country.

Besides, this thing with Kira is supposed to be *casual, like we agreed.* And no matter how much I might—*maybe*—want to consider otherwise . . . it's too soon to be clinging to another person. I can't go straight from being obsessed with Skylar for years to latching onto Kira. That's exactly what Skylar told me *not* to do.

Be your own anchor, I repeat in my head as I add the milk to the coffee with a dash of maple syrup. *Be your own anchor, not a sad barnacle on Kira's side.*

Despite the splattering, the coffee is perfect. I head back to my office with my head slightly clearer, finally ready for some science.

WHEN I ARRIVE HOME, EVERYTHING GETS CON-fusing all over again.

I stay late at work that evening to make up for my spacey, unproductive morning, so it's already getting dark when I walk in to find the table set with the nice dishes, candles burning in the center, and Kira bustling around in the kitchen.

"Hey, there you are!" she says, stopping on her way to the table to give me a kiss, glass dish of enchiladas in hand. "Perfect timing. Hungry?"

"Always," I say with a longing stare at the enchiladas. They smell *incredible*. But most of my brain is still lingering on that kiss a second ago. Automatic affection. A quick peck.

Felt . . . relationship-y. Not like something you do when your regular hookup comes home.

"This is fancy," I say warily, slipping my shoes off and throwing my keys on the counter. There's an open bottle of wine on the table. Kira's phone is humming a steady stream of quiet music.

"Well, you know, you're going back to your apartment, so I thought we should have a proper send-off," Kira says, peeking over her shoulder at me with soft eyes and a small smile. "Wanna go get changed? This'll be ready in a minute."

I drift off into the bedroom to strip out of my work clothes in a daze.

This is . . . weird, right? This whole thing is suddenly feeling very intimate. Maybe that's a weird thing to say, considering that my fingers and tongue have been on and in her so much lately, but this is on a different level. It feels like a date, way more than the night of the tarot reading did. With the look in Kira's eyes tonight . . .

I shove the thought out of my mind and pull-on sweatpants and an old T-shirt, deliberately going informal to tone down the atmosphere that's developing here. I'll just play ignorant. Feelings? What feelings? Nothing to talk about on that front for either of us. Why would I ever think otherwise?

But when I come back out, Kira pours me a glass of merlot and captures my mouth in a longer, slower kiss, our fingers intertwined around the wineglass stem. I lose myself in it for a long moment before snapping back to reality.

"I'm starving. Can we eat?" I say at an awkwardly loud volume, cringing at myself even as I flee to the safety of my chair. With a table between us, I can breathe a little easier. We dig in, and Kira starts in on a story about Grace, who is essentially living at the studio these days, crashing in a cot room so she can get right back to work—sadly, not all that unusual in the video game industry. As we talk, things . . . ease. I tell her about my silly complicated coffee and some minor drama between two of the engineering grad students, and the evening flows. It's fine. Nice.

Right up until the point where Kira lays her fork down and looks across the table at me, candlelight dancing in her eyes as her mouth quirks into a tiny affectionate smile.

"Nic, I . . . I wanted to talk you about something," she begins, and my body *slams* into fight-or-flight mode the second the words leave her mouth.

I knew it. I *knew* tonight felt different. I can't do this. I have to get out of here. I'm not ready. I don't want to hurt her. I don't want to *not* be with her. I just can't do . . . whatever *this* is. Panic, *panic*, PANIC.

I rack my brain for an excuse, *any* excuse that will get me out of here without having to hear the words I know are coming—

It's an honest relief when my phone lights up—with an actual *call*, no less—interrupting whatever terrifying thing Kira is building up to.

Then I see who it is.

"Oh," I say in surprise, a snake of dread coiling in my stomach. "It's my supervisor at the lab. I should take this."

Kira's brows knit in concern. "Yeah, of course. Hope everything's okay."

I dash into the bedroom, relieved to have a break from the Kira-related tension, at least, and answer the call.

"Hello?"

"Nic, it's Dr. Birk. I'm afraid I have some bad news."

The snake in my belly curls tighter, hissing a threat. Did I mess something up? Did I leave something dangerous out in the lab? No, I'm always meticulous in the lab; it's the one part of my life where I'm never a mess. What then? Dr. Birk clears his throat awkwardly, then sighs.

"We've been informed that our grant funding will not be renewed," he says, his light Danish accent softening the absolute destruction the words bring. "I'm afraid your contract will be ending in December instead of June. I'm so sorry, Nic. We've really enjoyed having you in the lab, and I'll let you know immediately if any other positions come up before December."

December.

Fuck.

I reply in a fog, somehow ending the conversation and hanging up without processing any of it.

December.

Everything is falling apart.

Skylar is leaving. Skylar and I are never happening. The job that lets me afford my apartment is gone. And . . .

I peek out the cracked door to see Kira clearing our dinner dishes from the table and bringing out dessert. The lit candle in the middle of the table flickers and flares, shining through the wineglass next to it. Kira hums quietly to herself, a small, private smile at the corner of her mouth. I love that smile. I want to kiss that smile.

But then I picture the look in her eyes just before I got the call, the words I could *feel* perched at the end of her tongue, and my heart leaps into a frantic race.

I should never have come back to Seattle. Maybe I was meant to stay in Maryland for my PhD after all. They wanted me to. I loved the research. I'd be so excited to work with my old advisor again. Maybe it's not too late.

But right now, Kira is waiting for me.

I step out of the bedroom and attempt to force a smile, but I'm deeply unsuccessful, judging by the way Kira's good mood falls away in an instant.

"What happened? Are you okay?" she asks.

Her eyes are so soft, her hands lifting to reach for me, and I can't help it—I flinch away. The hurt in her eyes, the flickering candlelight, the perfect little mini cakes waiting on the table, and those echoing, unspoken words from earlier, terrifying and wonderful and . . . god, I want to hear them.

I can admit it. I *want* to hear them.

But I can't repeat the past, can't cling to Kira just because Skylar is leaving. And maybe this *is* real, and I *should* give it a chance, should let Kira say those words . . . but I chicken out. I can't deal with it right now.

I'm not even sure I can stay in Seattle anymore.

"I'm not feeling well," I say, eyes fixed on my carbon atom socks. "I think I'm gonna go to bed early."

"O . . . kay," Kira says. "Did I do something wrong?"

"No!" I yelp, even as my brain screams, *Yes! You were too perfect, too kind, too talented, too beautiful, too loving, and I am absolutely not a person you should love. You've done everything wrong, Kira, and you have no idea.*

"Just feeling a bit sick," I say. "I'm sorry. Thank you for dinner and . . . everything. Good night."

I don't know why I don't tell her about my job ending.

I don't know why I don't mention the ten thousand contingency plans already running through my head.

I just lie down in our shared bed, fully clothed, and pretend to be asleep when Kira comes in to check on me.

THE NEXT DAY, AS I STAND IN MY·NEWLY cleaned apartment with my few meager boxes of belongings, I call up my advisor from my master's degree. She's always had office hours at the same time every Thursday, and I'm hoping she won't be meeting with a student, because I might *explode* if I don't talk about this. The phone rings once, twice . . .

There's a CLICK.

"Dr. Iyengar," the voice on the other end says.

"Oh, thank God," I say, then slap a hand over my mouth. "I mean, hi, Dr. Iyengar."

"Nic? Is that you?" she asks, a laugh in her voice. I wince.

"Right. I should have said that. Sorry. It's me. Nic. Nicole Wells."

Why am I like this? God, I did a whole master's thesis with this woman. I can talk to her like a human.

"Anyway," I say, desperate to get past my awkwardness. "I was hoping you had a few minutes to talk?"

"Well, if you're calling about coming back for a PhD like I asked you to, then you can have all the time you like," Dr. Iyengar says with a teasing tone. When I'm silent for a beat too long, she adds: "Wait, *are* you thinking about coming back?"

"I am," I say quickly before I can chicken out. "Yes. I just . . . I was wondering if it was too late to be considered for January enrollment. I'm not really sure how it works, but the website says applications are considered on a rolling basis, and . . ."

I ramble on about my lab losing its grant funding until Dr. Iyengar saves me. "Just send in your application materials as soon as possible. The committee meets regularly to review whatever applications have come in, and I'll make sure we meet soon enough to consider you for January. List me on your form for a recommendation letter, and I'll get that done as soon as I can."

"Wow," I say, stunned that it's this easy. "Why? I mean, thank you. But . . . yeah, why?"

Dr. Iyengar laughs. "We coauthored two papers together, Nic! I loved working with you, and our research interests overlap so well. Working with you on a doctoral thesis would be a blast. I can't promise anything, of course, but you'll have a strong advocate at the table."

"Wow," I say again, apparently unable to come up with anything else. "Thanks again, Dr. Iyengar. Really, it would be amazing to join your lab again. I'll get my application in by the end of the week."

Five minutes ago, I hadn't actually made up my mind about it, but after this short conversation with my old advisor,

I'm ready to hit Submit on that application right now. I was considering applying to a different school too, just to increase my chances. But there's not much choice when it comes to fire science programs, and I already know I love the University of Maryland and Dr. Iyengar. That's where I'll have my best shot.

I intend to sleep on it, to give it a few days and consider if it's really what I want.

Instead, I stay up late updating my CV, writing a statement of purpose, throwing together a description of research experience and interests, and digging up writing samples from my published journal articles. I'm technically applying to the materials science and engineering PhD program, since U of M only offers a Master's degree in fire protection engineering, but the two programs encourage crossover, and Dr. Iyengar serves as faculty in both. I already know exactly what they're looking for and which research project I'm interested in joining. I only just left my master's program a few months ago, so it's fresh. It's easy.

I hit Send at 2:00 a.m. and collapse into bed, determined not to think of how disappointed in me Kira will be.

There's nothing to tell yet, anyway.

If I get rejected, no one ever needs to know.

CHAPTER TWENTY

KIRA

Nic is being weird.

I mean, Nic is always a little off-kilter, which is one of the things I like so much about her. She can be kind of a space cadet, but in a way that's endearing rather than annoying. I mean, she's brilliant, and she listens when we're talking and has thoughtful things to say. She just . . . gets a little lost in her head sometimes, as if she's listening to a different song than everyone else.

That's not what's happening tonight, though. Tonight, Nic just seems . . . off. Spacey in a *bad* way. Through the first round of drinks, our toasts to Skylar, and Ian's harried late arrival, her mind is very much elsewhere—which is un-fortunate, because I wore this sheer glittery crop top and skin-tight skirt, hoping she'd be peeling me out of them at the end of the night. She's looking good too, in her under-stated way: straight-legged black slacks that make her ass look unbelievable and a vivid purple button-down with only the buttons right over the bust buttoned. Her hair is in a high ponytail that Willow clearly helped with, leaving her face and chest on full display and accentuating the lines of her neck. We haven't seen each other since she moved back to her apartment, or even spoken much, thanks to conflicting work schedules. Apparently I've gotten rather used to regular partnered orgasms.

"Make sure you mentally put her clothes back on before you talk to her," Grace shouts in my ear, to be heard over the music. I whip around with a glare to find her looking like the cat that got the cream.

"Shut up," I hiss, leaning in close. "I'm not . . . We're not—"

"Not what? Sleeping together?" Grace says with a laugh. "Because that's a goddamn lie. I am your *roommate* and you two are *not* subtle. I wasn't at the studio *every* night, you know."

I want to melt into a puddle and vanish through the cracks in the sticky club floor. Knights is not exactly the club I would have chosen for this event, but Marco insisted that Skylar would want her not-a-bachelorette party somewhere new, to see as much as she can before she leaves. I get his point, but . . . ugh. This place is a bit too phallic for my tastes. Unsubtle artwork about knights and their "lances" everywhere. Skylar thinks it's hilarious. I'm just wishing there was a quiet corner somewhere that I could pull Nic into and ask her what's wrong. But maybe that would be too not-subtle. We haven't told anyone about our arrangement other than, apparently, Grace (by accident).

I don't know. Maybe I'm just not built for hookups, or

maybe anyone would start to develop feelings after a month of sharing a bed, meals, friends, and quiet evenings—

I slap a hand over my eyes and face away from the group to get my expression under control.

"Hey, are you okay?" Grace asks, wrapping an arm around my waist and resting her head on my shoulder. "Shark mode disengaged. Serious Grace here. What's going on? Are you and Nic fighting or something?"

The words burst right through the dam I'd carefully constructed, apparently just waiting for someone to ask so I wouldn't be alone in this.

"We're not *anything*, Grace. We were just hooking up. Nothing serious. It's casual."

"Oooh," Grace says, rubbing my arm as I blink away the tears. "Lovey, you haven't done a single casual thing in the entire time I've known you. Granted, it's only been two years, but . . ."

"No, you're right," I say, sniffling. "You're right. I said the exact same thing to myself when all this started. I should have known better. This was always going to end badly for me."

Grace waggles her hand as if to say, *eh, kinda.*

"I'm not sure it *has*, actually," Grace says. "Nic's been staring at you every second you're facing away from her. But she's got that same miserable nauseated kangaroo look she had the night before she left for grad school. Something's up . . . but it's *not* that she's uninterested or whatever."

I'm not sure that makes me feel any better, but at least I can work with it. I give Grace a quick side hug and a murmured "thanks," then make my way back to the group. Before I can get too close to Nic, though, her eyes widen ever so slightly. She turns to Ian, fully interrupting his conversation with

Marco to launch into some in-depth discussion of a video game they once played.

O . . . kay. I hover for a second, unsure, until a new song starts and Skylar screeches.

"Kira, dance with me!" she screams over the music, grabbing me and Marco by the arm. We're unceremoniously dragged onto the dance floor, where Skylar plants herself between us and dances her heart out to some song she and Marco know that I've only vaguely heard of. But I can do this. I can have a good time, celebrate my friend, and talk out the weirdness with Nic some other night. Now's not the right time. We're here for Skylar.

The others join in, the whole group drawing closer and closer until the packed dance floor smashes us all together, laughing and shouting with our arms above our heads. Even Nic seems to loosen up after a song or two, tipping her forehead onto my shoulder when the shifting crowd around us shoves our bodies together. But just as the next song begins, Nic checks her phone . . . then slaps a hand over her mouth with a high-pitched squeak.

"Uh, what was that about?" Ian asks, his awkward dancing slowing to a halt. Everyone else follows suit, pausing in a huddle around Nic. Her eyes are wide, and her mouth is open in an extended "uhhh . . ." like she's been caught at something and can't figure out what to say. My heart gives a pang of warning.

"Yeah, Nic," I say, even as she avoids my eyes. "What is it?"

She hesitates a beat longer, eyes scanning around our group. But no one's giving her an out. Willow, Ian, Marco, Grace, Skylar and I wait until she finally cracks.

"I got accepted!" she shouts over the music, then shrinks back into herself.

My heart freezes, solid in my chest.

"You *what*?" I demand. Nic backs up a half-step from whatever she sees in my face, then gathers herself with a steady nod.

"I got accepted to the PhD program at the University of Maryland. They do rolling admissions. It goes pretty quick, apparently."

"You *what*?" I ask again. "When did you even apply?"

"Yeah, Nic, why is this the first we're hearing of it?" Skylar asks, sensing the tension. "Did anyone else know?"

Everyone else shakes their heads. At least I wasn't the only one out of the loop. Nic, to her credit, looks ashamed.

"I only just sent in my materials last week," she says. "My old advisor fast-tracked things for me. It's not a one hundred percent done deal yet. She personally recommended me to the committee and they still have to meet, but she says she talked to some people, and it's all but guaranteed. I loved working with her so much, and now I have the chance to research and write with her again."

"But what about your job?" Willow asks, their mouth set in a miserable frown.

Nic strangles her phone with her nervous fidgeting.

"That's what started the whole thing," Nic says. "I got a call from my supervisor last week saying that my position is getting cut short. It's ending in December. The perils of grant-funded employment, right?"

She gives a weak laugh, but no one laughs with her. I rack my brain for when, over the last week or so, she might have heard about this, something that might justify her not mentioning it. Then . . .

"Oh my god. The last day you spent in our apartment. We were having dinner. Then you ran off and said you weren't feeling well. That's when you found out, wasn't it?"

She doesn't immediately reply, but the answer is all over her face. I pounce again.

"Nic, why didn't you say something? I was *right there*. I would have been happy to talk it through, or—"

"I didn't *want* to talk it through!" Nic shouts. She bites the edge of her phone case, then shakes her head. "That night was already . . . weird, and hard, and then I got hit with that news, and I was just . . ."

"Why *was* it weird that night, though?" I demand. I'm fully sticking my hand into an open flame at this point—I get that—but we've been dancing around this, and I'm tired of it. I'm tired of people jerking me around, dangling the things I want in front of me, only to snatch them away and blame *me* for it. If she's going to do this, I'm going to make her *say* it.

"Why was it weird, Nic?" I ask again. The others are edging away from us, leaving us to talk—to *fight*, because that's what this is. Our first fight as a not-couple, because we aren't together. Not like that. But we *could* be, if only we could *talk* about it. So yes, I'm pushing buttons. I'm forcing the issues. We're doing this right here, right now, in the middle of this dance floor.

Nic finally explodes.

"This was supposed to be casual!" she says, her eyes shining in the dim light. "That's what we agreed on. I can't be getting into something new right now. Skylar said—"

"Oh my *god,* Nic, you don't have to live your life by these rules like someone's going to arrest you for sticking a toe out of line!" I say, sounding so desperate. "You can decide for yourself if something works. You're doing exactly what you said you wouldn't do. You're just doing what Skylar told you to do without stopping to think for yourself about what *you* want, what's right for *you*."

Nic rears back like she's been slapped, her mouth agape. I should stop, I should just leave it there, but I can't. I've been boiling over with the need to tell her how I feel for weeks, and she's never given me the chance. If this is going to be it for us, then I at least need to know I told her.

"Yes, we agreed to keep things chill, I know," I say. "But I've been *trying* to tell you, Nic—"

I cut off, my throat going thick with emotion. I close my eyes and take a breath, then force them open again, heart hammering.

"I've been trying to tell you that I want more," I say, as quietly as I can and still be heard. "I want to be with you for real. And maybe you don't feel that way about me. I can take it. But I have to at least tell you: I love—"

"Come with me, then," Nic says. Her fists are clenched at her sides, her eyes darting wildly around the room like she's looking for an escape. "If you want to give this a real try, then come to Maryland with me."

I laugh. I can't help it. It's cruel, maybe, but it's just ironic—this girl, the only person I've felt anything for in years, is asking me for the one thing I unequivocally can't do. And truly? I think that's *why* she's offering it. It's a safe bet, because she knows it's one I'll never take.

"You know why I can't leave Seattle," I say, shaking my head.

Nic throws her hands in the air. "You're never going to get anywhere here, Kira. You've said that yourself. Even your teacher said so. How many promotions do you have to lose out on before you admit that it's never going to happen for you here?"

I press my lips into a thin, hard line.

"And when are *you* going to stop grasping for something

to give your life meaning? You can't just run away to grad school every time you don't know what to do next!" I shout.

Nic folds her arms and lifts her chin in defiance.

"Watch me," she says.

And she walks away. Away from me, from Skylar, from everyone, straight out the front door and into the night.

It's over.

It's *over*.

CHAPTER TWENTY-ONE

NIC

The lab is the only place I can set things on fire without hurting anyone or getting arrested, and so the lab is where I head directly from Skylar's not-a-bachelorette party.

I have a change of clothes stashed in my office, so I pull off the fancy outfit I wore half hoping it would make Kira want to hook up in the club bathroom, and pull on my "in case of singed clothes or chemical spills" joggers and T-shirt.

Then, I set fires.

There are a few grad students and assistants still in the lab despite it being nearly midnight on a Friday, but they don't stick around long once I start burning things. Maybe it's the dead look in my eyes, or my absolute silence, or the dried tears on my face.

Whatever it is, they all flee, and I ignite.

I don't even keep track of what I'm burning, what supplies I'm using, what the results are. What are they going to do—

fire me? It's not like I'm going to try to burn the building down or anything. Besides, with the amount of fire suppression in this lab, I'd just end up as a drowned, foamy, miserable rat with a lot of explaining to do.

Hours go by.

Skylar is pissed at me. *Burn.*

Kira hates me. *Burn.*

I'm stuck here for another three months. *Burn.*

Here I am, once again, right back where I started three years ago: desperate to get out of town because it's too hard to face everyone. It's too hard to ask for what I want. It's too hard to love someone.

Only this time, that someone is Kira.

Burn.

Times like this, I really wish my mom was alive to talk things out. I was so young when she died; I don't even know what she would be like in a situation like this, but in my memory, she was warm. Comforting. Always happy to see me, ready to give hugs, excited to hear about my little kid treasures and experiences. It really sucks *all* the time, not having a mom anymore, but now more than ever, my heart aches for the empty space in my life where she should be.

Then I remember . . . I *do* have a mom I could talk to. My adoptive mom. *Skylar's* mom.

Assuming she doesn't hate me now.

I pull out my phone and open our text thread, then pour the entire mess into it without a second's hesitation. If she's going to stop talking to me, it's better if I find out now. Rip all the bandages off at once, torch everything so at least in the aftermath, it'll be easy to see what, if anything, remains.

I sink into the chair at one of the low workbenches and flop forward, pressing my cheek into the cool stainless steel tabletop, rambling at Mama Clark via talk-to-text and not even bothering to correct any of the errors. It's 2:45 a.m. I've got nothing left.

I fall into an exhausted sleep on the bench.

"HEY, MS. WELLS?"

I jerk awake, barely grabbing the edge of the workbench in time to keep myself from toppling off my stool. Jerry the security guard stands at the other end of the bench, his fist still resting on the table from knocking on it.

I gasp, clutching a hand over my heart.

"Geez, Jerry, you scared the hell out of me!" My breath burns in my chest as I try to coax myself down off the ceiling from the sudden flood of adrenaline. Jerry grimaces.

"Real sorry about that. Just came here to tell you, there's someone out front asking to see you, said you weren't answering your phone. Skylar Clark?"

I sit up straighter, grabbing my phone to see the time (10:32 a.m., whoops) and the excessive number of notifications: fifteen from Skylar, eleven from Mama Clark, four from Willow, two each from Ian and Grace, and one from Marco.

None from Kira.

Not surprising, I guess.

"Thanks for letting me know. I'll just, uh . . ." I glance around the lab; wow, I *really* made a mess in here last night. "I'll be out in ten minutes. So sorry."

"No worries. I'll let her know," Jerry says. "Hope everything's okay."

He leaves me standing in the wreckage of my terrible coping, frozen in place. No, Jerry, everything is *not* okay. But I need to at least get this lab in shape before I leave. As quickly as I can, I clear out the ignition chamber of all remaining debris, return my personal protective equipment, and do a general tidy so the place looks halfway presentable. Not as pristine as I'd normally like it, but also not out of line with what we typically see after someone pulls an all-nighter. It'll have to do.

I hang up my lab coat and safety goggles in my office, shove last night's clothes in my bag, and run for the front door, giving myself a subtle sniff along the way. Not the freshest. Some toxic cross between bar stink (must be my hair) and lab stink (my clothes). But it is what it is at this point. I burst through the door with a wave of thanks for Jerry, then spot Skylar leaning against a light pole right out front.

Skylar—and her mom.

Mama Clark is here.

My eyes fill with tears, and Mama Clark steps forward to wrap me in her arms, cooing comforting nonsense at me. Sobs wrack my body as she holds me together at the seams, my brain screaming the same thing over and over again: *I'm a mess, I'm a mess, I'm an absolute fucking mess and no one should have to put up with me.*

Skylar attaches herself to us both, rocking with us in a big family hug until my sobs die down to sniffles. Mama Clark leans back and wipes away my tears, then fixes my (probably disastrous) hair.

"Come on, lovey," she says, guiding me into the parking lot. "We've moved brunch up to today. Thought you might need it."

My stomach gives an audible growl. I haven't eaten anything since before the party last night.

"I do," I say, carefully watching Skylar from the corner of my eye. "Thank you. For, you know, coming out here."

"Of course, Nic. This is what family does," Mama Clark says.

That threatens to set me off all over again. I press my tongue hard against the roof of my mouth to keep myself from crying all the way to the car, where I slide into the back seat for the ride to brunch. To my surprise, Skylar climbs in the back with me instead of riding up front with her mom. She doesn't say anything, just rides in silence by my side, staring out the window until we arrive at our favorite brunch place. It's a total dive, grimy enough that the food blogs haven't managed to find it yet, but the food is excellent. We grab a booth, Skylar and her mom on one side and me on the other, and a server pops over before we've even gotten settled.

"Morning! Drinks?" she asks, brusque but not unkind, tucking her hands in the front pockets of her pale lavender apron.

"Mimosas for the two of us and a glass of orange juice for that one," Mama Clark says. "And waters all around, please."

"You got it," the server says, then disappears into the back.

"No mimosa for me?" I ask, pouting.

"These are intervention mimosas," Skylar says. "Drink your orange juice and prepare yourself. Once you have some food in your stomach and sense in your skull, maybe we'll get another round."

I wince at the harsh (yet totally deserved) words. So much for a cozy family brunch to help me feel better.

Mama Clark watches me from across the table in that way moms do, scanning every inch of me that she can see to evaluate my general health and sanity. I haven't looked in a mirror since yesterday, but I have some idea of what she's seeing, and it isn't good.

"I'm so sorry for all those texts last night. I hope they

didn't wake you up. I was deliriously tired and . . . clearly not thinking straight. At least they filled you in on everything that happened? I guess?"

Mama Clark clicks her tongue disapprovingly. "What I could read of them. Half of it was nonsense. Skylar translated for me this morning, so I think I've got everything now."

Our mimosas arrive, and I give a half-hearted "cheers" when prompted, then slump back against the booth.

"Are . . . you angry with me?" I ask, sounding miserable and pathetic and childish. I hate this about myself, this horrible *neediness* that I'm sure is all about my dad, and that makes it even *worse*.

"Yes, sweetie," Skylar says, reaching for my hand across the table. "I'm mad. You hurt my friend."

I wince, looking away at the fading news articles and Polaroids haphazardly taped up around the bottom of the bar.

"I'm sorry. I never meant to hurt Kira. Things just got so confusing, and I was trying to do the right thing. But you're right. I hurt her in the process, and that's on me."

Skylar pokes my hand until I look back at her.

"Not just Kira, you goof. *You*," she says. "You hurt *you*, too. Yes, Kira is really hurting, and we'll talk about that in a minute. But I want you to know that I care about *you* in this situation, too."

She pauses, head cocked, then shrugs. "And hey, I care about me as well. I'm leaving in a week, and things are terrible. I don't want to be selfish, but it'd be really great if we could work all this out before the party. I want to leave knowing everyone is in a good place. And you, my love, are not in a good place. Neither is Kira."

"Yes, let's not completely let Kira off the hook here," Mama Clark says, bristling. "If I interpreted the text mishmash correctly, Nic *did* offer for Kira to move to Maryland with her. That's something."

Skylar nods, conceding the point. "It's true. Kira's going through her own thing, and her life is burning down around her just as much as yours is, which I'm sure you'll find out about soon. She's been clinging to her *own* toxic ideas about how things *have* to be. You two are awfully similar in that respect."

We pause for a moment while our server reappears to take our orders. I let Skylar order me some kind of very sweet waffle thing, since my brain is in no shape to make decisions. I study the lamp hanging over our table, an old, weathered thing that looks like it was scavenged from a '60s-era diner. Somehow it's both meticulously clean and looking ready to break down at any moment.

"Here's the part that I don't get," Mama Clark says as soon as the server leaves, resting her elbows on the table and propping her chin on her laced fingers. "Why wouldn't you just let Kira tell you how she feels about you?"

I open my mouth to spout my automatic response, then catch myself, giving my brain a minute to sort through all my swirling feelings and fears. Why *wouldn't* I let her say it? There were so many moments we could have had a conversation— "Hey, I know this is supposed to be just sex, but can we talk about that?"—but every time I caught the tiniest whiff of *feelings* talk approaching, I bolted like a frightened rabbit from a forest fire. I know the reason I've been *telling* myself, but is it the real one? How do I even know what's true anymore when I'm so practiced at lying to myself?

"Skylar, you told me I needed to be my own anchor," I say slowly, trying to parse as I go. "I was worried that if I let things get serious too quickly, I'd just move from . . ."

I cut my eyes back over to Skylar's mom, unsure if it's awkward to talk about my decade-long fantasy of marrying into her family.

"Well, I thought I'd be going from clinging to one person right into clinging to another," I finish. "I was really trying to follow the advice you gave me. You were right. I need to not define my entire life by other people and think about what *I* want."

"And . . . what *do* you want?"

Images from the past months flood through my brain. The tarot date. Those lazy weekend mornings in bed with Kira while living at her place. Home-cooked dinners with her. Washing her hair for her and massaging her sore muscles after her long shifts. Being comatose on the couch with her while we snacked on one of my baking fails. Hanging out together with all our friends, hooking pinkies together when no one was looking.

"Do you think that maybe the thing you were clinging to was my advice?" Skylar says, eyebrow raised, as if I had spoken any of those thoughts out loud. "Or your interpretation of what *I* wanted, or something?"

I grimace. "That's what Kira said."

Skylar's mom reaches across the table and lays her hand over mine.

"My dear," she says, "if you'll permit me to steal the therapist hat from my sweet daughter for a moment here, I think the overall problem is less any specific thing you're clinging to and more this overall pattern of black-and-white, rigid thinking you keep falling into."

Skylar looks up at her mom with pure love in her eyes. "*Yes*, Mom. Yes. That is fully *it*. Nic, it feels like you're waiting for someone to pass down a rule book that will tell you how to structure your life. And that makes sense, considering your past—you didn't have a sturdy adult figure for most of your life to provide you with any structure or teach you how to stand on your own. Not that it's bad to rely on others or have a community to lean on when you need it, of course, but you can't just completely outsource your decision-making, either. There's a balance to be had here. I'm not gonna say you're wrong about not jumping in too fast. It's smart to be cautious after going through a massive paradigm shift."

Mama Clark holds up a finger to chime in. "*But*, you shouldn't say no to something you know, deep in your heart, is what you want. *Definitely* not for the sake of following what someone else told you is right. You've got to learn to trust yourself, my love. Trust your heart and your instincts the way you trust your brain in the lab. You don't second-guess yourself when you're reacting to a lab situation with all your fire and chemicals and stuff, right?"

I shake my head. "That's how you lose your eyebrows or end up tripping the suppression system. Fire can be unpredictable, and the situation can change in milliseconds."

I aggressively do *not* think about how unsafe I was in the lab last night.

Mama Clark raises her mimosa to me and winks. "Well, then, you already know what it feels like to trust yourself. Can you imagine what it would feel like to expand that to your personal life?"

I blink. The honest answer is . . . no. No, I can't.

But I think I'd like to.

That's what I've wanted all along, actually. Some stability and confidence. Some sense that the world won't give way under my feet like a collapsing platform in a Mario game. It's sad that I've never even considered I could provide that feeling for *myself*.

Our food arrives, giving me a little time to process as I scarf like a . . . well, like a person who hasn't eaten in sixteen hours. But Skylar doesn't let me off the hook for long.

"So, here's what it comes down to, friend," she says, pointing at me with a piece of stabbed omelet on her fork. "It's not your fault that you have trauma. It makes sense. Your childhood was a mess. But it *is* your responsibility to take care of yourself and learn to work through your trauma, and to make sure you don't hurt others in the process. You need a therapist, Nic. Not me, obviously, but one of the ones I sent you the *last* time we had this talk. You have a lot to deal with, and you deserve to feel good about yourself and your life."

My gut reaction to that is very telling. Something in me immediately questions: *Do* I deserve that? Is it possible for me?

But that's just proving Skylar's point, isn't it?

"You're right," I say, staring down at the puddle of syrup on my plate. "If I'm going to be worthy of Kira—"

"Reframe that, please," Mama Clark says with a *tsk*.

I pause, thinking through my words, then wince and nod.

"Right, sorry. What I mean is . . . if I'm going to show up in a relationship with Kira the way she and I both deserve, if I'm going to be a good partner, then I need to work on all this. And it's not fair or ethical of me to treat *you* like my therapist, Skylar, which I think I have at times. I'm really sorry about that."

I hesitate before blurting out the next part, checking to make sure my words are coming from the right place.

"I don't want pity," I begin, speaking slowly and with care. "And I don't want cheering or validation here. I'm just genuinely wondering—do you think Kira and I are good together? How do I know if this thing between us is real?"

Skylar and her mom look at each other and bust out laughing.

"Oh, Nic. My sweet Nic. Let me put it this way," Skylar says. She pushes her plate aside so she can rest both hands on the tabletop.

"You're free-flowing where Kira is rigid," she says, slicing down on the table with her left hand for me and her right for Kira, repeating the gesture for each point. "She's organized where you're chaotic. You bring out her goofy side. She brings out your inner caretaker. She's in awe of your brain and passion. You're in awe of her bravery and determination. You make each other better."

At that, she clasps her two hands together and shakes them for emphasis.

"You take care of one another. You both want the same things long-term: marriage, kids, and careers you love. *And*—please cover your ears, Mom—there is absolutely blistering chemistry that we can *all* see, and I *know* you've slept together multiple times, so it must have been good. You literally fucked in the bridal shop the other day because you're *so* into each other."

"How did you *know* about that?" I ask, horrified.

She waves the question away. "You're fantastic *together*. So, like . . . what exactly is the problem here?"

I open my mouth to respond, but no sound comes out . . . because I don't have a single thing to say. For so long, my whole idea of love has just been "Skylar." Not even specific traits or associated feelings or anything. Just . . . Skylar. But hearing her list all those things about me and Kira makes me want to leap out of this booth and shout, *Yes, that's what I want!*

Skylar, looking awfully smug, continues. "I feel like you

keep trying to invent a problem, or some kind of reason to justify not having to take a scary leap. You feel like you're breaking a rule or something. But there's no rule against being happy, Nic."

Even still, my mind tries to resist, tries to dredge up more reasons this can't possibly work out. Finally I give voice to the thing I'm truly, deeply afraid of.

"But will she forgive me?" I whisper, tears springing to the corners of my eyes. "Do I even have a chance?"

Skylar taps her bottom lip, thoughtful, not rushing to quick reassurance, which I appreciate. After a moment, she meets my eyes, expression solemn.

"Kira is careful with her feelings. Once she gives them, she can't easily take them back. You owe her one *hell* of an apology, but I think you have a solid chance. The question is, are you going to take it? Preferably in the next week, before my goodbye party?"

I nearly laugh in her face, the question is so absurd. I didn't realize how committed I was until this moment.

"Oh, I'm taking it," I say, making an obligatory grab for the check before Mama Clark slaps my hand away. "Thank you for everything. Both of you. I gotta go make some plans. I'll let you know how it goes, okay?"

"You better!" Skylar calls, but I'm already out the door and dialing my phone. It only rings once before there's an answer.

"Nic? You okay?"

"Will," I say, "I need your help. Are you off in the woods somewhere, or can you come scheme with me?"

CHAPTER TWENTY-TWO

KIRA

The Toyonda Civry finally gave up the ghost at the worst possible time, of course. I was nursing a broken heart, in a rut at work, and deeply *exhausted*, so it was almost anticlimactic when it finally blew a head gasket and stranded me (at the DMV, of all places) earlier this morning. Renewing my Washington State driver's license felt like an almost defiant act at the time—I'm not leaving, I'm *not*—so it felt like punishment for my hubris when I got a repair estimate higher than a down payment on a new car would be. Figures.

As a result, I'm riding in the passenger seat of Grace's car, on the way to the firehouse, when a notification pops on my phone with a headline:

SEATTLE INFLUENCER TO ABANDON ALL ACCOUNTS, START FARM IN FIJI
Internet relationship counselor Skylar Clark is reportedly fleeing the country

"Oh, shit," I say, eyes wide. "Pull over. We're close enough to the station. Here's fine. You gotta read this."

Grace yanks the wheel to the right way too quickly, parallel parking around the corner from the fire station, then practically crawls into my seat.

"This is a straight-up media massacre," she says, reading over my shoulder as I skim the article on a trashy Seattle gossip website. One of many articles, I'm now seeing. I nod, lips pursed in sympathy.

"A true roasting. I never expected it to be this bad. They sure know how to take something innocuous and make it sound sinister."

"Right?" Grace says. "'Fleeing the country,' they say, as if she's some kind of fugitive criminal on the run from the law."

The source of the rumor is someone who claims to have overheard us at the club on Friday night, though why it's only now hitting on Monday, I can't say. I don't know how someone managed to lurk close enough to hear us, but they have the basic details correct, down to Skylar's plans to farm taro and run a vacation rental property.

"Sounds like self-indulgent privileged millennial bullshit to me," the anonymous source is quoted as saying.

"People are so quick to run their mouths when they feel anonymous," Grace says, shaking her head. "They know I'd teleport in and punch them in the throat if I found out who they were."

The story has been picked up by every local culture and lifestyle outlet, from blogs to podcasts to the back page of an actual real-life newspaper, with varying levels of viciousness. How is this *news*? Must be a slow week.

My phone buzzes, and a notification pops up: @DoctorSky is going live!

"Oh, here we go," I say, tapping the notification. I have to be at the station for a 5:00 p.m. meeting in twenty minutes, but we're here plenty early, and I, at least, want to see what Skylar's strategy is going to be. My phone fills with the image of Skylar curled up on the bed in her childhood room, attempting to look like she just woke up, but in a way I know means she's already brushed her hair, washed her face, and changed into something "cozy yet accessible—that's the vibe, Kira."

"Hey, Skylings. I wanted to post a quick video here so you can get the truth straight from me before wild speculation completely takes over the narrative. And of course, I owe you all an apology."

Grace clutches my arm so tight that her nails dig into my biceps. "Oh my god, she's doing an Internet Apology Video. This is wild. I'm so excited right now."

Skylar smiles on the screen, so sweet and sincere that it's impossible not to forgive her. "This isn't how I wanted you to find out about my plans, obviously, and I'm genuinely sorry for the way this news has gotten out."

"The apology that isn't really an apology, check," Grace murmurs, holding up a finger for *one point*.

"I actually had a whole big announcement video recorded and scheduled for next week!" Skylar continues. "But so it goes. One of the best skills you can cultivate in life is adaptability, and through it, resiliency."

"Slipping in a little counselor speak there. Nice," Grace says, ticking off another point.

Skylar shrugs on the screen with a helpless little grin as if to say, *What can you do?*

"So, to make sure things are absolutely clear, I'll tell you which of the wild rumors flying around right now are true. Number one: yes, I *was* planning to delete all my social media accounts in the near future. Since then, however, I've talked things over with a few friends and have instead decided to leave my accounts up as an archive. One thing remains the same, though: I won't be here anymore, and I won't have access to my accounts. All my old posts will remain available as a mental health resource, but I will no longer be creating new content or responding to messages and comments."

Her smile turns wry, somehow managing to make it feel like every one of her hundreds of thousands of followers is in on a joke.

"Now, let's talk about this Farmer Skylar business. Come on, folks. I have more solid plans than 'run halfway across the world and start a farm.' I can't tell you what they are *yet*, but I will soon. That's not a tease, I promise. There's just one thing that hasn't been announced publicly yet, and I can't tell you about it until it is. For now, just know: yes, I'm gonna play around with learning to grow taro and rent out my house whenever I'm not using it, but that's just for fun on the side. I have one *big* reason for going . . . and it's a really good one, too. Not 'good' as in like, 'oooh, it's a juicy secret' and I'm teasing you about it. Good as in . . . joyful. And important. Yeah, I'm really happy about this."

The live reaction chat is a flood of speculation.

She's totally marrying someone and moving to Fiji to be with her. Remember when she said she was "off the market?"

She's joined some kind of exclusive influencer cult where they lay around on the beach all day and sell skin care products right???

#SkylarsSecret is that she's a tool

Maybe it's a commune and she's doing one of those digital detox cleanse things?

"I'm literally watching her follower count skyrocket," Grace says, constantly reloading Skylar's socials on her own phone to watch the numbers change. "If I didn't know for sure that Skylar is following through on all of this, I'd say it was a brilliant PR stunt."

As if replying directly to Grace, Skylar continues.

"I know some of you will believe this is a stunt for attention or something, which is okay. Time will show my sincerity, and I can endure a week of the inevitable harassment until then. As always, I ask that all of you be kind to each other in the comment sections, even as things get complicated and hard. This community has always been a space for productive dialogue and healing, and I hope we can keep it that way throughout this final week. I'll have some content coming in a day or two on parasocial relationships and some recommendations for other counselors I trust and vouch for, who you can follow for all your relationship advice needs."

Skylar yanks her artfully slouching sweater back up over her shoulder and blows her viewers a kiss.

"And of course, I do still have that one last secret . . . and it's one I hope will give everyone something to think about. Hopefully you'll all allow me this one indulgence while I get everything in order for my big move. Don't worry, my dearest Skylings. You'll hear the rest very, very soon."

The livestream ends, and the silence in the aftermath feels echoing and strange.

Well, I guess there's no shoving this feral cat back in the bag. It's out there now, and that makes it more real than ever.

It's happening, publicly confessed and everything. Skylar is leaving. And now Nic is, too.

Without the distraction of the livestream, reality comes slipping back in. I fought with Nic. She doesn't want to be with me. She's leaving and we're over. Skylar's mad about the whole thing and basically said "go fix it before the party." Then *she's* leaving. And now, the car my dad gave me is dead and gone. Just like he is.

And who knows, my career might be dead, too.

"Hey, you look like you went to a bad place," Grace says, poking me in the arm. "Go, do your meeting thing, and then let's get dinner. My treat. I'll be right up the street at the library until you're done, okay?"

"Okay. Thanks, Grace. You're the best."

"Don't tell anyone," she says with a wink.

I steel myself with a deep breath, then climb out of the car, shoulders back and eyes forward.

Being called into the chief's office on my day off would be worrying any time. Today, when I'm dragging a broken heart around like a lead weight around my neck, I feel like I'm walking toward my own execution.

I have *no* idea what this meeting could be about. Did I screw something up? Are they afraid I'm going to sue the department because I got passed over for the promotion *again*, and there's going to be some kind of "we swear it's not about gender" mediator there to talk me down? If so, they've way overestimated my energy. I am *tired*, down to my bones and soul. All I want right now is to grab food with Grace and get through Skylar's goodbye party with my dignity intact, then take a few days to go visit my mom in Vancouver. She'll fuss over me, get angry on my behalf, tell me all about whatever new miracle curly hair care products she's discovered, and take me on a tour of every single public art project I've already seen.

It's exactly what I need right now.

I walk through the door to the station with ten minutes to spare—early as always—so I take some time to give my locker a good clean and scroll through my social feeds while lounging on my bunk. It only takes two swipes for photos of Friday night to pop up, posted by Marco, Grace, Ian, and Skylar. They're pre-fight photos, of course, so Nic and I are glued to each other's sides in the group photo, grinning at the camera. I perfectly remember the feel of her pressing into me, the heat bleeding through my dress . . . I shove it all away. No point in wallowing. I give Skylar's accounts a quick glance— yep, completely on fire—then make my way to the chief's office now that it's *acceptably early* instead of *annoyingly early*.

I stop outside his office door and close my eyes, centering myself. Finding that calm, resilient place in me that can withstand whatever they throw at me. My father's ghost whispers in my ear, his words from the years before his death running on constant replay: "Don't be a firefighter, Kira. They'll never let you make it. There's no point in you doing this. Why are you doing this?"

And, the coup de grace, the thing he never said while he was alive, but for sure would if he were still here today: "Why do you keep trying? They've made it obvious enough that you're never going to get ahead here. Just give up and move on with your life."

I loved my father, but his words always hurt me way more than any challenge I faced at work. If he'd believed in me, would I be a better firefighter than I am today? Would I be good enough?

I lift my fist and knock just under the name plate: Kip

Barnes, Battalion Chief. When the chief calls for me to come in, I turn the knob and walk in with my head held high, my father's voice in my ear the whole way.

"Have a seat, McKinney," Chief says.

This is looking worse by the minute. His face is serious and sympathetic, and sure enough, there's the mediator from the city office. What *is* this?

The mediator, a white lady with lightly curling hair the same shade of blond as Skylar's, gives me a serene smile and holds out her hands.

"I'm Anna Markland, and I work in human resources for the City of Seattle. I'm just here to answer any questions you may have and facilitate any discussion that arises."

I feel the hot rush behind my eyes but fight to keep it back. I will not cry. I will *not*. Not even when I'm apparently being fired for *no reason* from the job I've given everything to since I was eighteen years old. I take a slow, calming breath in through my nose, then pull myself together.

"Nice to meet you, Anna. Chief, what's this about?"

He lifts a pen from his desk, shiny and red like our vehicles, and fiddles with it for a moment before he realizes what he's doing and lays it back down.

"McKinney, a transfer request has come down from the ops chief. They want to move you to Station 37. I'm approving the transfer, effective September 1."

I blink, stunned on so many levels I can't even process. I'm not being fired, it seems, which is good. But I'm being transferred to a fire station all the way across the city, as far from this station and my apartment as you can get. And even worse . . .

"Isn't Higgs the chief over there?" I ask.

Chief grimaces, because he knows exactly what I'm getting at. "Yes, he is."

Great. Higgs *hated* my father. They butted heads for fifteen years, and when my dad made assistant fire chief of operations, it was all-out war. This is a punishment. Or an attempt to run me off. Possibly both.

"And do you know why that station specifically, when I've been serving this neighborhood for almost ten years?"

Mediator lady Anne opens her mouth to say something soothing, but the chief speaks up first.

"The ops chief did not share his reasons with me. I know it's a big shift, and you'll probably want to move across town to be closer to your new station."

I close my eyes against the stab of pain the thought provokes. I've lived in this neighborhood my whole life. It means something to me, to be here. Maybe too much. I think back to the tarot reading, to that figure on the Ten of Swords, run through and bleeding out. Maybe it *is* time for a change.

Just not the kind of change they're looking for.

"We hate to lose you here, McKinney. You're a good firefighter and a well-respected leader."

I snort, and both the chief and Anna from HR tense, like they expect me to shout at them, or throw things, or get violent.

Instead, I stand and hold out my hand to the chief.

"It's been a pleasure working with you, sir. I know this area better than anyone else currently on staff, and I'm sorry that I can't continue to serve the neighborhood I grew up in. But I'll give my all to my new station. I look forward to meeting my new colleagues."

That is some of the fakest bullshit I've ever spoken, but one lesson I learned from my dad early on is to never burn your bridges, no matter how desperate you are to reach for the lighter fluid, strike a match, and watch everything crumble to ash. Today's enemy might be tomorrow's colleague or job reference. I want to crawl across this desk and scream in his face, tell him what a shitty job he does running this station and all the ways I would improve it if I had his job. I want to tell him he's making the biggest mistake of his career, denying me promotions, letting me go to another station. I want to say it all.

I don't say a word.

I turn to leave, but the chief's last-ditch effort at smoothing things over gives me pause.

"McKinney, this new station . . . it looks like there'll be a lieutenant posting opening up soon, and more after that, plus lots of young green recruits who could benefit from your experience. It's a good posting, with room for advancement, and you might have better chances—"

Bridges be damned, I can't listen to this.

"Don't make promises you can't keep," I say, cutting him off.

His mouth tightens. Then he nods.

Asshole.

Despite all the pleasant talk, I know he's one of the people who's been keeping me down. I know his history in the service. I see him being all buddy-buddy with the male firefighters, and with the folks higher up in the service who hated my dad. He's never wanted me to have a permanent place here. Now, through some backdoor deal with the ops chief, he got his wish.

It's no matter. I'll put in my resignation letter first thing tomorrow morning.

There's no point in staying here any longer.

I turn, march out the door with my head held high, and make it all the way back to Grace's car before I break into wracking sobs.

Now this is over, too.

I've lost the thing that mattered most to me in this world, the thing that I've arranged my entire life around—that I wanted more than anything.

The thing that lost me Nic.

If I'd just agreed to go with her, I could have left this department on my own terms *and* had her. Well, maybe. In hindsight, I'm not sure her offer was sincere anyway. She doesn't seem to know *what* she wants, and I refuse to be an afterthought.

I fill Grace in on everything once my sobs die down. After a fierce hug and much swearing, she drops me back at our apartment with a promise to return with the good mochi and a bubble tea. I wash my face, then stare at myself in the mirror, picturing that Ten of Swords card once again.

"There's nowhere to go but up when you've got ten swords in your back," Gabe said.

With my tears dried, a strange lightness fills my body. It's a little like taking off all my gear after a fire call, the absence of all that weight, the feel of the cool air on my skin, sweat evaporating. Every day has been another battle, a constant struggle, pushing, pushing . . .

I'm not going to push anymore.

I've gotten a definitive sign that my path forward is not with this fire department. And since Skylar is leaving, and I've burned things to the ground with Nic . . . I'm completely free. I can forge a new path. I have so many options available to me, and nothing stopping me from choosing any of them.

I do a few jumping jacks to get the excess tension out of

my body, then sit down at my computer and search for that email from my FEMA instructor. She offered me mentorship and guidance in finding a new department where I'd be welcomed, and it's past time I took her up on it. If they can't see me here in Seattle, can't see what I'm worth, then they don't deserve me. I'll go somewhere I'll be valued, where I can do good work and make the kind of real change I've always dreamed of. And if I have to leave Seattle, the place I've lived all my life, to make that happen? Well, so it goes. Everything here is a disaster anyway.

I'll go to Skylar's party. I'll get through it without making a scene with Nic. I'll watch the girl I fell in love with run away to grad school again.

And when it's all over, I'll be okay. I'll do what Skylar's doing and go pursue my dream somewhere far away. I'll have a new direction and new opportunities. I'm strong enough to handle this, and brave enough to make it happen.

For the first time in a long time, I feel . . . hopeful.

There are so many good things on the horizon.

CHAPTER TWENTY-THREE

KIRA

Two days later, my cooler head has prevailed. Ultimately, I opted *not* to immediately spike a flaming resignation letter through the chief's office door, and the decision pains me. It's technically a good thing: I'm following my mentor's advice and holding off until she gives me some good job leads to follow. I've never not had a job before, and the idea of not having one lined up before I resign is just too scary. I have bills to pay.

There's just a whole lot of pride-swallowing that has to happen in the meantime. The flaming resignation is *so* tempting.

Yesterday was my last day at my old firehouse. There was a cake. There were a lot of insincere well-wishes. We don't normally do that kind of stuff for someone who's just transferring, but I basically grew up in this firehouse. I've worked here for almost ten years, since I was eighteen. It's weird, and it matters, and everyone knows it even as their eyes betray their guilt. They're glad I'm leaving.

Well, I'm glad to *be* leaving. Or so I tell myself. I'm just not going where they think I am.

I head home, determined to enjoy the five days off I have before reporting to my new fire station on Monday morning. September 1. The end of the weirdest, hardest, most painful summer of my life since my dad died. I haven't had five days off in a row in . . . well, I can't remember. But I'd already put in for one of my many unused vacation days for the day before Skylar's party—didn't want to be dead on my feet for it—and the rest is just how the scheduling worked out for my new shift crew. It's for the best, anyway; I definitely don't want to report at 8:00 a.m. the day after the party, which is sure to go late.

Unfortunately, five days off is also a lot of time to stew in my feelings. It's been a long week of silence from Nic, and I've basically lost hope of things working out. I'm mad—of *course* I'm mad—but the past few days have given me time to realize my own mistakes, too. I should be the bigger person here, should call her up and apologize, but I don't trust myself not to make a mess of it right now. I still feel raw, like I have emotional road rash from that giant wreck of a fight we had.

I fall into a fitful sleep, napping from when I get home at 8:30 a.m. until almost noon. I would have slept longer, but my phone buzzes from its resting place on my breastbone, pulling me back toward consciousness.

WILLOW: Hey, I'm gonna be in the neighborhood around 7. What's that coffee shop you love right near your place? Wanna meet me there?

On the one hand, my soul feels incapable of leaving this bed. On the other . . . something chocolaty and caffeinated. Mmm. I send Will a map pin for the coffee shop and drag myself up. If I wallow for one whole day, chances are I'll wallow for my whole vacation. Better to set a good precedent early.

ME: Meet you there.

Will and I haven't spent much time hanging out one-on-one, but I do adore them. And hey, since both Skylar *and* Nic are now leaving, guess I'd better put more effort into my friendships with the others.

We're barely at the coffee shop for ten minutes that evening, though—just long enough to order drinks—when Will looks down at their phone and grimaces.

"I'm sorry! I gotta go. Something came up. I'll see you at Skylar's party, though, yeah?" they say, walking backward out of the shop as they speak.

"Okay, but . . ."

The door closes, and they turn to jog back up the street, presumably toward their car.

That was . . . weird. Okay.

I take my time walking back to the apartment, enjoying the darkness and fresh air. Maybe I should go for a walk tomorrow morning. An infusion of sunshine might help me feel human again. I'm not a wallower. I don't sit in my feelings and do nothing. I act. I work hard. I make change. What can I do to move forward today?

I'm so lost in thought that I miss getting the key in the lock of my apartment door. Twice. With a swear, I finally get the door open—and immediately smell burning.

There's fire *everywhere*.

Tiny flickering candle flames. Over a hundred of them, sitting on every surface. Pillars, jars, votives, tea lights, and even some long tapered candlesticks.

And in the middle of it all . . . is Nic. Holding a pie.

"Grace let me in," she says, looking like she'd be wringing her hands in front of her if not for the frankly enormous pie. "I hope that's okay."

Grace. Of course. And Willow was the distraction to get me out of the apartment. My heart executes a series of complicated flips, even as my brain rings every alarm.

She's here. My brain can't formulate any other thoughts. Just . . . her.

Nic.

My emotions are such a messy jumble that my face can't figure out what to do. I'm angry. Hurt. *So* frustrated and confused.

But . . . still so in love. So glad she's here.

Terrified.

"Yes, it's fine," I finally manage when Nic starts to look nervous at my silence. "Did . . . I mean . . . What . . ."

Wow, this is going *great*.

"Isn't this a fire hazard?" I finally ask with a helpless laugh. Nic holds up a finger, then sets the pie down and pulls a small fire extinguisher from behind the dining table.

"I wanted you to be able to hear what I have to say," she says, waggling the mini extinguisher at me, then holding it out for me to take. "Which means eliminating the thing that I thought might cause you some . . . distraction. So there. If something bursts into flames, you can put it out and save us. Or you can hit me over the head with it and run away, if you feel like it. I would deserve it. Just take the pie with you, okay, because I worked really hard on it, and it's the best one I've ever made."

"Nic—" I begin, but she waves me off.

"Please, let me say this first. Kira, I am *so sorry*." She steps forward and takes my free hand, squeezing it gently. "I have been oblivious, and hurtful, and cowardly, and just . . . generally terrible. I thought I was avoiding my Three of Swords moment by keeping you at arm's length, but it was the complete opposite. I hurt you. I kept secrets, and said all the wrong things, and didn't let *you* say the *right* things. I overthought everything and found my way into yet another rigid worldview that . . . well, it fucked everything up pretty good. *I* fucked up."

Nic rubs at her eyes, which glisten with moisture, then blinks at the ceiling before she continues.

"And honestly, I think it was just another way of clinging to Skylar. I get now that I was never into her romantically. Now that I know how it feels with *you*, I can see the difference clear as day. I've fully let that go. But it's almost like I needed to replace that framework with something else. Otherwise, the whole thing—my life—would be structurally unsound. No foundation. The entire methodology of my life was wrong, but instead of scrapping everything and starting fresh like I should have, I kept trying to bend the data to fit my conclusions. And that's just bad science. That's the shit that gets you fired in academia."

I give a weak chuckle, feeling almost lightheaded as the reality sets in. She's apologizing. She lit all these candles. She made me a pie. She's *here*. But does she mean it? Can she really stick with something new?

"Good thing it was just *your entire life* and not a lab experiment," I say with a weird, giddy sort of laugh. I'm so afraid to hope this might actually work out. My hesitance must show, because Nic drops my hand and gives me some space.

"I went to my first ever therapy appointment this week," she says.

I blink. "How have you been friends with Skylar this long and not been to therapy? I mean, not because she makes people *need* therapy, though, *maybe* . . . well, I mean, just because she's such an advocate."

She shakes her head with a huff of laughter. "I know, right? Not for lack of her trying. I just kept putting it off, and she probably thought I'd never go if she pushed too hard. Which, fair. But I finally went, because I wanted to make sure I could do this."

"Do . . . what?"

She smiles, though it's tinged with sadness.

"Be with you, if you'll have me. Deserve you. Treat you the way you should be treated, and be with you as my own whole person instead of just a weird barnacle stuck to you. One therapy session didn't work *all* that out, of course, but we had two pretty intense double sessions that laid some good groundwork. Enough to convince me that I'm not the weird, empty, desperate shell of a human I sometimes feel like. There's . . . more to me, I guess."

"Of *course* there is," I say, eyes wide in shock. I knew Nic had some self-worth issues, but I didn't realize she thought so little of herself. "Nic, I wouldn't love you if there weren't more to you. You're brilliant. You're *so* funny. You help me find my chill. You love your friends so fiercely. God, you're not a barnacle, Nic. You're a whole person, and you're *great*."

Nic collapses into me, burying her face in my shoulder. My arms come up around her, holding her to me like I've been aching to do all week, and I feel her trembling, feel her tears soaking into my shirt, feel the warmth of her body against mine, and *breathe*. All I've wanted all week is to be close to her, to sort out this awful mess so we could get back to where I *knew* we belonged. Like this. *Just* like this, with her a little messy and me a little too uptight and finding our perfect balance somewhere in the middle. Nic mumbles something into my skin that I don't catch, and I press a kiss to her temple.

"What was that? Didn't hear you."

She pulls back, flicking her eyes up to mine for just a second before looking right back down at the floor.

"You . . . love me, you said?"

I give a disbelieving laugh.

"Nic, this whole fight was because you *knew* I'd fallen for you, and you wouldn't let me say it. Of *course* I'm in love with you."

Nic's bottom lip goes wobbly, and she just nods, unable to speak. She falls back into me, freely weeping. I run my hands through her hair, whispering over and over that I love her, I love her, I want to be with her . . . I *love* her.

"I love you," she finally whispers, strangled and hoarse against my skin, her whole body shaking. She pulls back with a watery smile, shaking her head in disbelief.

"I'm gonna be honest," she says, steeling herself. "I feel like I'm not allowed to say that. Like I haven't earned the right. I only just unlearned my old definition for love, and . . ."

She trails off, visibly losing her confidence. I pull her to me and kiss the salty tears from her cheeks with long, lingering presses.

"I don't care. We have a chance now, and that's all that

matters. As long as you want to try this, as long as you feel something for me that matches your new definitions, then I'm happy. I just want us to have a shot."

Nic nods again until she recovers her voice.

"I feel . . . *so much* for you," she says through her tears.

Those words tell me more than an "I love you" ever could. *That* is Nic's real "I love you." But there's one thing that still needs to be said.

"I owe you an apology too," I say, brushing the hair out of her eyes and behind her ears. "We set boundaries for our relationship, and I pushed things further than you were comfortable with. That's on me, and I'm really sorry for putting you in that position."

Nic starts to deny it, but I shake my head.

"Hey, don't let me off the hook. I just want you to know that if we're going to be together, I'll respect you and any limits we agree to. Okay?"

She smiles, red-cheeked and teary, nodding. Then her smile fades.

"There's just one more thing," she says, hesitant, some of the pain creeping back into her eyes.

"The PhD?" I ask. She nods.

"I really do want to go," she says, drawing back away from me, her gaze downcast. "The more I talk to my advisor, the more I realize how much I want this. Academia is hard, and it sucks in a lot of ways, but there are things I want to research. I can't imagine anything else I really want to do. I can defer for a semester, or even a year, and try to find another job in town to give us a chance, you know? To see if—"

"I'm leaving the SFD," I blurt out.

Nic blinks. "Uh . . . what?"

I recount the whole situation with the transfer, my commitment to finding a department that will appreciate me, and the grief I'm still wrestling with over it all. Nic nods, squeezing my hand in sympathy as I choke up near the end.

"Anyway," I say, clearing my throat. "The point is that Maryland is as good a place as any to look for a new department. I'll ask my mentor to put out some feelers, and I can deal with my situation here until December. Like you said, that'll give us some time to see how things go . . . with us."

Nic takes a shaky breath, a smile tentatively curling at the corner of her mouth.

"So . . . we are?" Nic asks, eyes shining with hope. "Going to be together, I mean?"

I pull her to me, melding our bodies together from thigh to cheek, reveling in the press of her soft curves to mine.

"If you agree, then yes. Absolutely."

She fully breaks down crying then, and my own tears mix with hers as I hold her tight, stunned by my luck. At the beginning of this week, everything was going wrong. My future was so uncertain. Big parts of it still are, actually. But there's one steady, sure thing now, at least. And I feel like with Nic by my side, I can weather the rest. We'll figure it out.

We'll pick a new direction together.

Our embrace turns to kisses, then deeper kisses, our bodies beginning the slow spin-up dance they've gotten so good at over the last two months. Hands graze hips and necks, slide up the backs of shirts, and as soon as she brushes the side of my breast, the spark in my belly ignites.

"Make-up sex?" I murmur against her lips.

"Make-up sex," she agrees, yanking me back toward my bedroom. We stumble around the dining table, narrowly avoid tumbling over the couch, and I'm about to hoist her up on the bed when she suddenly pulls away.

"Wait, wait, hold on," she says, darting around me to run out of the room. My heart drops right through the floor. Did I do something wrong? Did she change her mind . . . ?

But no, she's just frantically blowing out hundreds of candles.

"Fire safety and all," she says before blowing out the next batch.

I fall even more in love.

It's hours before we remember the pie on the counter. But when we do finally go back for it—Nic's right.

It's her best one yet.

CHAPTER TWENTY-FOUR

KIRA

The decor for Skylar's party matches the invitation boxes she sent us months ago, because of course it does. I'm sure she had all of this perfectly envisioned even then.

Each table has a glass cylinder filled with layers of eco-friendly, compostable glitter in bands of color, surrounded by wires of twinkle lights that make the glitter shine like fire in the late evening dark. There are tropical drinks with little umbrellas ready to be passed around, and taro bubble tea to represent her Farmer Skylar ambitions, but inevitably, there will be a few people who opt for Skylar's custom cocktail for the night: The Solo, straight whiskey, just like we talked about. A giant table holds little gift bags with a small goodbye token from Skylar for each guest, including a photo of her sweet, smiling self in the back of a U-Haul. She actually did it.

And, adorning every spare bit of table and floor are the

plants Nic and I bought for her, all perfectly healthy and ready to be killed for real by whoever takes them home.

"I guess Skylar really does have a green thumb," I say, leaning in close to Nic so my breath ghosts over her ear. She shivers, her next words coming out in a jumble.

"Yeah. Green. Stuff. Good," she babbles, leaning her head back on my shoulder to expose her neck . . . and giving me a perfect view down the front of her top. *Nice.* I foresee a *very* good night in our near future.

Ian, Marco, Grace, Willow, and Skylar are all already here, chattering in a little cluster near one of the space heaters, because even though it's late August, it's still Seattle. The barn doors are thrown wide open to let in the fresh night air—*and* the prying eyes of every passerby on the street. It worries me, considering the way Skylar's fan base and the local media reacted to the news of her departure, but she's planning to livestream this whole thing anyway, so I guess privacy is a moot point. As we approach, a flare of nerves makes me squeeze Nic's hand tighter. We texted the group ahead of time to let them know we were okay and everything would be good for the party . . . but we didn't tell them that we're officially together. We wanted to save that news for in person.

Ian spots us first, followed by Willow, then the others, and the conversation falls silent, replaced by a hum of tension in the air. I force a weak smile as Nic squeezes my hand.

"I've got my head out of my ass this time, folks, promise," she says. "It's for real now."

To prove the point, I lean over and press a kiss to the side of Nic's head, pulling a bright smile from her, and all the wariness goes out of the group in an instant. In the space of a blink, we're surrounded by our five closest friends, a giant clump of hugging, squealing human. Skylar's mom materializes from nowhere, joining the group and wrapping Nic in her love.

"It's about damn time," Grace says, the first one to break away. "I was about to concoct some kind of scheme of my own to get you two to wake up."

Marco lays a hand on Grace's shoulder with a solemn, sympathetic nod. "It must have been so hard to hear them fucking under your very own roof while knowing their incompetence with feelings. Thank you for your service."

My cheeks go flaming red as I slap both hands over my face with a groan. Skylar's mom—who is also Nic's mom—just heard that. And yet, rather than making it awkward, she laughs louder than anyone. Skylar insists on capturing the moment for posterity—*and* because, as part of her agreement with the bridal shop, she needs to post all our fabulous outfits to her feed before she's locked out of her accounts.

Through it all, Skylar looks stunning. The dress she chose for the event is not at all what I would have expected. Normally, Skylar is all free-flowing, gauzy boho style with soft edges and a trail of fluttering fabric wherever she goes. Tonight's look is more structured and mature, a reflection of the Skylar she's becoming. She wears a sleek, clean-lined sheath in purest white, but the real eye-catching drama is at the top: an asymmetrical neckline that goes up over one shoulder, leaving one arm bare. The *other* arm is encased in a full shoulder-to-wrist sleeve dotted with tiny white buttons on the forearm. A running embroidery of flowers where the hem sweeps the floor completes the look, bringing in a touch of the old Skylar. It's perfect, and Skylar wears it with effortless grace.

"Okay, okay," her mom says, shooing everyone back toward the bar once we're done hamming for the camera. "The guests will be arriving any minute. Skylar, are you ready for this?"

For just a second, I catch a glimpse of the version of Skylar she keeps hidden from the world—a vulnerable, nervous woman who, for all her accomplishments, still worries she'll never be truly competent. Then she takes a breath, brushes her hair off her shoulders, and smiles—confident Skylar again, ready to take on the world.

"I'm ready."

Skylar hands her phone to Marco, always her unofficial videographer when they're out together, then waves to get everyone's attention.

"Excuse me, everyone! Yes, thanks, hi, I . . . have a few announcements I'd like to make, and I'm going to livestream them to my social media, so I wanted to give you all a heads-up that if you aren't comfortable being seen by hundreds of thousands of people, you might not want to walk behind me right now!"

There's a general chuckle, and then Skylar nods to Marco. As soon as he taps the phone, Skylar's off.

"Good evening, everyone!" Skylar says with a wave. "I'm so glad all of you could be here with me tonight—both those in this room right now and my dear Skylings joining via livestream. I have some news to share, some people to thank, and as I announced yesterday, some social media accounts to lock up once we're done.

"First things first: to my Skylings, I need to reinforce an important point that I try to reiterate as often as possible. Social media is not reality. The version of myself I present to you is not a complete picture. The truth is this: I am both the PhD-holding therapist you love and the somewhat messy pseudo-entrepreneur you love to hate. And underneath it all, I am also an anxious, imperfect human terrified of failing at the things that really matter to me. All my pet projects—they're just experiments, something for me to hyperfixate on when my brain gets squirrely. But there's one thing I've been working on for the past two years that I've not told a soul about, other than my family and those directly involved."

Skylar takes a breath and blows it out, centering herself. I feel Nic's hand slip into mine, and she squeezes, resting her head against my shoulder.

"I'm proud of her," she whispers. I nod my agreement as Skylar continues.

"I've been collaborating with my former PhD advisor on some research that is close to my heart: the effects of climate change on interpersonal relationships. I can finally announce that we've just had a paper published in the most recent *Nature Human Behaviour* . . . and my upcoming move to Fiji is actually because I'll be continuing that research with other psychologists from around the world. We'll be studying community mental health needs, centered in one of the areas that will be most impacted by climate change in the coming years."

Nic glances down at her phone, which is open to the livestream chat. There's a near-constant stream of hearts and shocked screaming face emojis, a few dickish comments about Skylar "getting political," as if they haven't already been following a queer woman advocating for mental health all this time—but mostly just love. Lots and lots of it. Skylar gives a little self-deprecating smile and shrugs.

"It's been . . . hard to take myself seriously as a researcher. Even though I've accomplished a lot, I've also burned many projects to the ground over the past few years, and I know that. But this is work that deeply matters to me, that I've loved pursuing, and climate change affects us all. If nothing else, I hope you will take this as a call to learn more about the ways climate change is affecting people's lives in life-or-death ways *right now.* Not in fifty or a hundred years, not once the oceans cross a certain temperature threshold, but *right now.* I've put together a list of resources on my website, and I hope you'll take the time to look. I owe so many thanks to my advisors and fellow researchers, who are all cited there, and some of whom are here tonight. I appreciate all your support, and I hope we'll help many more people together in the coming years."

I glance back down at Nic's phone. The comments are scrolling almost too fast to read, but apparently, people are already on the site, checking out the resources. At least a few fellow academics in her community are impressed, proclaiming her "the real deal." Good. She deserves some recognition and respect.

Skylar takes an unsteady breath and shakes out her hands to release some nerves.

"And, finally, as promised . . ." she begins, letting the tension hang for a beat. "Tonight, I am locking myself out of my social media accounts. Once again, I *will* be leaving my old content up as an archived resource, but I will no longer have access and will not be posting anything new going forward. I've asked my wonderful friend Grace, who is known for her . . . hmm, what's a kind way of saying 'bull-like stubbornness'?"

"Steadfast and reliable!" Marco says with a wink.

"Damn right!" Grace calls up. A chuckle rumbles through the room.

"Right. My *steadfast and reliable* friend Grace is going to join me up here to change my passwords and delete the apps off my phone. Grace?"

Grace practically bounds up to the front, grinning her delighted shark grin. "Reporting for duty!"

Skylar gives her a quick side hug, then turns back to the live stream on her phone.

"Well, my dear Skylings, this is where I bid you adieu. Be kind to each other, take care of yourselves, go to therapy, and as always: have compassion for yourself and for others who are nothing like you. This world is on fire, and its people need your love—and *action*—now more than ever."

Finally, with a glint of tears in her eyes, she waves.

"Goodbye, my friends."

She blows the screen a kiss, then ends the livestream and hands the phone to Grace like it's a hot potato. Marco stands by, filming them both as Grace taps into the settings, changes the password, deletes the app . . . and then it's done. A hundred pounds of weight falls off Skylar's shoulders, and her smile is enough to light up the night sky.

"It's done!"

Then she breaks down into tears—but not of regret, or sadness even. She looks so *free*. We all join in, smushing her in a giant hug and getting tears all over each other. Ian smothers me from one side, Willow from the other, Nic behind me, and Skylar in the center of it all. It's the end of an era. The beginning of so many good things too, of course, but this whole phase of our lives is ending. What an incredible thing that we all got to be together for this moment. I guess Skylar knew what she was doing all along. I should've known.

All in all, the party is—to *everyone's* surprise—a simple and beautiful affair. The evening concludes with hors d'oeuvres, more drinks, a cake that does *not* have a seven-hundred-dollar topper on it—Skylar was fully fucking with us by that point—and the distribution of the houseplants. Nic and I end up with two each somehow. Punishment, probably. It'll be embarrassing if, after all this, we can't keep them alive . . . but I suppose we'll deserve it.

And finally, when the party winds down and it's just our group left at the end, we say our private goodbyes to Skylar. She's getting on a plane first thing in the morning. There's a tiny part of me that's been bracing for this moment. For my own painful goodbye to my best friend, the woman who helped me through some of the hardest times of my life. And for Nic's goodbye, too. After everything, I've been worried . . . but I shouldn't have been. They hug each other so tight, and there are tears and quiet words. The word *sister* is whispered between them.

Then, we leave—together—and Nic takes me home to her place and pulls me out of the dress that tempted her so at the bridal boutique.

When you have a big, emotional ending in life, it helps to have a new beginning to look forward to. I think back to Gabe, to the tarot reading, and to that Ace of Cups at the end of my spread—new love, a cup overflowing.

I look down at my Ace of Cups, her cheeks flushed and hair spilling over the pillow . . . and I drink deeply.

I have a feeling my cup will never be empty again.

CHAPTER TWENTY-FIVE

NIC

Four months later

Kira could afford to be a U-Haul bi on her firefighter salary, but I'm more of a Budget truck lesbian, myself. Or at least I would be, if I had any interest in driving a giant truck cross-country. I'm leaving that one to Kira, who actually has experience driving something bigger than my little Mazda3.

It's Sunday morning, and I'm in the parking lot of our apartment building, trying to shove a few final things into the mini moving truck we rented while Kira scrubs the baseboards of our apartment in an effort to get our security deposit back. *Our* apartment because, to save money for our new place in Maryland, Kira moved out of Grace's apartment and into mine at the beginning of October. It happened to coincide with Grace mysteriously saying, out of the blue, that she could afford the place on her own and needed "some alone time right now anyway."

It was also a bit of a trial run for us. We didn't think it was smart to move across the country together without test driving what it actually felt like to live together in a more permanent way, not just me crashing while my apartment got fixed. It went *mostly* well, though there was an adjustment period. After all, Kira is the neatly tabbed binder, and I'm the newspaper no one could ever figure out how to refold that's also maybe missing a few pages. She's got the logistics of life *down*, and I . . . well, speaking *generously*, I get out the door most days with my keys, shoes, and head. But we found our balance. She's an excellent cook, and I am excellent at ordering takeout. I'm good with money—all those years of high-level math and statistics classes—and stay on top of our bills and budget. She's good at making sure we don't run out of toilet paper and edible food. And hey, I'm becoming a not-so-bad baker. I can give her a steady supply of mediocre pies for as long as she wants them.

I can admit that I'm having some mixed feelings about leaving Seattle again so soon after returning. The two years I was at grad school the first time around, all I could think about was getting back home to Seattle. To my friends and chosen family. I could never shake the feeling that it was all temporary, and I never put any effort into making it a home. But this time, it'll be different. I'm going for a PhD, which will take anywhere from four to six years—let's be real, probably six.

And this time, I'll have Kira with me.

I'm going to miss my family and the friends who are still here, but Kira and I will be back for holidays all the time. We'll stay in touch. And we'll build a whole new life together, too.

It feels unreal, standing on the precipice of this huge step forward. I can hardly believe I made it here. It's *thrilling* in a strange way, this whole "knowing what you want and really going for it" thing. When I arrived back home seven or eight months ago, I was a wreck. I was so out of touch with my own feelings, I had no idea what I wanted, and I felt sorry for myself all the time. Intolerable, really. I don't know how Kira fell in love with me. But damn, she did, and I couldn't be more grateful.

And hey, that therapist Skylar recommended has done me wonders over the past four months—and will continue to via telehealth, thankfully. Everyone should go to therapy at least once in their life. It's amazing how much bullshit we manage to convince ourselves of.

Our friends are dropping by to see us off this morning, one last big group hug before we hit the road. Ian arrives first, parking on the street just in front of our apartment building and trudging toward me like a zombie lumberjack. His eyes have dark circles under them, and his body language *screams* exhaustion.

"Ian, my dude, I mean this in the most loving way possible," I say, wrapping him in a hug. "You look like shit. Did you sleep?"

He gives a half-hearted chuckle.

"No, I definitely did not."

"Ah, I'm sorry, friend," I say, patting his arm consolingly. "Can you go back home and sleep more after this?"

He shakes his head.

"Nah, I'm heading out to brunch with Mar—uh, my . . . roommate."

He grimaces at his slip, and a puzzle piece drops neatly into place in my brain. *Click.*

"Oh my god," I sputter, the truth dawning on me. "*You're* Marco's brunch guy!"

"What? No! I'm not! I . . . uh . . ."

To my complete and utter surprise, a glint of tears appears in his near-panicked eyes. Oh *shit*.

"Hey, hey, it's okay, I'm sorry," I say in a soft tone, going into damage control mode. I don't want to jump to conclusions, but we're in really delicate territory here. "I didn't mean to push, or . . . out you, or whatever. If that's what this is. You don't have to tell me anything if you don't want to."

Ian's shoulders slump in defeat, and he rubs a hand over his eyes.

"No, it's okay, I . . . Skylar's the only one I've ever talked to about this, and even then only because she guessed. And since she's been gone . . . I haven't really had anyone to talk to. It's hard to get her on the phone with the time difference."

He sounds so *lost*. My heart aches for him.

"And now I know, and I'm leaving, too. Oh, my sweet friend." I grab his giant mountain man arm and squeeze it tight. "At least we'll only have a three-hour time difference, not nineteen. We talked all the time when I was in Maryland last time. I'll do my best to be here for you."

Be here for him for . . . *what*, exactly, he hasn't said yet, but I'm getting the general idea.

But Ian, being the big, soft, brave teddy bear of a man he is, works himself up to it all on his own.

"I've been having brunch with Marco every other week for like eight months. And it's the best part of my week. And I . . . *think* I've developed feelings for him."

"But you've always said you embrace the 'confused straight guy' label—oh."

"Yeah. Emphasis on 'confused.'"

"But . . ." I trail off. Ian has always been one of our group's Token Straights™, and my brain is having a hard time shifting him to a new category. "No '*but*,' obviously. I love you forever, and my brain will catch up in like, thirty seconds, promise. Wow."

"Hey, I don't blame you. My brain *still* hasn't caught up," Ian says, looking down at his feet. "There was one time before, in college, at a party before I met you all. But it was so random and, well, *short*, if you know what I mean."

His cheeks redden, and he hurries on.

"I never thought of it afterward. Even being around you all constantly and knowing what I know, I still never really thought it meant anything. I figured I was just, you know . . . a modern, evolved dude who could admit a guy was good-looking without it threatening my masculinity or whatever. And for lots of guys, I'm sure that's true, but . . ."

"But not for you," I say, *so* gently. His bottom lip wobbles for a second. Then he takes a big, deep breath and blows it out slowly.

"Not for me, I think," he says. "I started hanging out with Marco one-on-one a few weeks before you came back to Seattle, and I hadn't thought about that *one* time in college in ages. But being with Marco made me remember it. Then think about it again. And again. And I realized . . . you know, if you have to keep asking yourself the same question, maybe there's something to it."

I grab his hand and squeeze so tight because I understand that *completely*. My heart aches for him.

"Friend, we're here for you no matter what. Have you talked to Marco about it?"

Ian shakes his head. "No. I think he really does see our brunch days as just two bros enjoying delicious food that isn't served any other time of the week. You know how Marco moves. If he wants something, he goes for it. He's not shy about it."

"Well, yeah, but that's for rando guys. You're his friend, and you've *been* his friend since college. That's a big risk."

"Believe me, I know," Ian says, his eyes serious.

"Yeah, I guess you do, huh?"

I give him a small smile and pull him in for a hug. He really is in this deep.

"Now I wish we weren't leaving just yet, so we'd be here for you while you go through this," I say, rocking us back and forth in the hug. "You should really talk to Kira, though. Since she's bi, she might have some different insight for you on processing this stuff. Not to slap a label on you or anything, just that she's been through a similar . . . awakening?"

I give him one last squeeze, then hold him at arm's length.

"I wish you all the good things in the world, my love. I hope this works out for you."

Ian shrugs, expression miserable, obviously already resigned to his fate.

"I wouldn't count on it, but I appreciate the thought," he says, squeezing my hands. I stand up on tiptoe to press a kiss to his bearded cheek.

"Love you, Lumberjack. Take care of yourself."

"You too," he replies. "Or more like, don't drive Kira nuts as she attempts to prevent you from sleeping in your lab and starving yourself."

I bark a laugh, shooting a glance over at Kira, who has since come downstairs and is trying to force the door of the car closed after adding one box too many. Hopefully I'll still be able to see out the back window once we get on the road.

"How right you are. Not gonna lie—this week has been hellish," I say. "Moving is always stressful, and even the shiniest of couples are ready to bite each other's head off by moving day. I have a feeling things are about to turn around, though."

Willow pops up next to me, glancing over their shoulder like they're expecting to be spotted. "Nic, you gotta lose that super obvious scheming face or she'll catch on."

"Catch on to what?" Ian says immediately, and I slap a hand over his mouth with more force than I intended.

"Shush your face!" I hiss. "You'll spoil the surprise. Stick around and you'll see. When did you even get here, Will?"

They shrug. "A minute ago. I parked around the corner."

Grace and Marco pull up right next to us and climb out of the car, no shits given for the Permit Required sign. Eh, they'll only be here for a few minutes anyway.

"I can't believe you're leaving this early," Grace moans, not for the first time. She's wearing pajama pants with little hamburgers on them, slippers, and a hoodie from a K-pop band she's not yet exposed me to. On a spiritual level, she's clearly still in bed. Marco pats her on the head lovingly.

"I'll drop you right back home after this. Don't worry, your dearest love in the world will still be waiting for you."

"Fuck yeah, I *do* love that bed," Grace says with a solemn nod. "If this were a podcast, I'd be giving you a referral code for ten percent off that bed right now. That's how much I stand behind it."

My phone chimes the ringtone for an incoming video call, and with a smile, I pull it out of my pocket and answer. The last member of our group has arrived.

"Hey Sky! We're—"

"HAPPY MOVING DAAAAY!" Skylar shouts over the

phone, steamrolling my greeting. We all bust out laughing, crowding around the phone so everyone can get in the camera shot.

"How's your research going?" I ask, and she makes a face.

"Fabulous, obviously, but we're not here to talk about *me*. We're here to see you and Kira off as you drive into the sunset together!"

Everyone makes an obnoxious chorus of "awwww," and I roll my eyes. Kira throws an arm around me and leans in toward the phone.

"You are way too chipper for whatever the hell o'clock in the morning it is for you. I'm gonna need you to tone it down *several* notches."

"It is 4:30 a.m. of *tomorrow* for you all. I'm a time traveler! You're worth it, my loves," Skylar says with an excited clap.

I silently agree with Kira. Too. Early. For. That. Yet another reason Skylar and I could never have worked out. There's no way I could wake up to *that* every morning. I'd much rather have Kira's hair in my mouth as she starfishes over me until noon. I smile to myself at the memory of having to literally pull her out of bed this morning at 7:30 a.m. She and Grace made good roommates for a reason. Without a shift at the fire department to shape her schedule for the past week, she's reverted to her natural night owl ways. We have to get on the road ASAP, though; the drive to Maryland is going to take us six days, and we've got a reservation at a hotel this evening along the route. At least the route looks clear of snowstorms . . . for now. I tilt the camera back toward me and raise my eyebrows at Skylar.

"I'd thank you for getting up early to see us off," I say, "but I'm sure you get up at four every day for sunrise yoga

on the beach and homemade chia seed goat milk yogurt par-
faits or something."

"Um, it was a coconut milk and taro blend, thanks," she
replies with a flip of her hair. Everyone laughs.

Okay, fine, that actually sounds delicious.

"Anyway," Skylar says. "I actually don't have long. We're
heading to Taveuni for a week to meet with some of the in-
digenous communities there, so I have a boat to catch! I just
wanted to make sure I got to see your faces and wish you well,
my lovelies. Please keep us updated on your drive!"

"We will. You be safe too, Sky," Kira says.

"Stay away from the edges of the boat!" Marco adds, to
which Skylar sticks out her tongue.

"Okay, I love you all, byeee!" she says, blowing us all a
kiss before the call ends. I put away my phone and turn to
my friends, my bright "talking to Skylar" smile fading into
something more wobbly. Grace spots my impending tears and
launches herself at me with her signature rib-cracking hug.

"Don't you dare make me cry right before I have to sneak
off and make chaos," she whispers in my ear. I hug her back
and plant a giant smacking kiss on the side of her head.

"Thanks again for your help with that," I say. "Gonna miss
your very unique brand of piranha energy."

"Damn right you will," she says, then raises her voice for
the others to hear. "And if anyone fucks with you or Kira at
your new jobs, I'll fly to Maryland and eat them."

"Thanks, I guess?" Kira says, taking over the Grace hug
so Marco can throw his arms around me.

"I'll do better this time, I promise," he says, squeezing me
tight. "I know I sucked last time, but I'm almost done with
my NP degree. I'm gonna start existing more."

His eyes slide briefly to Ian, then snap back to me, almost guilty-looking.

"I really hope so," I reply, nuzzling my head against his. "I missed you. Talk soon, okay?"

"You got it," he says, his smile small but sincere as he pulls away. I actually believe him.

Ian slides in for one last hug, not saying anything this time, just holding me close.

"I'm here for you," I whisper, then kiss him on the cheek. He nods, turning to Kira as Willow dives in, squeezing the life out of me.

"Proud of you, Nic," they say. "You've come a long way."

I plant a giant smacking kiss on the side of their head and back up to arm's length.

"My only disappointment is that I'm leaving before I got to solve your mystery."

"My mystery?" they reply, all wide, innocent eyes. I level them with a frank stare.

"Yes, your *mystery*. Whatever you've been disappearing to do."

They shrug, totally nonchalant. "I go on a lot of hikes. You know this."

"I do. *And* I know that you've been disappearing way more often, for way longer, and seem to have no cell signal or internet for days at a time. Besides, I *know* you, Will. I can tell you're hiding something. But I also know that you'll tell us when you're ready." I lean in for one last hug, then squeeze their hand. "Just be careful, and ask for help when you need it, okay?"

"That's rich, coming from you," Will says, but their small smile takes any sting out of it. "I will. Safe travels, friend."

With all the hugs given and final goodbyes said, Grace

herds everyone out of the way, over toward Marco's car, as I follow Kira to the moving truck.

"Please be *super* careful on the road with this giant thing," I say.

"I've driven a fire truck in a snowstorm in emergency circumstances. I'm pretty sure I can handle the smallest moving truck on the market," Kira says. She hauls herself up into the cab of the truck, then gasps. I grin, hopping up onto the step by the driver's side of the door to watch her reaction.

A ring dangles from the rearview mirror of the truck, tied there with a shiny purple ribbon. Candles line the passenger side dashboard and seat, lit by my partner-in-chaos, Grace. She can be super sneaky when she's on a mission, and she had no problem slinking away while we were all chatting with Skylar. The ring glints in the combination of morning sunlight and flickering candlelight, the purple amethysts accented with white sapphires and beautifully detailed metalwork in white gold.

"What do you think?" I ask, reaching over Kira to tap the ring so it swings gently back and forth. "Will you marry me, Kira?"

It's a formality, I know that—but my heart races all the same, the muscles in my arms shaking with nervous tension as I hold on to the truck. We've already decided to come back to Seattle sometime next year to get married. Kira's a romantic, though, and secretly quite proper about some things. I worked hard to find this ring, and eventually found a seller on Etsy who creates handcrafted rings with ethically sourced or lab-grown gems for a reasonable price, like I knew Kira would want. When I told her our story, the seller even offered to customize the ring for free with little curling flame patterns in the metalwork. It's perfect, in my opinion. I just hope Kira agrees.

Kira turns to me with wet eyes, her lips pressed together in that way she does when she's trying not to straight-up bawl her face off.

"How in the hell did you manage this without me noticing?" she asks with a laughing sob, her mouth stretching into a wide smile.

I take her hand and bring it to my lips, pressing a lingering kiss to her soft skin.

"Grace is an evil genius, and I can be sneaky when properly motivated. And you are the best motivation of all."

She launches herself at me. I have to grab the door of the truck to avoid being knocked down by the force of her kiss. She seizes me around the waist to keep me from falling, and I cradle her face in my hands, taking kiss after kiss from her sweet, soft mouth. When she finally pulls back, her eyes are wet and shining.

"I don't want to look away from you, but I also really want to look at this ring, and I'm so conflicted."

With a laugh, I reach past her to pull the ring down. I untie the ribbon and drape it over her head. She bats it away, giving me the chance to grab her other hand and slip the ring onto her fourth finger, breathing a silent sigh of relief when it fits. It took a lot of sleuthing on Grace's part to get her ring size, and a small part of me was still afraid it would be wrong. The ring glows beautifully on her finger, though, bright and colorful and perfectly hers.

"So, uh, not to rush you or anything . . ." I say, drawing the hand with the ring to my mouth for a kiss, and Kira lets out a startled "oh!"

"Yes, obviously!" she says, gripping my hands and yanking me in for another deep kiss. "Also, these candles are a total fire hazard and need to be put out immediately."

"Yes!" I say, leaping down to sprint to the passenger side and open the door. "I didn't actually intend for these to be burning for so long, but you kept me in suspense *forever*, so—"

"Oh, stop. I was basking in the romance of the moment and admiring my gorgeous new ring. Should I have rushed right through? Quick and efficient proposal and acceptance? Record the results, write the lab report—"

"Oh, *shush*, you," I say, then blow out a bunch of the candles with dramatic effort. It feels weirdly like my birthday, in more ways than one. My gorgeous, brave, brilliant girlfriend is now my fiancée, we're moving across the country to start a whole new era of our lives together, I'm pursuing the research that I love, and life has never been better.

I gather all the candles into the box I'd left in the passenger seat of my car for this specific reason while our friends descend on Kira to coo over the ring, which most of them have already seen pictures of anyway. Once I'm done, I'm absorbed into the group and passed around for a repeat of the whole hug queue again.

Finally, when the excitement dies down, we settle into one giant group hug, falling completely silent. It's like we're in a bubble of frozen space-time, existing just for the six of us, with Skylar here in spirit. It feels like an echo of Skylar's goodbye party, the feeling of this being the last time we're all together. Maybe Grace will move next, or Willow will meet someone, or Marco's new nurse practitioner qualifications will pull him somewhere else. Our lives are taking us in new directions.

But for the first time, I'm not afraid of it. I'm not fighting it. It's a *good* thing. Nothing can last forever—and nothing *should*. That's how you get stuck, and that's an experience neither Kira nor I would ever recommend. I'll always be grateful for the time we've had as a group—and most importantly, I can accept now that we don't have to keep living in each other's pocket to be important to one another.

We can walk our own paths, secure in the knowledge that we can always come home.

I walk Kira back to the moving truck, placing a kiss just below her new ring as we go.

"I can't believe I have to ride in a vehicle separated from you *all day*, just staring at this ring," she says, affronted. "Did you design this proposal with torture in mind?"

"I didn't, but now that you mention it, it *is* an entertaining side effect," I say with a wicked grin. I lean in and nip her ear. "By the time we get to the hotel, you'll be *dying* to get in my pants."

"Oh, you are *evil*," Kira says, burying a hand in my hair to pull me in for a deep, slow kiss that sets my blood on fire. I'm half a second from pushing her up against the side of the moving truck when Marco's voice calls out.

"Okay, now you're just dragging this out. Get lost!"

We break off, laughing, and I swat Kira on the ass as she climbs into the cab of the truck. Once I'm settled in my car, the cheap two-way radio we bought for the trip beeps.

"Ready to go, love?" Kira asks over the radio.

I take one last look out the window at our gathered friends and smile.

"Yeah. I'm ready."

I'd follow this woman into the fire any day.

★ ★ ★ ★ ★

ACKNOWLEDGMENTS

This book has been a hell of a journey.

I wrote the first few chapters of *All Fired Up* in the summer of 2018 while anxiously awaiting the release of my debut YA novel, *The Disasters*. The following summer, I finished the whole first half. And then . . . nothing until 2022. I changed agents, had several things under contract that took priority, 2020 happened, I had my wonderful kiddo, and I *couldn't figure out how to make this book work*. Something just wasn't right.

Thankfully, my incredible agent, Eric Smith, was there to help me puzzle it out. Through many emails and a brainstorming call or two, we got it working enough to attract the attention of my lovely editor, Cat Clyne. Cat's insight shaped the book into its final form, which you hold in your hands. More than any other book I've written, this one really was a team effort. Thank you, everyone. I appreciate you so very much. Special shout-out to my first agent, Barbara Poelle, who first encouraged me to try my hand at a rom-com, believed in this book and its characters, and gave it its title.

A note: I am neither a firefighter nor a scientist studying fire. I did plenty of research, but no amount of research can match lived experience, and I made a lot of stuff up. My apologies for any errors. I write *always* with admiration, and I think you're all total badasses.

Thanks as always to my friends who keep me sane and bounce ideas around, most especially Jamie. You've been here for this book from its earliest days, and I so appreciate you! Rosiee, Leigh, Steph, all the usual crew—I'm so glad you're in my life.

Final thanks always go to my partner, N, and my little one, F: you two are my world. Thank you for your love and support, even when this job takes me away from you. I adore you both.

CREDITS

Thank you to everyone who made this book possible:

Publisher: Loriana Sacilotto
Editor: Cat Clyne
Managing Editor: Stephanie Choo
Art Director: Tara Scarcello
Cover Artist: Sarah Long
Publicity: Kamille Carreras Pereira
Marketing: Lindsey Reeder
Sales: Bailey Thomas
Copy Editor: Jennifer Stimson
Proofreader: Leigh Teetzel